RACHEL NEUBURGER REYNOLDS

Drowning Lessons

RED FROG BEACH 🐸 MYSTERY SERIES #1

www.rachelneuburger.com

ISBN: 978-1-7338378-4-2 (PRINT)
ISBN: 978-1-7338378-1-1 (MOBI)
ISBN: 978-1-7338378-2-8 (EPUB)

Cover design by Tim Marrs

This book is dedicated to John Reynolds, my everything...

ACKNOWLEDGMENTS

I'm so excited that I am finally getting to write an acknowledgments page. I've been waiting for this a long time…

I've had a lot of helping hands on this one. Thanks to Joe Roland and Marianna Kulukundis for their help at the beginning. Big love to my early readers: Mary Syler Lange, Peter Breger, Laurence Paone, and Colleen O'Donnell. Huge developmental thanks to Gordon Dahlquist and Michael McDonough. The lesson I learned from Michael, is that if someone like him pokes a small hole in a mystery, it all unravels. It's come a long way from there.

Thanks for the support and encouragement from my agents, Sharon Belcastro and Ella Marie Shupe, of the Belcastro Agency. Big ups to my original editor, Brenda Heald. And a million extra thanks to my copy editor, Meredith Rodriguez.

For guiding me through insecurities and answering so many more questions than anyone should ever be required to answer, thanks to Gary Sunshine, Roland Scahill, Katerina Baker and Ned Livingston.

Thanks to my amazing mother, Evelyn, who introduced me to mysteries, typewriters, and most importantly the confidence to know I could do this. And very grateful to my father, Alfred, as well, for always encouraging me to do what I loved. Lastly, thanks to my husband, John, for his love, support, and belief in me… and for walking with me on this journey, from one beach to the next.

.

~

DAY ONE

~

1

FAKE IT 'TIL YOU MAKE IT

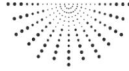

*O*ur captain cut the motor of the speedboat about 300 feet from Cinco Puntos Beach and sat there, staring into the crystal waters off the Caribbean coast of Panama.

The beach was one of the most magical places I had ever seen. It was a gorgeous, empty white sand beach lined with starfish so big that it would take two hands to pick one up.

A good swimmer could have easily made it quickly to shore, but, as we sat under the noonday sun, the captain lied to my fellow passengers, muttering, "Piranhas."

The captain was lying at my personal misguided request. My next action wasn't going to make anyone happy, and I wanted all the help I could get.

Feeling relatively comfortable in my safety vest, I rose to look my guests in the eyes, teetering a bit due to my fear of water. "Welcome to Bocas del Toro," I nervously said.

As the Maid of Honor for my dearest friend Olivia's wedding, I was one of four attendants put in charge of small groups of guests. Each group of invitees was scattered over four eco-resorts on two neighboring islands.

The bridal party had flown down on Saturday to get the lay of the land, to indulge in a little relaxation, and to prep for the additional thirty-five guests who'd be joining us for the ultra-luxurious destination wedding.

The other three bridesmaids and I were responsible for the constant entertainment of our little flocks. They were a high maintenance contingency. Entertaining them on a regular day would have been hard enough, but an all too recent break-up with Salty, my ridiculously-named ex of five years, made it all feel like a Herculean task.

Currently it was my duty to ready these guests for the first in a packed schedule of five days of decadent events. The problem was just that it simply wasn't going to start well.

The five guests began sweating away, waiting for whatever I was going to say before I led them out of the perils of the piranhas (in my extensive research of safety of all the sea dwellers of the archipelago, piranhas were far from the worse, but I wasn't going to get into that just then).

"Come on, Lexie," Dave, the groom Walter's brother, said, "why aren't we going to shore?"

Good question.

It's because I have to perform my first official duty as a bridesmaid.

Olivia was starting to get a bit out of control, I might be correct in saying. She'd given me a script to recite along the way to the first event, and it wasn't going to be pretty.

Olivia had been my best friend since I was five. Last year, she was adorably thrilled, like a toddler, when she had learned she could have a destination wedding. Then, slowly over the course of the year, she started losing sight of reality. For the last month, she had been transforming into a bona fide Bridezilla.

I just kept tight-lipped about most of her behavior. You only get married once (some may say). She'd come back to her normal self after this all became a memory. She always came back for Earth after she got a little alpha.

I tried to keep a bright smile and sunny disposition, reaching down to open a waterproof lockbox. I knew I looked ridiculous, being the only one wearing a safety vest while also shoved into a cute little blood-red dress that fit four weeks ago and was now resembling sausage casing.

My split with Salty had hit me way harder than I thought. The ten pounds I had added since certainly weren't doing me any favors on this beach vacation.

"Fake it 'til you make it, Lexie," a wise-ish woman once said to me.

"So," I said, "on behalf of Olivia and Walter, would you please surrender your phones, computers, and all mobile technology to me for the duration of your stay on Bocas Del Toro?"

Five baffled and irked guests stared back at me, making no move to hand anything over to me. Checking a phone at the door of a club or a party for a few hours was a concept that was getting some traction back in the States, but it wasn't going to catch on for an entire five days in Panama.

I went on to mutter that it was for the best, and that, in any case, they weren't going to get any phone service on the island. Besides, when was the last time they had been really free of technology? This was ultimately going to be the couple's gift to them.

More in hopes to get away from the non-existent piranhas and out of the sun, they began to accept defeat.

First, Walter's brother, Dave, and his girlfriend, Georgie, tossed their matching iPhones in the box. Pretty much everything about them matched: dirty blond hair, dark blue eyes, color-coordinated outfits perfectly tailored for their lanky bodies.

Becky, Walter's long-term assistant, gave up her phone next. She had an envious head of wild beautiful red curls that seemed to be constantly bouncing. I'd only met her once before, but with hair like hers, she wasn't easy to forget.

When it became obvious that I wasn't playing games, Josh, one of Walter's groomsmen, frowned but followed suit.

I'd read he'd be quiet in the ridiculously large wedding binder we were to have with us at all times. "Unassuming," was written, followed by, "Just there."

The book said that if you did get him talking, he'd become a mile-a-minute snooze fest. Olivia had made us laugh, smirking after meeting him at the engagement party. "What did he do? Go to the barber and ask for the 'regular guy' haircut?"

She hadn't always been quite so snarky.

Looking at him now, I saw he had a friendly smile. There was something about him. Deep hazel eyes glanced back at me when I briefly caught his gaze. And yes, though I guess he did have the regular guy haircut, it had the charm of just starting to go grey through the light brown. And the kind smile? I hadn't seen one of them for a while.

One of the people I was supposed to wrangle from the airport had ceased to get off the plane, thank god.

Olivia's very estranged younger sister, Emma, surprised everyone when her response card came, devoid of any answers to the questions about dietary restrictions and flip-flop size. The RSVP, hastily scrawled with a green Sharpie, announced, "Your sister and some dude will attend. Surprise!"

Classic Emma, always making things at best inconvenient, and at worst horrid. It was the best moment of my day when I didn't see her get off that flight.

One man remained, staring me down, phone held tightly in his hand. Last but anything but least was Nico - tall, dark, and mean. As the heir to a Greek shipping fortune and a hedge fund genius, he had more money than I could even begin to comprehend, and access to a world that I never thought I would see.

When first being introduced to the Walter and Nico wealthy crowd through Olivia, I had learned that there were three distinctive categories of wealth. There were those with money, those with real money, and then there was Nico.

His gift to the happy couple was paying for the over the top wedding, which I knew had already hit the low six-figures. I had always tried to be positive about people, but he was simply a Class-A bastard. He could simultaneously piss off, and then charm, everyone in the room. He was rotten.

He shoved his phone down his pants. "I dare you," he said. He looked up at the sun in glory, then said with condescension, "I'm Greek. We Greeks love the sun. I could stand here all day."

And I went for it, hand down his pants, trying to avoid his intimate areas, while he made a point to attempt the opposite. Quickly reaching deeply into his luxuriously soft boxer briefs, I gave his phone a heave-ho overboard, made-up piranhas cheering me on.

His eyes bore into, and I was possibly shivering waiting for his response. He knew just the below-the-belt thing to say. "No wonder that writer of yours left you."

I left him, but I wasn't going to get into it with someone like Nico.

Count to ten.

Count to ten twice.

Count to ten backwards.

Then breathe and resume my hostess duties.

The captain started up the motor and we were off to the landing. Avoiding Nico's stare, I tried to return to my scripted TV hostess positivity.

"Okay, before we check into the hotel, please join us for an early lunch at Red Frog Beach, hosted by the charming bridegroom, Walter! Following your feast, we'll head out on a fun-filled snorkeling trip before we shuttle you to your luxury accommodations."

~

RED FROG BEACH was on Isla Bastimentos, a half hour boat ride from the major island of Isla Colon. It was home to the resort where only Walter and his parents were staying. The bride would be staying at one of the other resorts until their wedding night.

I helped everyone off the boat into two feet of warm Caribbean water so I could give the folks my requisite welcome speech before lunch. I handed each of them an official blood-red wedding towel, the intense shade being one of many small homages to Olivia's gothic past. It was going to be blood-red up the wazoo.

Looking on the bright side, a week out of New York was a week out of New York. We were off-grid, in the Bocas del Toro archipelago, off the Caribbean coast of Panama; 6 islands, 52 cays, and over 200 small islets.

Though there was a marina we could have used at the Red Frog Beach resort, it hadn't been built when Olivia and Walter had first visited the beach three years ago. They wanted to share the experience of their original discovery of the great expanse of the virtually empty, white sand Red Frog Beach. Thus, I lead my charges off the beach through a rugged path up the coast.

Becky, Walter's faithful assistant, walked closely behind me, smiling and always looking like she was about to say something. She giggled often in a coquettish way. She had enough energy and happiness for all of us.

A few moments in, I returned to my performance. "Welcome to Bocas del Toro, which translated means Mouth of the Bull. Not far away, we also have beaches like Bocas del Drago, which is Mouth of the Dragon. This very island was discovered by Columbus on his fourth and last trip to the new world in 1502…"

Nico, financial master of industry and best man, chimed in, "Did he have to conquer the imaginary piranhas first? That must have been a sight."

Rather quickly people stopped listening to me, but I knew how to reel them back in. I skipped ahead to my favorite part as a trio of minuscule red frogs hopped across our path. I reached down, carefully picking one up.

The group was talking among themselves. Georgie was repeatedly asking her boyfriend, Dave, when she'd be getting a cocktail. I'd been told in advance that she and Walter's brother were good friends with the bottle. Knowing I was losing them to the promise of a tropical tipple, I spiced things up.

"Please, guys, hold on. This is going to blow your mind. These are strawberry poison-dart frogs, used to make blow darts a hundred years ago. Once upon a time, the natives used to sharpen slivers of wood with the jaw of a sawfish, dip them in frog poison, and blow them through bamboo shoots. A master assassin could hit a target from thirty feet."

The group took a few steps back as I held out the adorably lethal two-centimeter frog.

Georgie buried her face in Dave's shoulder, mumbling, "Save me."

"Don't worry. You can't die by touching it. You'd have to actually put it in your mouth and suck on it."

Nico raised an eyebrow.

"You would have to agitate the frog," I continued. "You would have to get its defenses up, get the poison glands working overtime, and then roll your dart on the frog's back. Alternatively, you can puncture a gland to extract the poison."

Becky hadn't said much yet, but she put her hand near mine, wanting to hold the frog herself. "He's pretty. This red is pretty," she said, smiling goofily.

I further explained, "That's how larger animals know to stay away. Bright colors like this mean danger. It's their only line of defense against these little red guys."

Nico raised his arms in the universal "So what?" gesture, walking off from the group, while the frog still rested comfortably on Becky's hand.

Dave got a little closer, and snickered, "I'd take a picture, but, huh, no discernable camera..."

We cleared the jungle, arriving on the stunning beach with mighty waves crashing into the glassy waters. Pristine and sun-drenched, it was arguably the most beautiful and serene place I'd ever seen.

Walter greeted us with open arms, *"Bienvenidos al Paraiso!* Let the party begin!"

Like Olivia, he had an enviable body, complete with a six-pack shimmering in the rays of sun.

Olivia's success had come from Femme Fit-all, her lady's

boutique gym business. That was how they had met. Not that Walter was lazy or a lady; he too owned gyms, only his was a nationwide chain. And he had wanted to buy hers. He'd been unsuccessful.

The rest of the wedding guests were already on the beach having a beautiful party, which warmed my broken heart. The huge snorkeling catamaran had already docked at the marina, waiting patiently for us down the beach.

We were just close enough to see Olivia waiting on the boat, long blond hair casually blowing in the soft tropical breeze. She was waiting for her grand entrance. There was nothing she loved more than a grand entrance. Except Walter. And possibly me.

Just beyond the lapping waves was the biggest grand shellfish and champagne feast I'd ever seen. Two bartenders walked through the revelers, taking orders. When done with demolishing local langoustines and similar island treats, everyone ran into the waves, ignoring my warning that one should take a twenty-minute break to digest food before taking a swim.

Walter held back with me for a moment, turning to look at me fondly.

There was no arguing that he was a good-looking man, one of the few people I knew who were naturally light blond. I'd always thought he resembled someone in one those old photos of the football team at Yale in the 20's. Very classic.

We always got along in groups, but never had much to say one-on-one. We both stared at Olivia, talking to one of the snorkeling crew, going over some list in her binder. She then looked up and smiled at the man before giving him a little hug.

Through all her Bridezilla tendencies, she had a glow

about her. She exuded the kind of charisma that made you feel like you were the only person in the room. Her laugh could cheer up any gloomy space. Over thirty years of friendship, her laugh and smile had saved me on more than one occasion.

She waved to us from the boat, sending kisses our way.

Walter stared at her adoringly before he said, "Lexie, you're being a real champ about all this. I know how hard what you are going through is. I also know that she's got a little over enthusiastic about this wedding. She might not show it right now, but she is so grateful for you. You're her biggest cheerleader. Maybe she'll calm down a little now that everyone's here and all is in motion," he said hopefully.

We could both wish.

"You know Olivia." I blew a kiss back to her. "You have to cut her a break sometimes. I love her. It's her week."

My focus slowly turned to what in my opinion were rather large waves. Like an overprotective mother, I was already concerned with the swimmers, the riptide, and bubbly champagne brains.

Together we walked down to the water in silence, wading in ankle deep, and I felt the riptide even there. From what seemed like miles off, my new friends were body surfing, and it certainly looked really fun and carefree.

I stopped as Walter confidently walked further into the ocean towards his group of his romping friends. Finally, he turned to me and asked, "Aren't you coming?"

"Nah, thanks. I'm going to play with the poison frogs."

He didn't understand if my comment was humor or just strangeness. He turned his back on me to join his friends in the big bad ocean.

As Walter ran towards his friends in the sea, I was able to

stop smiling for the first time since I'd picked up my group from the airport. As determined as I was to be strong and to be the best hostess ever to grace the waters of Bocas Del Toro, I realized I was going to be in for one hell of a week.

Fake it 'til you make it.

2

SAFETY FIRST

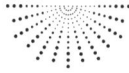

$\mathcal{N}$ever having snorkeled, I had still done extensive research to make myself the resident expert. Before we embarked at precisely 2:10 on our marine adventure, I tried to give my safety talk as everyone boarded.

Olivia graciously greeted all her guests before they reached with double kisses on the cheek. I wasn't too far behind her. Different bridesmaids were responsible for different events, and though I wasn't in charge of this event per se, I was very serious about safety and wanted to do the best for the folks who were putting their lives on the line by participating in water activities.

"Now I want you all to have fun, but there are a few things to keep in mind. People die every week from snorkeling, so be careful. Yes, every week. And note that it is most definitely overcast. If it starts to rain, I want everyone out of the water. Salt water conducts energy like nobody's business. When I say "out," everyone is out. I won't be in the water, so if you have a problem, make eye contact with me. I see that some of you have chosen not to put on your life vest...."

Amanda, the bridesmaid in charge of the event, took over, placing herself between me and Olivia. "This Debbie Downer is not being serious. It's just for insurance! So everyone put your red vests on and get ready to party!"

Amanda was Olivia's business partner in their boutique gym industry, and a model turned personal trainer. They met when the bride was an obsessed client, crazy to diminish from a soft size 10 to a tight 2. They were both excellent spokesmen for the gym.

Rounding out the bridesmaid quartet were Marianna, who had competed with me for the title of Olivia's BFF since kindergarten, and "Phil the Gay Bridesmaid."

Phil took little offense to the moniker. He was a literary agent who had represented Olivia when she was a struggling but super talented novelist. He gave her his blessing when she decided to become a boutique gym mogul. She wasn't making him any money anyway. I'd asked him if the nickname bothered him, to which he replied, "I'm gay. I'm a bridesmaid. What's to be offended by?"

Amanda was an enviable hostess, welcoming everyone in her elegant manner, as if she was hosting a luxury dinner party and not a water sport excursion. She remembered everyone names, while handing them glasses of watered-down rum punch as if it was Dom Perignon. When I voiced my concerns about drunk snorkeling to her, she replied, "Don't worry Lexie. One watered down rum drink never killed anyone."

I hadn't googled that particular statistic.

Nico commented in passing me, "Walter is spending an awful lot of my money on a wedding that feels like spring break in Cancun."

Motoring to our first dive spot, Bridesmaid Phil put his

arm around me, handing me a plastic cup of the Hawaiian punch/cheap rum mixture, toasting, "It's 5 p.m. somewhere."

"Yes," I replied, "that would be the Ukraine, where I'm sure they aren't snorkeling."

"Though," he smirked, "they are drinking down on the beach on the French Riviera. I'm sure of it."

He liked to go tit-for-tat on any subject at any time, and he was very good at baiting me.

"They aren't really. It's February and it's about fifty degrees there. And it's three o'clock, so no one in France is going to dinner."

So I'd heard. I'd never been to France.

A half hour later we arrived at our snorkeling destination - a pristine coral reef teeming with sea turtles, parrot fish, and perhaps a nurse shark. Carlos from the snorkeling company gave his own safety talk before everyone jumped in, finishing with the confidence building statement, "There has never been a human death by nurse shark attack unless they are provoked, so stay away from them. If they see you, they will generally run off."

Generally?

As Carlos dismissed everyone to have fun, he turned to me and said, "You don't have to know how to swim to snorkel, tall girl. We have a Styrofoam surfboard with ropes for you to hold onto. Big Al, over there, will be with you. It's really quite amazing in there. You kind of can't help but to fall in love a little."

"That's okay. Thanks." I stood at the rear of the boat, as the wedding party waited for their chance to go fins first, single file, into the warm tropical water.

Olivia, fins already on, ready to topple at any moment, put her arm around me before she made her way in. "Are you okay? How are you holding up? I just want to make sure that you are okay."

"Yes…?"

"Really?" She turned my head to look at her eye to eye. "I know you too well. You never need to lie to me. I'll ask you again, are you okay?"

"Of course I am," I lied. "Now go avoid a jellyfish."

I wasn't the only person not partaking in the fun; Walter's mother took her book out and sat in the shade, as Marianna rhetorically questioned, "Do you know what salt water does to your hair and skin?" Both were happy sticking to the rum punch.

Olivia had really scored with the wedding photographer, Migs, who was getting ready with his underwater camera and wet-suit. He had grown up in Panama City and went to New York to study photography at Cooper Union. No small feat in itself, for sure.

His name was Miguel, but he adopted his New York nickname permanently. Lack of opportunity and aversion to the winters had sent him back towards the equator, where he could make piles of money photographing beach weddings and snapping for travel publications.

The fact that he had been published in *National Geographic* allowed his rates to skyrocket. The fact that he was incredibly easy on the eyes did not hurt. Green eyes, I noted, which were a nice surprise.

Did I mention he was easy on the eyes?

I knew how much he was getting paid for this job and he was worth every penny, dealing with the ever more demanding Olivia.

Everyone looked dead as they floated above whatever beautiful sea creature had transfixed them. Before Migs jumped in, he commented, "They look ridiculous, right?"

"Like a school of dead red snappers, currently in season."

With a healthy guffaw, Migs turned and said, "You've got a great, dark sense of humor when you aren't being blue."

"You go after that nurse shark, Migs," I said with a smile. "Get a nice picture for me."

$\sim$

FORTY-FIVE MINUTES LATER, Carlos had his crew start signaling the snorkelers to come back to the ship. A few people had grown bored enough that they had already rejoined the vessel, but most were still out there. Slowly people returned.

"I saw a stingray!" exclaimed Amanda, as she grabbed the ladder and took her fins off.

Following her was a man named Lloyd, muttering, "It wasn't a stingray, it was a bat fish. Never speak without certainty."

Lloyd was the man of my recent nightmares. Back at the Midwestern College he'd gone to with Walter and the gang, there had been a small plague of murders, the victims being pretty blonde coeds. The investigation at one point had been focused on Lloyd. The police never made an arrest, let alone a conviction on the murders.

Granted I wasn't blonde, but I remembered what had been written about him in our binders, in bold, underlined, and all caps: BEWARE. HE IS DANGEROUS AND SMARTER THAN ANY OF US.

The last stragglers came, while the rest were already toweled off and enjoying more rum punch at the front of the boat. One more guest still floated in the ocean. At first glance, he might've been transfixed by a turtle, but I knew that something was very wrong.

I blew my personal whistle in a panic. Who wasn't there? I spotted the photographer, three bridesmaids and Lloyd the serial killer. The father of the bride. I couldn't remember the faces of half the people on the trip. I counted off my campers. Dave and Georgie. Quiet Josh. Nico hadn't come back.

Oh my god. More importantly, where was Walter?

No one had taken notice of what was happening, so I grabbed Migs and yelled at the top of my voice, "Everyone to the front of the ship for more rum punch and group photographs!"

Olivia turned her back to me before she noticed anything wrong. She danced off with the rest of the party. "Yes! I love it. Maybe we can get everyone to put their masks back on for the photo. It will be adorable."

Only Lloyd remained with us, joining us to watch in detached curiosity.

"*Mierda*," Carlos said and dove off the boat. I watched him move through the water as if in slow motion. He moved quickly to the seemingly unconscious snorkeler.

I prayed it was just someone who drank one too many glasses of rum punch and was transfixed on a school of gorgeous strawberry groupers. Carlos turned them over in the water and it was clear that it was a man. My mind raced, trying to remember who I'd seen return.

Please, not Walter. Please, not Walter.

Lloyd helped get the body out of the water, while Carlos pulled off the snorkel mask, revealing the face of Nico.

I'd seen this scene a thousand times in movies - the lifeguard pulled a lifeless swimmer back to shore for mouth-to-mouth resuscitation, bringing them back from the brink of death. Surely, he'd be fine.

Carlos repeated the process time and again.

"Is he okay?" I asked, to no response.

"No, he's dead," Lloyd said to me. "Know what I mean?"

Lloyd looked me directly in the eye and a chill ran down my spine, which was half to do with Nico and half to do with Lloyd's preternaturally blue eyes. Match those peepers with his black hair and 6'4" sinewy body, and he was every bit of a vampire who just happened to have a tan.

Carlos and Lloyd brought Nico down to a cabin, while one of the deck crew called ahead to Bocas Town Marina to say that we'd need an ambulance to drive us less than half a mile to the hospital.

"I suppose we should tell Walter," Lloyd dryly said, clinically looking over the body. "I'm not this kind of doctor, I suppose, but I'd say massive coronary. Drowning?" He tenderly touched Nico's face. "Good night, dear friend."

We abstained from speech, as drunken revelers stomped around above us. Carlos paced and let us know that we'd need to give the ambulance driver cash when we arrived, as soon as someone could find him. The driver also had a cab that went to Bluff Beach and back, where sometimes he'd spend the day if business was slow. It was unclear whether the vehicle was technically an ambulance at all.

"Of course it is," Carlos said with a bad poker face.

"Lexie," I heard Olivia sing from the top of the stairs. "We need you! Migs has a very particular concept for this photo—"

"Can you come down here, Olivia," I meekly asked.

"Migs has a concept for disembarking very artfully, taking photos while…" she continued, walking into the room and laying eyes upon the corpse. "This is not happening. God damn, this is not happening. What happened? Is he okay?"

Lloyd lit a cigarette.

Of course he did.

"I'm not that kind of doctor," he said for the second time, stopping when Walter walked into the room.

Walter appeared not to believe what he saw; his dear friend laying still on the bed.

Olivia looked wildly around the room.

The boat docked at the key side and I heard footsteps as our partygoers disembarked above us. Carlos had his crew tempting people away from the ship, making the masses forget that they hadn't moved on to a second snorkeling spot.

Walter sat silent, head in his hands, elbows on his knees. Olivia, Carlos, and Lloyd heatedly discussed what would happen next. The room went silent when the next thing that Olivia said was, "Let's keep this quiet until we know what happened. I want to have all the information before we tell the guests."

Oh no. She's up to something.

When the group started talking again, Lloyd nodded and motioned towards Carlos and said, "Just let the captain there tell them there was an unfortunate snorkeling incident. I get it, Olivia. Ducks in a row and all that."

"I'm not saying snorkeling incident," Carlos chided. "I've got insurance to worry about. Unfortunate snorkeling incident? What's wrong with you?"

"You want a list?" Lloyd calmly asked.

How could you fault a man for being crazy when he so casually owned it?

Did they have a point? I suppose that it might have been wise to wait until it was clear what had happened. Lloyd looked at her, in what I can only describe as clinical bemusement, and gifted her with enough rope to hang herself. He abruptly offered to remove himself from the boat and treat the remaining guests to a late afternoon cocktail at the Pickled Parrot, five minutes across the bay on Isla Carenero.

Walter made a b-line for the bathroom, hand clasped over his mouth.

Lloyd ran his hand through his thick dark hair as he put his sunglasses on, lighting another cigarette, smirking at everyone remaining through his dark lenses.

He handed me a wad of cash for whatever corrupt local might need it and left, turning back to cynically say to Olivia, "I'm so very sorry for your loss."

3

DR. NOLAN AT YOUR SERVICE

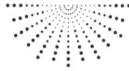

*T*he hospital was in a state of general disrepair, but as there were just about 10,000 people living on the island, I guess it was workable. Besides the carnage of a serial killer named Jackson Landis back in 2016, who had gone on a homicidal real estate inspired spree, there wasn't a lot of death that went on in the hospital.

There was hardly any violent crime to speak of, except the predictable drunken American tourist brawls. It was really more of an out-patient clinic, and if the problem was any bigger than an infected ear or an epic hangover, the patient would be flown to Panama City.

Nico's body was brought into the rarely used morgue. I say morgue, but they had never autopsied anyone there, and it was filled with outdated machinery and tools. The victims of the Landis crime had been flown to Panama City, which I assume would be Nico's next port of call. It was really more of a dead person's way station.

Dr. Nolan was ridiculously cute and could have been

mistaken for a surfer. He was easily under thirty and told me he had gone to medical school in Panama, as he couldn't get into a decent American one.

He added the fact that this was not for academic reasons and that was he was fine with that because it allowed him to work on alternative cancer treatments that the US wouldn't approve due to the "cancer economy."

Dr. Nolan stated, "If the head of the American Cancer Society won't put his wife through chemo, you have to wonder if something is very wrong."

He continued fantasizing about the clinic he yearned for until it dawned on him that he was talking to three people flanking their dead friend on an autopsy table. He scrunched up his nose, never having needed much of a bedside manner, and said, "Oh, I'm sorry for your loss."

Walter put his hand on his dead friend's arm. "I have to go," he whispered, his eyes filling with tears as he quickly left the room. "I think I'm going to be sick."

Dr. Nolan whipped the blanket off of Nico's body and went through the routine of checking his pulse and listening to his non-existent heartbeat. He said to his nurse, "Note: time of death is 4:46 p.m."

"It wasn't actually," I noted.

"Well, what do you want me to do? This is what goes on the death certificate. We'll ship him to Panama City and then you can arrange to transport him back to America. We can start the paperwork, but we don't have the capabilities on the island to keep him on ice. Who's in charge of this guy?" Again, as his bedside manner left something to be desired, he added, "Anyway, sorry for your loss."

"Well…technically not my loss," Olivia said. "But it's very very sad."

Dr. Nolan looked at me, "For the record, can you identify this man?"

"Yes?" It felt wrong. Someone who liked him should be identifying him.

Olivia was quickly losing her cool, eyes dashing between Nico's body and the door. She pulled me out of the room and down the poorly lit hall to the exit. It was the middle of the week, so the streets were still fairly empty; a few locals making their way to their hospitality jobs, and a couple of tourists window shopping while others dipped in and out of bars.

She bummed a cigarette from a hungover couple walking down the street. After five years of abstinence, she still lit up like a pro.

We'd smoked our first cigarettes together at the age of 13, hiding behind the cork trees in the tree sanctuary. For me, it was the one and only cigarette. Thanks, but no thanks. For Olivia, it had been a hard-to-break habit now rearing its ugly head.

Olivia also held her copy of the wedding binder tightly under her arm, pages dog-eared and worn. We'd been working from an enormous version of a planner for a year now, with all the documents you'd expect; schedules, contracts, individual bridesmaid responsibilities and the standard wedding nitpicking.

I always had mine close by, now in a commemorative red wedding tote, of course. Within the overstuffed, constantly updated planner was the equivalent of an 8th-grade slam book.

It had been designed to give us pictures and basic info on all the guests and their dietary restrictions, but had devolved to a nasty book of secrets and judgments, and I now knew far more than I wanted to about anyone. It was worth hiding.

I gave everyone in my book a nickname, or I'd never have remembered. Princeton Colleen. Little Joe. Walter's uncle who become known as Commando Gordon. Photographer Migs had tested me on the names just that morning and I'd aced it.

Olivia's voice was gravelly. "I need to find Walter. Is that cool? I'm sorry to leave you here, but... I've just never seen him like this. His friend's dead – I mean, what can I do? That was horrible. But just please keep this between you and I... and Lloyd, god help us."

"Olivia, we need to tell people. People need to make arrangement to get back home,"

"No one's going home. That's why we have to wait to tell anyone. I need to figure this out."

"What?" I assumed the event would be called off.

"Not until we know what happened. I mean... obviously Nico would want the wedding to go on..." She was counting on her hand, quickly calculating. "I'm thinking that maybe you can handle this morgue stuff for a bit? I'm far too emotional, obviously, and have to calm Walter down. I've got seventy-two hours before the wedding to make things cool."

"Olivia..."

She frantically rattled off all the reasons why the wedding was impossible to cancel. In addition to the fact that Nico wouldn't be around to foot the bill in the future, there were the schedules of the rich and powerful to consider, and the impossibility of ever getting her parents in the same room again.

She took a long final wet drag of her cigarette and said, "So you see, this wedding is going to happen. Not a question in my mind. I have to tell Walter before he... I have to find Walter." In a state of confusion, she slowly walked away, working out step one in her quest to find broken-hearted

Walter. Eventually looking back at my shell-shocked expression, she added, "I love you, Lexie."

She threw the cigarette and her binder carelessly on the ground, taking a momentary break, stretching her perfectly sculptured arms defiantly above her head. She quickly picked up her beloved binder and was off.

Where are you about to do, Olivia?

I missed the old, dark, hilarious, struggling writer version of her. I loved her success, her confidence, and humor, but running a business like hers, I guess you'd have to change.

Five years ago, she and Bridesmaid Amanda had opened Femme Fit-all. They ran a showroom, not really a gym, where clients would meet model-attractive trainers who would make house calls, showing clients how to work out in their homes with whatever they had: candlesticks, half-gallon jugs of milk, the seven volumes of Harry Potter. They'd learned early on that recommending jump ropes and hula-hoops in NYC apartments was a recipe for disaster.

Clients could have trainers "update" with them in their homes as often as they needed. The most popular package was the gift of the 4-session quarterly visit. 75% of the unfit, slightly-bloated New Yorkers only used it once, if ever.

All gyms counted on the post New Year's resolution drop off, but Olivia had almost zero overhead, and the laziest of all gym rats would all soon disappear into the un-muscled masses. All gyms work on the model that only a fraction of people with memberships show up and exercise, but Olivia and Amanda didn't even go through the pretense of having locations.

We were still as close as ever, but slowly but surely over the last five years, since she'd partnered with Amanda, things were just a little different, just a little less lovely. Sometimes it was like old times, and sometimes it was like I never knew her at all.

~

BACK IN THE MORGUE, Dr. Nolan worked with the nurse in silence. I sat uncomfortably on one of the wobbly chairs in the room, trying to conjure up some sympathy. Truth be told, I went through my mental filing cabinet of memories of Nico and could not think of one where he was truly kind to me. When I'd tried to sit down at one of their poker games last summer, he had shooed me away, saying, "Just for the big boys, little girl. Tall little girl."

My thoughts were interrupted by the nurse, softly asking me, "Are you next of kin?"

"Me?" I exclaimed, as if it was the most ridiculous thing I'd ever heard. As if someone could tell, as he lay dead on a table, that he thought he was far too important to go near me with a ten-foot pole. "No."

"Do you know who that would be, and how we can contact her?"

"Max," I said, as I watched the doctor. "I don't know how to find her." I didn't even know her last name.

Please don't make me call Max.

Nico's estranged wife, Max (short for what, no one knew), would most definitely not be attending. She was inhumanly beautiful with sleek long red hair and granite eyes, and a nastiness to rival that of her husband's.

Max was of British aristocracy, which was one step above socialite, I had recently learned. I was told that Princess Di had been her eightieth cousin, thirty-six times removed, or something ridiculous like that, which made her about three-thousandth in line for the throne.

Late into the few evenings that we were at the same parties, Max would corner me, drunk and sad, confiding the same things every time; how much she missed Europe, how much she hated Nico, and how her and motherhood were a match made in hell.

Every so often, she was charming and sometimes even thankful for hearing her out without any pretense of judgment. Men would pass us, drool over the unthinkable beauty, then give me a quick once over, returning their focus to Max as they kept on walking. She never acknowledged they existed.

Max and Nico finally had enough of each other and split last May, with a heinous divorce currently in progress. Neither would leave their Gramercy Park townhouse, perhaps because of the possibility of losing custody of their six-yearold terror of a son. My guess was the atmosphere stayed as pleasant as their sunny dispositions.

He had money. She not-so-secretly had none, but she had beauty, youth, and indisputable jet-set bona fide aristocrat status.

"Anita, *ves esto?*" Dr. Nolan looked shaken, as the nurse joined him on the other side of the table. His latex-clad hand was frozen on Nico's well-formed triceps and he moved the examination light over his arm.

Oh no. This can't be good.

He rolled a surgical instrument trolley over and grabbed small forceps. The nurse joined him by his side.

"Do you see this?" he asked her. There was a small but very inflamed spot, which looked like a bad spider bite. With forceps, the doctor removed what looked like a tip of pencil lead. "Well, well," the good doctor said. "Look at that. How does a needle break like that?" He paused. He was going to say something big. "I don't think that this

29

was a heart attack. Right into the brachial vein. Assassin style."

Assassin? Did he really say, "assassin?"

He became excited and curious, like a mad scientist, and decided to go to the police. Maybe he'd finally get to do an autopsy after all.

4
BOCAS, PD

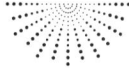

*Y*ou could walk the length of Bocas Town in ten minutes, so the police department was close. The streets were lined with clean but rickety three-story buildings; hostels and low budget hotels, markets, and restaurants. Only a few looked like homes.

Most people who worked on the island lived on the mainland and traveled by ferry or speedboat. There was also a community of Americans working here, those who had come down for vacation and never left.

Land was cheap and so was everything else on the island; 60 cents max on a water taxi, $12 for a gourmet meal, and the waterfront property cost a fraction of the price of neighboring Costa Rica. With modest savings and a job at a hotel or a water sports company, you could live like a king, or at least maintain a fine middle-class lifestyle.

Dr. Nolan had put the tip of the needle in a ziplock baggie. We had spent thirty minutes in his musty office, with an administrator trying to get the island's police detectives on the phone.

"Let's just walk over there. But seriously, fifty percent chance they're even there. Just as possible that they're off surfing. It's pretty standard," he said, rummaging through his small volume of English and Spanish medical books, finally finding what he was looking for.

No one looked twice as the doctor walked familiarly through the station; just a few waves and nods. We entered an office with two casually dressed officers.

"Lexie, this is our crack team of island detectives, Alajandro LaGuardia and Juan McDonough. Not answering your phone today? This is a serious emergency," the doc scolded.

"If you don't dial in on 104, it's not really an emergency. Everyone knows that," La Guardia said, with minimal accent.

Dr. Nolan kicked his chair. "Then why give me a private number?"

"Simple. If it's not really an emergency, you'll go away." They both laughed.

The doc tossed the baggie on their cluttered desk. "I figured it would be easier to bring this than to wait three days for you to get back to me."

McDonough picked it up and examined it through the baggie. "What do you have there?"

"One of the guys from the big wedding is dead. I don't think it was of natural causes. I think this guy has been killed," the doc gravely said.

He dramatically stated this, as if it was the first time he may have uttered the words. He came off more like a bad medical soap opera than concerned doctor. LaGuardia almost looked as if he was going to giggle, which struck me as strange.

"Always a bit of the drama with you. I'll see when we can

get a helicopter from Panama City to pick him up," La Guardia said, reaching for the desk phone.

"Just listen to me for a few minutes and check this out before you call. Come down to the hospital for five minutes," Doc pleaded.

They put on their flip-flops and led the way. "Okay dude, but I think we've worked enough in the solving of murders department. The Landis case was all us, not Panama City. That was all us."

The Doc just said, trailing after them like a mascot, "This is something you are going to want to see. If I'm right, I've never seen this in my ten years here."

In his most pensive state, it was hard to take him seriously. Ten years on the job? He couldn't have been more than 30 at best. But then again, the cops looked like they might have been even younger.

The three of them crowded around Nico's inanimate form. Dr. Nolan held up the baggie with the needle tip. "Look at that wound. I'm near positive that he was killed with this needle. I read about this when I moved down here. This kind of lesion around the needle entry means it was, well, you know, essentially a poison dart."

Poison dart? Impossible.

The doctor opened an old book on the table next to Nico's feet, turning the musty pages until he found what he was looking for. McDonough looked the page over studiously and commented, "Red frog poison? I've never seen it here. But everyone knows...."

Who'd want to kill Nico? Besides everyone.

We only taught everyone at this wedding about red frog poison. That narrows it down.

LaGuardia said, "You know as well as I do that we have to get the body to Panama City tonight. We don't have the facilities. He's going to start stinking up your place really soon. And, who's footing that bill to get him there?"

I dug into my tote pulling out Lloyd's roll of cash.

"Get the body back, fine, but we have this needle tip." Dr. Nolan held up the baggy and shook it in LaGuardia's face. "We have the facilities. Can't you take it up to the research station? Please?"

La Guardia looked at the small wound with increasing curiosity, pulling his longish black hair into a ponytail. "Hmm. That would be something. When was the last death like this on record?"

"The records aren't great. I can't find a report of it," Dr. Nolan said, looking through the book.

"It's foggy, but I'm a little curious, to tell you the truth," McDonough stated.

Doc continued, "Could you just ask this one little favor? I'm just dying to know. Not literally."

Around the coast and up the island was the Bocas Research Station, a field location of the Smithsonian Research Institute, systematically examining "interactions between diet and toxicity in dart poison frogs."

McDonough was excited to tell us that he had a good friend up there, who might look at it for them. He was getting excited, smiling like a little boy. "Wouldn't that be something?"

He went on to explain that he might have missed his scientific calling of herpetology and spent a good deal of time with the traveling researchers up the west coast.

La Guardia sighed and sat down in an examination chair, lighting up. "Hey, McDonough. Do you think we should close the airport?"

No one seemed to be bothered by indoor smoking.

Casually, McDonough answered, "Yeah, why not? Until we know what we have."

They seem to get a kick out of this. It's as if they did it just for laughs on a fairly regular basis, pleasantly speaking with the guys from air traffic control.

"This is very exciting," Dr. Nolan said. He was trying to be low key, but he was desperate to be part of this investigative clique.

I think he had wanted to be one of the cool kids his whole life. Now maybe he was a part of something big.

McDonough was on hold for a long time while we all waited, silently watching and listening. The conversation was in Spanish, so I had to wait with bated breath, listening to any word that I could understand.

He finally said, "They'll look at it. We should know by tomorrow."

LaGuardia seemed satisfied. "Okay, airport closed. Keep it closed until tomorrow if we see we need to investigate."

I meekly said, "Is there still a chance it was a heart attack? Or just a regular drowning?"

The police looked at Nolan, who bit the inside of his cheek, thinking. "I mean," he said like a twelve-year-old, "it's possible. But, I don't know, call it a hunch. I think we know exactly what it is."

I took a deep breath and closed my eyes, to escape for a moment. I was terrified. Not at the fact that there might be a killer in our midst, but at the thought having to face telling the close to unraveling bride.

5

SALTY TEARS

*L*aGuardia drove me home in a police boat, which I thought was actually very cool and important. I offered to take myself home in a water taxi, but he thought that I might be shaken and upset by Nico's death, and gallantly wanted to make sure that I got home safely.

No one had seemed to want to say "murder" out loud until the research facility could analyze what they had, most likely by tomorrow. I had a feeling they weren't being 100% kosher on not contacting Panama City yet. He casually asked me about Nico, what he was like, and if there was anyone in the wedding party who had any feelings of ill will for the deceased.

What could I say? I'd met him a dozen unpleasant times and that's all I know.

Before I got off the boat, he offered me a beer and he sat down next to me, commenting, "We'll let you know about the toxicology results when we hear back tomorrow. I don't think I really believe it, but if you see anything strange, let us know, tall girl."

If I saw something? What would I see? What would I be looking for?

I watched the boat pull away from the dock and head south, quickly out of sight and earshot.

The resort was empty, thankfully, with the rest of my guests obviously still living it up with Lloyd at the Pickled Parrot. Of the four bridesmaids, I'd definitely won out on the digs, laying my hat at Mariposa del Mar on the main island of Isla Colon.

Six luxury bungalows had been built over the clear shallow water near a mangrove. The rooms were connected by a long walkway, which continued on to a reception area and a mellow, elegant restaurant, now empty. The website described the resort as "constructed using the traditional methods of the archipelago: each handcrafted cabin is built upon stilts over the water and covered by a palm leaf roof – an unforgettable habitat congruent with the native communities of the region."

Not too shabby.

Walking past the bored bartender, it felt rude not to get a drink, so I ordered Soberana beer. I joked with the bartender at how funny it was that a beer had the word "sober" in it. The irony was lost on her.

I walked straight through the cabin and onto my terrace, which had been my home and respite since Saturday. One could dive directly off the deck, if they were the kind of person who swam. *Not me.*

I pulled my phone out, expecting a dozen voicemails from Olivia, but there was only one text message: WALTER AND I CAN KEEP A SECRET.

She's got to be kidding.

I tried to call her. How was I going to tell her that

however bad it now was, it might get a whole lot worse? Maybe it would go to voicemail.

"Lexie. Ok. Fill me in," she urgently said. Taking a turn for the sweeter, she cooed to Walter, "Baby, will you check what's keeping the martinis?"

Is that what you drink when your friend dies?

"Olivia, I don't know how…" I stuttered.

"Spit it out."

"Well, it looks like it might not be a heart attack. Or drowning."

I could imagine her face; lips pursed and furrowed brow. "What do you mean? Of course it was."

"They think it could be venom from a poison frog. They are analyzing a puncture wound and a needle now."

"Are you messing with me?"

I heard Walter return in the background, most likely two martinis in hand. "Who's messing with you, baby?"

"No one, Walter," she dismissively said. "Lexie says that these backwoods cops still can't figure out if Nico drowned or had a heart attack. So we'll have to wait to make any decisions until tomorrow."

I didn't follow that logic.

I wasn't going to be able to get through to her. "You understand we're probably talking about a murder. You have to think of the safety…"

She was done with the conversation. "You worry too much, Lexie. You are going to be the best host a cocktail party has ever seen tonight. Don't worry. Now I've got to get going. We're just trying to process things over here."

"Don't hang up!"

But she did.

I tried to call back repeatedly. The first two calls weren't answered, and the subsequent ones went to the voicemail of a turned off phone.

Take a break, Lexie.

Look at where you are. When's the next time you're going to see a dolphin?

I tried to appreciate the magic of the scenery. To say that it was common to see dolphins dash by was an understatement. They were constantly frolicking along the coral reef at the edge of the resort.

Watching them made me doubt the hype that they were the smartest animals in existence. If they were truly brilliant, they wouldn't be playing around like eight-year-olds during the last days of summer vacation. If they really were as smart as everyone claimed, they'd operate more like the deep-sea hatchet fish, with underbite fangs and existential scowls. Bottom feeders. Vertical migrators. Silhouette hunters. At that particular moment, I stood behind the theory that intelligence bred misery.

Stop it now. Chin up. Be a good bridesmaid.

I pulled out the slam book, hurrying to find Nico's page. As the best man, his page opened like a centerfold; a close-up of a handsome, imposing man, with his default expression of condescension, looking much more mafia than Wall Street. Next to him was the scribbled-out face of ice princess Max, with comments written over her white evening gown that I'd rather not repeat.

On the bottom of the page, Olivia had written in her blood red sharpie, "You scullion! You rampallian! You fustilarian! I'll tickle your catastrophe!" *Henry IV*.

She may have abandoned literature, but she'd always keep Shakespeare's Henries close to her heart. We'd spent a summer sure we would become stars of stage and screen, yelling across the yard, random lines from *The Complete*

Works of Shakespeare. But Max was a fustilarian for sure, whatever that was.

Re-reading all that I had forgotten, I saw Nico had still been a good friend to some. He'd invested in Walter's gym business, Lloyd's medical research, and the supercomputing start-up of Edgar, another groomsman.

Those facts didn't make him a good person, they made him a wealthier person. No mention of charm, charisma, or real charity.

Nico once came up behind me at a fundraiser he was throwing for a museum that didn't really need the money. "What about giving some money to a charity that's actually helping people in need?" I had asked, going on to ask if they donated any of their money to a real cause.

He didn't respond, but later in the evening grabbed my bottom and said, "You have a butt like a twelve- year- old boy."

Wanting to slap him, I merely walked off.

He had called after me, as I hurried into a different room, "What? That's a good thing!"

Please just have died of a heart attack.

I skimmed over the pages of the guests, most of whom I only knew in passing. Then I landed on Salty, guest no longer, face crossed out with various Shakespearian insults scribbled across his visage.

I'm not going to make it.

I never thought that I'd miss Salty, with his stupid name and passive-aggressive confidence. But the hole he had left was closing more slowly than anticipated.

It wasn't the crying fits of my college years, hyperventilating and dry heaving - a bond that Olivia and I had unfortunately shared for many years during destructions of the heart; it was a dull ache, aware of how long a day could be. *Blah.*

After four years with Salty, lying on the couch after he delivered me the perfect cup of tea, I simply said, "I can't do this anymore."

I ended up hating a lot of silly and meaningless things about Salty. I hated that he didn't use a Mac, wore his pants a little too short, and that his ears stuck out. I hated that he ironed his jeans and t-shirts and had abandoned rare steak for kale and beet juice.

I hated that he retreated to another room when my friends were over, and said things like, "Who else would be stupid enough to love you?" He'd turn, walk a few steps, then turn back and say, "I don't mean that," but the damage was done.

I felt conspicuously alone, even when we were together. Three days before, I'd received a text from him, stating, "As of late, I seem to have taken a full-time job regretting years of taking you for granted."

Day late. Dollar short.

Moving on takes time.

So, I'd go on faking it 'til I made it, but the wedding week was going to be challenge enough, and now with Nico.... I was exhausted and went inside. I stretched out across the couch, finally giving up trying to get the bride on the phone. Even if she hadn't been avoiding me, service was spotty at best.

What was she doing? Her wedding plans had morphed from Princess Diana in a train of ivory to the Countess of the Dark Side. I gave Olivia credit for abandoning the traditional princess theme, but I wasn't sure how the rest of the guests would feel about her witching hour fantasies. She'd joked for life that she wanted a wedding on an underwater Monopoly board we saw in *Cosmopolitan*. The humble dream I'd shared with her was a roller-skating wedding at our childhood rink, Spin Off.

We weren't Cinderella, she'd say. We weren't princesses in everyday life, so why dress up like one and have a mediocre dinner with the choices of chicken, steak, or pasta primavera? Sometimes salmon was added to the mix. But that wasn't any of our lives and weddings should represent who we were, or who Olivia was.

~

WHEN OLIVIA ASKED me to be her maid of honor, eons before Salty and I sunk south to Hades, I declined (there actually is a place called Tartarus south of Hades. It's really terrible there. Look it up).

"Please don't think it wouldn't be an honor," I respectfully stated, "but I'm not a good choice. I should be the last on your list. Last. What about Phil?"

"No," she said, as we sucked down PBRs in our dive bar, which she had pretty much abandoned for Soho House by that point. "But no. No, no, no. I choose you. We're blood sisters!"

Olivia held her scarred knuckle up, pointing at it dramatically, conspicuous enough for anyone around to take a gander. When we were eight, we scraped our knuckles with rocks down on Cape Cod, pressed them together for a few minutes, and from then on we were theoretically one.

"Blood." She put her hand, partially obscured by the 4-carat ring, on my bare one and pensively said, "Seriously Lexie. I just need two things and I will leave you alone after. One, you need to make sure I look gorgeous and two, throw me an epic bachelorette party. Phil and Amanda can do the rest. Wait, okay. There is a number three. Three, a good speech. A good toast. Most importantly I need an epic toast."

"I love you, but it's never three things with you," I replied.

"It's me and you, Lex. There's no one else who could hold a candle."

What could I do but say yes?

"Yes!" she exclaimed and ticked something off in her book.

Check. Moving on.

Yes, my responsibilities ended up being far greater than those three things she listed after she got the gift of a lifetime. After Nico offered to pick up the bill, the skies opened, so naturally, Olivia had planned for the moon.

I had my own mantra. I could close my eyes, breathe deeply, and think of my new Greenwich Village apartment that I would return to in five days. Small. Tiny, really, but affordable. And alone.

Olivia wasn't the only one who had written a book. I penned my own once too, a self-help volume of sorts called *Left Behind*, which encouraged you to have your friends verbally rip you apart, mentioning every flaw from the insignificant to the major, to inspire you to be a better person.

It was kind of a big deal for a while and I was paid a very respectable advance for a first-time author, certainly enough to quit my job and write full time for a stretch. At the time, I had thought that in publishing a semi-successful book, my days of working for someone else were over. Not so. The fad soared and then nose-dived pretty quickly. Two more books had been published, but they'd been so ignored that no one knew they even existed, and I was repeatedly asked what my follow up to *Left Behind* would be.

Money runs out pretty quickly in New York City, even

when you're cautious, and sooner rather than later I was back to theatre marketing. It was the least scientific of all marketing, where student interns were still sent out to Times Square with sandwich boards, shoving flyers in people's faces with promises of 40% off the Lion King, Tuesday through Thursday only.

If you don't like your life, change it. That's what they say. Five years ago, I thought that I had entered a better chapter two. That was when I hit 30. I guess that 35 meant chapter three. How many chapters were left?

Romance is not dead, but it is bastardized. It's a little bitter and a lot cautious.

I was exhausted and ready for a nap.

6

MURPHY'S LAW: ANYTHING THAT CAN GO WRONG, WILL GO WRONG

I was having one of those dreams, where you think you hear the voice of someone you know. Maybe a friend you haven't seen in twenty years, maybe a dead grandparent, maybe a rock star you'd never met but for some reason, you are buddy-buddy with in your dreams. You can never tell who it is, but the voice gets increasingly familiar. You quietly follow, eventually turning the corner, catching view of their shoes, the back of their head, the silhouette of their body, and then wake up...

It wasn't a dream.

I had taken an unheard of two-hour nap, still not having heard back from Olivia.

I trudged over to the closet. Ten blood red outfits hung side by side; one for every event, fitted for the pre-breakup Lexie of two months prior, who was ten pounds lighter. Granted, the wardrobe was all a lovely gift, but there was no chance of me blending into the crowd (forget about fading into the wall-less scenery).

Having identified the dress assigned to the party, I

47

squeezed myself into it. I looked like a red sailor in the Gothic US Navy, sucking my gut in, hoping the zipper would hold me in the heinous frock. Now constantly identifiable as crimson wedding concierge.

I was regular everywhere but my stomach, able to see the outline of my belly button through the fitted dress. *How offending.*

The very familiar but unidentifiable voices, which I'd thought had been from my dream, continued laughing and frolicking, having a great time splashing around. The scream and the laughter of a woman pushing a man into the water.

I can't place these voices, but they are making me nervous.

I don't need any more nervous right now.

Is it Nico's ghost? Is it someone else? Is it my NYC constant paranoia?

I settled on the most amorphous outfit that I had and walked back out to my terrace to see what was going on, and saw the body that went with the whimsical laughter: Emma, Olivia's younger sister. She had got off a plane after all.

God, how those sisters despised each other. The event that had been the final straw was still a mystery, but they hadn't spoken in over five years.

Olivia's father had put his foot down with Olivia to stop the ridiculousness. He wouldn't come unless the bride at least invited her sister. Olivia wasn't up for much tradition but needed to have her father-of-the-bride dance. It was one of the few traditions that she wanted to abide by for superstition's sake. No one thought Emma would reply. I don't think their dad was even happy that she did, to be honest.

Emma had been a terror for years. To say that they had seen each other twelve times in as many years would be an exaggeration. Emma had attempted to ruin all her older sister's triumphs; the publishing and flop of Olivia's poorly received novel, the opening of Femme Fit-all, the cover story of *Shape Magazine*. Though a murder wasn't going to stop the wedding, Emma certainly could.

She gushed from the next deck over, blowing inauthentic kisses with grand gestures. "Lexie, Lexie, Lexie! It has been way too long."

"You look beautiful," I commented, and she did; five years younger than her sister, and a lot more deceptively charming. Emma's genes were just a tiny bit nicer, a little smoother.

"I brought a surprise!" she chirped as her "random dude" materialized through the water, propping himself up on his elbows. He shook the water out of his hair like a shaggy dog and redirected his gaze towards me. Ryan Michael Lawler.

Knock me over with a feather.

The little clueless sibling had brought Olivia's high school boyfriend and the first "love of her life". She'd been ripped apart when Ryan dumped her three months into his freshman year of college. I spent hours hogging up the hallway phone at NYU (How did we exist without cell phones? And how did we pay exorbitant long-distance bills as college freshmen?), nursing her through her first heartbreak, the one you think isn't going to end and that might literally kill you.

Her roommate, who hardly knew or liked her, had begged me to come down to New Jersey to help, where I took her to the hospital; dry heaving, dehydrated, sleepless and unable to keep food down. She was able to compartmentalize, but she never forgot him. *You never forget the first one.*

I certainly never did. Forgot Ryan that is… He was the major secret of my life. He was my first love, before Olivia knew he existed. I met him the first day he transferred to Brookline High from Huntington Beach, CA.

He was a surfer, dreamy but demoted to riding a Boston

skateboard. We had a week together, keeping him secret because I didn't want to share him, and gave him my virginity. *Gave? Threw it at him.*

Try how I might to keep him to myself, all it took was one solo trip down the corridors of BHS for the lady hawks to descend. Then he had a virtual cornucopia of virginities to take, but he fell for Olivia. It wasn't her fault I was crushed; I never told her what happened. I had mistakenly kept us a secret. I didn't want to ruin it for Olivia, but I did my fair share of secret dry heaving in my own right.

Ryan, baffled, confounded really, looked at me, pulling himself onto the dock and grabbing a blood red towel. "Lexie?"

His movie star eyes repeatedly darted between Emma, myself, and an escape route he was obviously looking for.

"Lexie…come over here and talk to us. I'll explain." She beckoned me with her little finger.

I held my hand up to her, flabbergasted, gob smacked, knocked for a loop. "You, young lady, stay in your room. Ryan?!"

"You are here for the wedding too…?" Ryan began.

"Olivia's wedding."

"Crap," was his simple but suitable response. "I had no idea."

"Ryan, meet me in the bar, now!"

I held my stomach in as we walked.

Not a beauty contest, Lexie. Just get him out of here.

The sooner the better.

How was I going to say anything to him without lipstick? Ryan was walking behind me, looking like he just realized he was on bad reality TV. Emma started to come over to us, but I put my finger up again and hissed, "Back in your room."

The solution should have been simple - put them on a water taxi back to the airport so they could leave on the next flight out of there. Except that the airport was closed for the foreseeable future. A murder on a tiny island trapped us all. Their departure was more than I could fit on my plate. Yet another secret to hide.

~

BEFORE I COULD SAY A WORD, he had ordered two glasses of wine, handing me one as if an offer of apology. I walked quickly to the furthest table, like a bickering honeymoon couple, realizing we'd made a huge mistake by being together at all.

"Emma. Really? You knew her when she was six," I scolded.

Uncomfortable silence followed. The conversation couldn't be over quickly enough.

"What are you doing trolling around like that? What's wrong with you?"

"I just thought I was going on a slightly sordid, no strings attached vacation with an old friend. There was no ill will. Trust me, if I had know…"

"Old friend? Emma? You should be settled down and married. With kids or something. You should…"

"Should what? Miss Left Behind?" Twenty years later and his smile hadn't changed.

"Don't." No one could mention my book or the Left Behind Club except me. And I didn't mention it anymore, ever.

"What? I liked your book. I was so impressed and proud. So proud. So cool. I thought about writing you and telling you that. But, the road to hell and all…"

You shouldn't be here, Ryan. You should never have been anywhere.

"We'll go, Lexie. We can get on a plane and go. This is a stunning place, but I don't want to ruin Olivia's wedding." He offered an apologetic smile. "I don't want to do this to you."

How was I supposed to tell them that they couldn't leave the island; the airport was closed on the off chance there was a murderer on the island. I walked up to the owner standing behind the bar and tried to get her to find me a room for them, far away from the resort. As soon as the airport was open, they'd be gone.

We had an account at the "staff hotel," so it would be the most likely choice. It was difficult explaining to her that they were not leaving because they didn't like the resort, but that we just didn't want them here.

"Flozzie," I put my hand on hers, "this is the most beautiful hotel in the world, but those people…they are bad."

Flozzie called a water taxi. Before gathering up Emma, Ryan grabbed my hand, "Lexie. Trust me. All I can say is I'm sorry."

I won't lie. I won't say that I didn't have a compulsion to hijack a fishing boat to head down the canal with him, drinking rum punch and making out like a pair of lust-struck teenagers, hiding in the dark waters off the Panama Canal, living the high life until they turned off my AmEx.

Like always, though, my loyalty to Olivia and moral compass would never let me go down that avenue. That train of thought quickly left the station.

But, what if? The most nagging question of all time.

While arranging his exodus, I learned that, of course, he hadn't been Left Behind at all. Twice divorced, three kids, and currently single. Ryan owned a line of pseudo skate wear. He had done well.

THE WATER TAXI arrived and I went to grab Emma's luggage. She stumbled as she walked behind me, trying to apologize, "I see I went a little too far, maybe. But I was making a point. I was actually trying to do her a favor. Maybe this Mr. Wonderful who Olivia is marrying isn't so great after all. Maybe—"

"Emma. Shut up. As soon as I can get you off this island I will…"

She dropped her luggage and pouted like the spoiled brat I'd known so well growing up. "No, I won't leave. I was invited. My father is expecting me. My sister is getting married. You can't make me leave. You can't force me on to the plane."

She's right. Is there any rational thought in that narcissistic head?

"She would never do this to you."

"Wouldn't she?"

"What were you thinking, Emma? Bringing Ryan? That break-up almost killed her. And to be honest, I'd fear for your life. You're looking at, at best a knuckle sandwich, and at worst…."

This seemed to be enough convincing for her.

I happily sent them off in a water taxi to Tango Vista, the "staff's" third-rate hotel. There was no resistance on Ryan's part. Before he got on the boat, he whispered close in my ear, "I can't say that it hasn't been nice seeing you. Red has always been your color."

I clenched my jaw as I blushed, remembering the red underwear I had purchased at the Fall River Factory Outlets prior to my sweet cherry being plucked.

"You don't," I called after him, "ever date your high school girlfriend's sister."

He continued looking at me, taking me in completely, as they motored away.

How am I going to explain this one?

How am I going to deal with figuring out Nico's death when getting them off the island was becoming my first priority?

Help! Somebody. Anybody. I beg you.

I ran back to the bungalow, grabbing my phone and slam book, trying to call Olivia one last time.

I can't protect you if I can't find you.

There were three other resorts, Walter's bungalow and every restaurant on the two islands that I would have to visit, and a party to host. There was hardly time to visit even one resort.

I resolved myself to stick around the hotel and keep trying to call her. Worst case scenario, I'd wait for her at the end of the dock, quickly filling her in on the info. Olivia wouldn't make a scene at a party, would she? Old Olivia wouldn't, but new Olivia? The jury was still out...

7

NOBODY REALLY CARES IF YOU
DON'T GO TO THE PARTY

*T*he sun was starting to go down, and the first night's cocktail party would be beginning soon. There was still no sign or communication from the bride.

Migs had showed up early to set up lighting and the ridiculous addition of a step & repeat with the corporate logos of the bride and the groom, sandwiching the wedding's official logo. Another thing that seemed to come out of nowhere, clearly a later addition on Olivia's part.

Add hosting to the pile of things I am terrible at. Walking around a party, in my slightly socially awkward way, making sure everyone had a cocktail and a smile on their face, didn't exactly help my number one priority. But what Olivia wanted, Olivia got. That was the rule. *Always*.

Migs was being a terrible flirt, trying to get me in all kind of semi-suggestive poses, as well as surprise candid one. I gave him my poor excuse for a dirty look. "Migs, if you keep doing this, I'm throwing you and that $2800 camera right off this into the water."

"Take it easy." He took his camera out of reach and then rummaged through his bag, pulling out a fairly substantial double-sided document. "Don't bankrupt me. I get docked for every shot on this list I don't get. Do you understand this kind of pressure?"

I grabbed the list, another recent addition of Olivia's which I hadn't been privy to. "I never saw this." The list was a whole new level or ridiculousness. My lifelong ability to keep her in check was disappearing quickly before my weary eyes. What other surprise additions lay before us?

Right on schedule, the guests started arriving, one group after the next. I'd never be able to pry her away from her party.

I'm never going to get a moment alone with Olivia.

Maybe it's better that I just wait until morning.

Maybe it's the responsible thing to do.

I still waited on the dock, under the pretense of wanting to welcome everyone. The last to show up was a group with Olivia. The group skipped down the dock together, only stopping for a quick kiss on the cheek. She whispered in my ear, "Don't worry, it's going to be fine," before disappearing into the crowd.

My moment had passed.

≈

As we walked up the dock, dreading entering the party already in full swing, Migs started taking random pictures, mostly focusing on me.

"No posing. As is." Migs smiled. "Sorrowful, bitter, beautiful, broken-hearted."

I reminded him, "I broke up with him."

"Doesn't mean it doesn't hurt." A moment of sincerity before he continued, "But they do say that the best way to get over someone is to get under someone else."

The party was too crowded. Both Olivia and Walter were washed, revamped, and gussied up. Olivia glided easily back into charming hostess mode. She was in her element as center of attention. Walter looked like a cross between crying all day and a really bad flu. Olivia smiled at me and mouthed, "Thank you." Walter looked meek and lost.

What had Olivia whispered to him to keep him quiet?

Was she going to try to keep this secret through the wedding?

Has she really become so out of whack to lose any sympathy for a dead friend?

Maybe not friend. Benefactor.

And then I was ambushed by Marianna. She was another one of Olivia's pretty friends (though not as pretty as Olivia, who always had to be number one among her friends). While growing up, she and Olivia had gone skiing and horseback riding together; all the things I couldn't do. Dance clubs. Surf camps. Bungee jumping. Kung Fu.

She consistently reminded me of the all too familiar feeling of the humiliation I felt when I was dancing, one of the other simple pleasures I was not well-trained in. I had never learned to ride a bike, so the phrase "it's just like riding a bike" had no meaning to me. Throw in the lack of skiing, knitting, and tennis, and my activities were pretty much limited to bowling and reading books curled up in my favorite window.

A glass of champagne was quickly in hand, and Marianna was smiling like the most carefree of souls.

"Lexie, you are actually looking rather good with a little sun. Too bad you didn't have time to have those dresses let out a little. But you still look just…lovely," Marianna was the queen of the backhanded compliment.

I grasped for some witty and cutting comment and found none, simply saying, "Come on, Marianna. That's not very nice."

She gestured to handsome Migs, having a quick glass of champagne before he embarked on his tasks. "You don't know how to flirt. I mean, at all," she judged.

"Really? Well, neither do you." Boy, I had made my point.

"As a friend, my advice is to step up the wardrobe. You aren't going to snag a husband wearing the Target collection." For as long as I could remember, her one and only goal was to get married. And to marry rich. So far, no takers.

"Smile!" Migs said, bouncing out of nowhere, his flash momentarily blinding me. "Let's see your best Cheeseburgers in Paradise look. Come on Lexie. Flash me those fabulous choppers. I'm utterly hot for your canines."

How could you not give a little smile at that?

Marianna patted me on the back as if I were a puppy and quickly walked away, heading right towards the hors-d'oeuvres. I noticed Olivia alone and tried to make a beeline.

Amanda made her way over to me, looking infinitely better than me in our matching dresses. "Where were you? You and Nico? Have you seen him? There's fashionably late and then there's call the cops late."

Don't call the cops. Please. Whatever you do.

"It's a very long story." I was weary.

"Another time then. Get your hosting groove back on." She took my hand and pulled me over to an older man standing alone. Starting then, this party was back to being my responsibility. "Have you met Walter's Uncle Gordon?" Amanda graciously introduced us.

I attempted a few more interactions, looking for a group where I could be comfortable. No one seemed to want to be interrupted by the least personable island guide. Olivia was always my safe place at a party, never minding me standing next to her while I became comfortable. Her mother seemed like a safe choice, but as I started walking towards her, a finger tapped on my shoulder, revealing Becky, intent on talking to me.

Becky had been Walter's right-hand assistant, and she had traveled with Walter and Nico for twenty business weeks of the year. Nico had been very devoted to this investment and to his best friend.

Olivia went through a period of time where she was sure Walter was cheating on her with Becky. For a smart woman, she tended to make bad choices in men along the way. The fact that Becky, a work associate, was invited to this intimate gathering was not in Olivia's plan, but Walter put his foot down on that one.

"Great party," Becky said, launching into a mile-a-minute commentary. "Great atmosphere, great piña coladas, great sound of those nutterbutter howler monkeys in the distance, if you stand in the far corner near the kitchen.

"Cool island, cool people, not so cool weather, but that's okay. Hot, hot, hot! I mean better than New York where it's like 18 degrees and everyone's mascara is running down their face while you walk to the subways or even when you wait for a cab. You can never get a cab anymore, did you notice? Really kills your mascara and your shoes and your sanity, right? Don't even start me on Uber surge pricing.

"I talk too much and sound crazy, but you seem like a good person to talk to and I'm maximizing. You know? Have you seen Nico?"

Maybe she had been waiting to talk all day, but I agreed with her after every minute of her random observations, both entertained by her and waiting for my chance to exit. With her big, eager eyes and stream of consciousness conversation, she was terribly charming.

Charming but exhausting.

I needed a breather and headed to the outer boundaries of the bar. Regular Josh was the only one not attached to anyone in the group. I grabbed two glasses of champagne and approached him, remembering the kind smile. *Sometimes, kindness goes a long way.* I walked over to him. "Do you mind if I join you?"

"Sure." He took my drink offering.

"I'm Lexie."

"I know."

"You wrote a book," I stated, reaching for any conversation.

He nodded. "Yes. You wrote a book too." His smile from the afternoon was nowhere to be seen.

"So, we both wrote books," I said, hoping to seem interested and interesting.

He-half-heartedly held up his glass to meet mine. "The difference being, that people actually read your book. That must have been nice." He pointed across the room to a tall sinewy bespectacled man, looking at everyone as if they were part of a sociological research study.

Lloyd. Black hair, smirking, creepy, but when he dressed up, somehow he was magnetic. *Dangerous.*

"But what I'd really like to do is write a book about him. That's Lloyd," he said. "In college, we called him The Dissector."

"I know," I said in fear. "I know all about The Dissector."

I'd read about him in with slam book with complete

fascination. We'd been repeatedly reminded about him. He was a doctor and medical researcher. In college, he took his biology and anatomy classes very seriously and was lauded uncomfortably by his medical peers on his ease, precision and passion with the scalpel. He was now an MD, Ph.D., and whatever other Ds there were. The fact that he may or may not be have gone on a serial killing spree was just the icing on the cake. Eventually, it became a big joke between Walter and his friends, but Josh never stopped taking it seriously.

Medical research.

Serial killing.

Please don't let me put this two and two together.

"You're right. He would make a great book," I commented, nervously fixated on Lloyd and Nico's intense interaction I'd noticed on the beach early today when we all arrived for lunch at Red Frog Beach.

"I think he killed those girls. I thought it then and I still think it. It added up. I was on campus at the time and we were all scared still. Horror-stricken, even. Still am in a way. Though sometimes I think I'll drop the idea altogether."

"Glad he's not staying at our hotel…"

"Don't worry. You aren't his type anyway."

My problem, perhaps—that I wasn't a type at all.

I wanted to ask more, but Olivia yelled from across the room, "Pay attention to me! I've got something to say."

She was a woman who loved speeches. She'd get in front of a group and speak, sometimes for far too long; anytime, anywhere, any subject.

She started, "Walter was going to speak, but he now feels very strongly about waiting for the big day. So, here goes nothing. We kept this wedding small because we wanted to spend serious quality time with everyone, and for our close friends and families to get to meet the small group we love with all of our hearts."

Close friends? I wasn't so sure about that. They were a mixed bag of nuts for sure. Unusual for sure, charismatic undoubtedly, but I would never have used the word close.

Walter had his arm around Olivia's shoulder, pulling her close, both of Olivia's arms around his waist. She looked around the party, catching each guest's eye before she started.

"When I was writing this speech - yeah, not off the top of my head - I wrote the word love 22 times. How many times can I say love? A lot. A lot more than 22. I'm going to keep this short because you'll be hearing more of this from me probably every night. A lot. You know, after a month of dating Walter, I staggered away from a lunch with him, didn't go back to work, and wandered Manhattan, thinking that I had so much love for this man that I didn't even know how to process it. That I didn't know where to start." Olivia was glowing, staring at him with adoration. "It was the best day of my life at the time. It really was." Instead of kissing, they hugged, tightly, as if their lives depended on it.

Had anyone ever loved me a fraction of that much?

People clapped instead of toasting. Hooray for love.

Through my sad Salty breakup mode, I could still be so proud of her. Despite the last year, she was the closest thing to a sister I ever had. For better or for worse?

My conversation with Josh seemed to have unceremoniously run its course. "Well, I guess duty calls," I said, referring to nothing.

"Got it," Josh nodded to himself. As I walked away, he grabbed my arm. "Hey, by the way, I really understood your book. I didn't put two and two together at first, that you were the author, but I'm impressed. I didn't know you wrote it until Becky told me. We're here all week so maybe we'll have a chance to talk when you aren't on the clock."

I appreciated the enthusiasm, though I hated going through the whole story repeatedly. "Another time, I would happily talk about it."

After all, we'd be here for a week.

~

DAY TWO

~

8
LEFT BEHIND

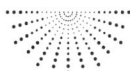

I was wide awake at the break of dawn, having tossed and turned over visions of Nico dead and an anonymous person snorkeling through the water with a huge needle in their fist. I turned over, thinking it was the normal time to get up, and had the horrible realization that it was 5:45.

It was pointless to try to go back to sleep. Dressing was a chore because I had hardly anything of my own to put on. Olivia had allowed only one carry-on suitcase from each member of the bridal party to ensure we'd stick to the prescribed garb. I headed out to my favorite hammock. It looked like rain, which wasn't a big deal in itself. Rain on the island was a twenty-minute downpour, and then a return to hours of sunlit paradise. Repeat. All day. We were officially in what was referred to as the rainy season.

Olivia's wedding was well on the way to being ruined. She'd be picking me up at 9 a.m. to go to the final breakfast summit of the bridesmaids, where I could finally try to talk some sense to her.

Olivia would freak out, and I somehow felt responsible. What could I do to bring her back to the semi-real world? I found myself paralyzed with fear of even starting a conversation. I stretched my hand down to the wooden deck and tried to sway myself a little in the beautiful hammock, seeking some kind of inspiration to help me delve into the mystery of Nico's snorkeling misadventure.

Left Behind. Ryan had also read my book, and that put a smile on my face. He had been one of three people to bring up the book to me in the last 24 hours, so it seemed that I'd have to suck it up and tell my story once again.

Five years ago, on my thirtieth birthday, thinking that life had passed me by, I cried at Olivia's apartment as she served a failed red velvet birthday cake. I sobbed into my hands, admitting my thoughts that I would be alone forever.

Now, at the advanced age of thirty-five, I could see it was ridiculous to feel that way at the age of thirty. I had spent almost five years living with someone I didn't care about, both of us wasting our time, though, hopefully, there was learning and growth. But now I found myself back in the same place. Would I feel the same about thirty-five, looking back from forty?

My desperation was what lead up to the beginning of the Left Behind Club, which was a very popular Friday night pity party. The gathering was based on a drunken metaphor I had conceived of - meeting at a joint called Loki on the Lower East Side.

Loki was named after the shape-shifting, wily, trickster Norse god. His attributes included complete lack of concern for the well-being of his fellow gods. He was solitary among the gods, which was the only thing in keeping with the Left Behind Club's philosophy.

My concept of the Left Behind Club had started after

someone had left the born-again sci-fi book of the same name at my apartment. I devoured it in about six hours, alone on a temperate night in May.

The storyline involved something about a 747 flying somewhere over Kansas City when all of a sudden all of the good, pure, churchgoing people disappeared in the blink of an eye. Including the pilot. Two and two were put together and it seems that those who disappeared had ascended to heaven in the Rapture, and all the folks of questionable worth and morals were left on earth to wander the lonely deserted streets.

Thanks to a benevolent god, you'll be relieved to know that two of the remaining passengers managed to land the plane, with help from the now skeleton crew at air traffic control. According to this book, the leftover Earth dwellers were given another seven years to get it right. Good people gone, dregs of society remaining.

At thirty, it dawned on me that I had closed my eyes for a second too long, just a fraction of a moment. All my contemporaries, now wedded, partnered and loved, had ascended to their secret little love coves, and the rest of us were in a tainted dirty pool of singles Left Behind. Lesser Beings. Alone and lonely, and still on the shelf, we were looked upon as suspicious spoiled goods. Defective.

No one is honest with friends about what is wrong with them, even in the simplicity of pretending not to see those giant pimples smack dab in the middle of your forehead. I started poking Olivia with truths about her and then had the biggest knock down argument of our friendship. We'd been cut to the bone by each other, but ultimately we emerged enlightened. In turn, I understood that I had to get to the gym, wear a little make-up, and generally not be so maudlin. I was askew, annoying, but maybe, just maybe, I was fixable.

Olivia and I decided this service could be of help to other people, so we called a dozen other singles who we knew to meet up for drinks a week later. With an all-night tone of no apology, we dissected the first volunteer, dear old Marianna. She was ripped apart aesthetically, philosophically, practically, down to her soul. Eventually, I couldn't decipher who said what, but it slowly worked into a tempered frenzy.

Olivia jumped ship after this first meeting. "I'm not like these losers," she said to me, referring to myself and her close circle of friends. "I don't need this to fix my life."

Determined as ever to prove she was right, she went off, abandoned writing, and opened her incredibly successful pseudo-gym. Two years later she was engaged to the perfect guy.

Not me. The meetings became a weekly thing, and I became the ringleader.

Around that time, Salty came on to the scene. He was a friend of a friend of one of the early members. His comments to the group were often too caustic and biting. When it came time for us to rip him to shreds, I was ready.

"Why don't I start?" I said, halfway into the ceremonial toast of the first shot of Jamieson's whiskey. "Firstly, your name is off-putting. It's stupid and seemingly not short for anything. And those glasses that you think make you look so smart? They don't. Unless it's Opposite Day.

"And this novel you are writing that no one has seen... I mean, what, where is it? This brilliant novel. You very well might be a brilliant copywriter. I mean, what you did with the Skittles campaign should get you a Pulitzer, but we are sick of hearing about the great American novel, which no one believes you have written. It doesn't exist and it bores everyone to death to have to hear about your literary genius.

Do you want to be a writer or do you want to write? Show it to someone or shut up about it."

We finished up with ritual applause, hugs, and pats on the back, and went into our normal cocktail hour. When I lowered my face to the bar for the first challenging sip of my martini, Salty attacked, pushing me through the small, weak crowd that surrounded me. He challenged, "You bitter, solipsistic wench."

Who says solipsistic in a fight? I pushed him back. He stumbled, regaining his stance, nostrils flaring like a bull.

We were separated by an excited group who had probably not participated in a fight since high school, if ever, and pulled us to our corners.

"You really don't think I've written anything? Come on." He grabbed my hand, leading me out the door. We cabbed it in silence to his apartment, a surprisingly nice doorman building on lower 5th Avenue. He took me into his office and said, "Sit." He sat me at his desk, opening a file on the computer. He grabbed my head and focused me on the screen, saying, "Read."

RESET BUTTON by Ezekial McManus.

With a name like that, I understood why he went by Salty.

He walked out of the room, so I read. It was funny, polished and complex. It was very good. He came back into his office as I was about thirty pages in. Somehow, I was embarrassed to look at him, knowing him far better than I did an hour ago.

Maybe though, no matter how you dress it up, your book is you.

He aggressively kissed my neck just long enough to know that I wasn't objecting, then pulled me off the chair and kissed me passionately in his arms. His kisses were too deep and too hard, teeth covered by lips grinding into my gums. I suppose you'd say we'd been together ever since, while we bided time until something better, hopefully, came along.

Soon after that Salty stopped going to meetings. He wanted me to stop as well, as we were no longer "Left Behind." He said that he thought that he probably loved me and that I had "characteristics which had become endearing."

I couldn't leave Left Behind. I had a responsibility. The club just kept getting bigger, proof enough that it worked. I had always been too scared to be ambitious, but an associate editor named Lanie approached me after a session and she convinced me to pitch the book concept with her. A book advance had followed, large enough to get me a year free of 9-5 office work, coupled with a two-book deal. Set for life, I thought.

Though Olivia had distanced herself from the concept that she was ever alone, she worked through draft after draft with me. The one caveat being that I wouldn't even mention her in the acknowledgments.

Left Behind had a decent response and a moment of success. The next book fizzled before it was even lit. My publisher dropped me, but I had a third chance with a fledgling imprint that took a last chance on me. To their major regret, the book ended up selling nothing, quickly in the 99-cent pile on the sidewalk in front of Borders, no one really caring if it was stolen or not. It wasn't worth the room it would take up in the warehouse. I was a one-hit wonder, as the latter two were so invisible that no one even knew they had failed, let alone existed.

Maybe if I could just waste away, swaying in the faint mist of the Panamanian rainfall, things would be okay.

"Lexie," Becky enthusiastically greeted me from her terrace, two cabins down. She was dressed and ready to go; bathing suit, cover-up, big white sunglasses, abs you only read about in books. "Join me for coffee?" she loudly said, not caring too much about who else she might wake. Three and a half hours until the next event and it looked like I was trapped until then.

"Sure." It was in the job description, after all. I walked back inside, and really just wanted to grab my cut off shorts and favorite t-shirt proclaiming *Whatever Happens in Transylvania, Stays in Transylvania*. It was red, which pleased Olivia, but she had ended with the caveat, "Please can you not wear it where anyone can see you?"

I quickly reread the notes about Becky from the slam book: 27, San Diego born and bred, studied business, and travels to Hong Kong once a year. "Don't get stuck next to her" was written in all caps. "And it is not super important to be nice to her either."

THE WALK to the restaurant was always a comforting view. The structure was built of deep stained local wood, completely open to the elements. No windows, no hammock to protect you from those sun showers; just ten tables always topped with some amazing local treat.

When I entered the restaurant, Becky waved, patting the seat of the chair next to her, as if there was a question of where I'd sit. She launched into a monologue about the flight, which quickly segued into a story about a pilot named Wrong Way Corrigan, who in the 1930's thought he was on route to California and ended up in Ireland.

"Anyway," she said, downing her coffee in one giant sip. "I've been wanting to talk to you since I found out that you were going to be here. Your book changed my life. Completely. Own it, own it, own it - you wrote that three times, and I did. My friends hung, drew and quartered me.

Sheesh! And I fixed it ALL. Except I did not get my ears pinned, but I've found a way to fix my hair to avoid that."

She held her hair above her head, showing off her elfin Prince Charles ears. "Wow! You are thinking, Wow! I know. So anyway, me and my friends got together and super trashed each other, but I think they were holding back, so I thought maybe you could call me out on what is wrong, wrong, wrong with me. I love how you write words three times in a row. Dissect me, please?"

A few years ago, at around the same time I decided I was too old for mini-skirts, I had retired my habit of repeating words three times in a row.

"I can't do that for you, Becky. It's just a very bad idea."

Over the years I learned that the theory of Left Behind didn't work. It made things worse. Illusion was good for people. So were flaws.

"Please, please, please. It's all I've been thinking about since I knew you were going to be here."

"I don't even know you. How can I tell you what's wrong with you?"

"Perfect. First impressions. That's what it's about. All, all, all."

There were only so many times, coming up with a dozen different reasons, that I could insist that a stranger ripping into her was a bad idea. Not willing to take no for an answer, she dug into herself once again. She said she knew, but could not stop, her crazy way of talking.

After blushing, she begged me to tear her apart physically. I still refused, and to be honest, there wasn't much to tear apart, so she took over again. She showed me how one eye was bigger than the other and her knock knees. She didn't need my to help rip her apart. She did well enough on her own. What a shame that such an eccentric gal couldn't see that her faults were what made her.

"Speaking of Nico?" she seriously asked. "Have you seen him?"

Thankfully, Walter's brother Dave and his girlfriend Georgie walked in for breakfast, and I excused myself and intruded on the couple's coffee and orange juice. After a few minutes of intelligent laughter, Georgie kindly asked, "Do you think that I could have my phone for a few minutes? Just a few?"

Dave smiled in a way to make clear he was seconding that suggestion.

"You know I would," I assuaged, "but I don't even know where they are. Olivia took them..."

He rolled his eyes. "Of course she did."

And the day had begun.

9

WHAT FRESH HELL IS THIS?
(DOROTHY PARKER)

*D*on't step on a crack or you'll break your mother's back. *Or something like that.*

Escaping from Becky and the quest for the phones, I wandered, looking down at my feet as I carefully strolled over the walkway. Though it was beautiful, and the other guests were happy to dive off their balconies into the calm clear sea, I was constantly concerned that someone was going to make that late night drunken stumble down the boardwalk. Two steps in the wrong direction and you'd be sleeping with the fishes.

Can't you just relax for once?

Looking forward to and desperately needing a still early morning nap, the once familiar, now noxious smell of cigarette smoke met me at the door of my bungalow.

The killer knows I know. And my days are numbered.

I hadn't seen anybody out since I was sitting with Becky. I carefully opened the door to find Olivia in a chair in the corner, smoking a butt, looking like the little girl with the little curl when she was horrid.

How did she get in here? I didn't hear her speedboat. I didn't see her sneaking down the dock.

"Jesus, Olivia!" I exclaimed. "You scared me half to death. Why are you still smoking?" I asked.

"I'm not smoking," she said while exhaling a toxic cloud of smoke.

The light through the wicker shades gave Olivia a kind of film noir look that unfortunately Migs was not around to capture. She was dressed to the nines, 1950's style. She was beautiful. Even by her normal extra harsh standards, she was easily a 9 out of 10.

"I couldn't reach you. This phone service is going to put me in an early grave. Do you think I need this? There's only so much I can take," Olivia spouted.

"Can you please be a little more specific?" I rubbed my eyes. What couldn't go wrong this trip?

"I know everything. I know absolutely everything. About them."

For the sake of her make-up, she held back her tears. To cry was a verb she had stricken from her vocabulary, but she was close to relapse, at the tipping point between sobbing and chopping someone's head off with an axe.

Not me, I could cry for everyone. I wondered if there was a crying saint, and if there was not, could I be she? St. Lexie cries so you don't have to?

"And how could she do this to me?" She threw her hands up in the air. "Forget about Emma, how could he do this to me? I feel more betrayed by Ryan. Am I in a nightmare? Pinch me quick."

So I pinched her. With her, it wasn't just a saying.

Her voice had become uncharacteristically quiet and high, like a whispering mouse. It reminded me of her one awkward year - glasses, braces, and a visor she wore over her terrible haircut. She took a year off from being popular, becoming the shyest thing you could imagine, before getting contacts and rising to the top of the social structure once again.

Groggy and guilty, I slowly composed my response. "He didn't know it was your wedding. I really believe he didn't know. And they're off the island as soon as the airport is open."

"The airport is closed?!"

I forgot to mention that one.

What could I do when she only gave me two minutes yesterday?

"Well, I took care of them." She said.

I'd seen a million different expressions on Olivia's face over the years, but this one was new and downright diabolical.

She killed them. Please don't tell me that in not what she means.

She started to chain smoke and got comfortable, telling me the tale of her run-in with the couple the night before.

After the party, she took the Walter for a quick martini at a place called the Wine Bar that served everything but wine. The bar featured rickety, old, busted chairs perched atop a potentially unsafe floating deck.

Eventually. Walter decided to go back to his villa and enjoy his late-night impromptu bachelor party. While he waited for his water taxi, who walks in but her beautiful sister and the never forgotten Ryan?

She nodded casually, as if it were her mother and I who had walked in, and not the ingredients of our broken hearts. So she sat at the bar, watching the uncomfortable non-couple.

"And I thought, what would Cleopatra do?" she asked, like it was a normal question.

"Cleopatra? No idea."

"Ok, here's how it went down. I believe it was a success. I walked over to them and sat down. I tried to order the most expensive thing they had, but that only came to like $12, so there you have it. Ryan apologized. Really apologized. But Emma? My sister, my flesh and blood, my genetically predisposed likeness? She said nothing.

"I said that maybe it was time to bury the hatchet, since they had once been the closest people to me, and offered for them to come on my boat for expensive champagne and a tour of the island. As a surfer, Ryan couldn't resist."

"After midnight? In your boat? I know Ryan likes to surf, but...is this the truth?" The thought of them circling the island in the dark gave me the shivers.

"I'm a good driver. And the boat has lights. I'll admit it would have been easier earlier in the day, but I didn't really give them too much of a choice."

What did that mean?

Once they got to the rougher waters on the eastern side of the island, Olivia named off all the beaches they sped by. Bluff Beach, not great but you might spot a leatherback turtle. La Curba, where the surf breaks both ways. Dumpers, named after the nearby garbage facilities.

She finally cut the motor at the most dangerous beach on the island, Paunch Beach. Waves broke both right and left. The riptide was vicious, and at high_tide the beach disappeared altogether.

Olivia continued, "They had no idea what was coming. But I told them that, oh no, the hatchet was not being buried, but maybe they were about to be."

That's a criminal mind if I ever heard one.

"I pulled out their passports, which believe me were not easy to procure, and told them that they better meet me at the airport in the morning so I could escort them on the noon flight out. If they didn't show, I'd take the passports, shred them, scatter them in the ocean, and wish them luck to ever getting off the island."

Great idea, if the airport wasn't closed.

"Come on," she said. "We've got a bridesmaid meeting to get to, and I'm ripping everyone a new one."

Would I be able to have her committed this far from America?

I grabbed my book and bag, wearing a terrible red eighties off the shoulder, sweat suit material mini-dress. As soon as we got on the boat, she launched into her recent mantra.

"Don't tell Walter about the frogs. Don't tell Walter until he needs to know. Okay?" She seemed to compose herself. "This is really not what I need. I've got pages full of terrible things to be remedied already. Really not what I need…"

She turned the key to the boat, turned to me, turned away. Repeat. "I'm going to say something really terrible. Really bad. Do you think that there's going to be a problem with Nico paying for the wedding still? I think everything was paid up front, but I can't cover what wasn't. Oh god, that's really terrible. Really terrible. Forget I said that. Please, forget I said that."

But you did.

Then she took off, lurching out into the water. Thankfully, this boat had seatbelts I could wear over my safety vest.

It wasn't in her nature to believe that she couldn't excel at something immediately. Sometimes this trait was annoying. Sometimes it was strangely and indefinably endearing. But that was Olivia. I'd seen twenty-five years of it, in various incarnations. The mold had been broken when she was born and, depending on the day and on her whimsical moods, I wasn't always sure if that was a good or bad thing.

She yelled for me to come up to sit with her, and cut the motor again, lurching off again as soon as I sat. She spelled out to me the latest crisis, nervously yelling over the running motor. "And you aren't going to believe it. It gets even worse. It's hair, teeth, and eyes all over the place," Olivia cried out, quoting our favorite seventh-grade teacher.

"I'm having what you might call an attack of the panic," she said as we headed off to Coral Cay, hands down our favorite restaurant, on the coast of, well, Coral Cay. Since we'd arrived on Saturday, we'd eaten lunch there three days out of four. You'd order, snorkel, eat and then were encouraged to throw your leftovers to the fish clamoring around the dock.

"Olivia. Just slow down. We can get through this together. We've gotten through worse." Technically, we hadn't, but... "Just slow down. Calmly tell me what is happening."

Olivia's immediate crisis was merely about a woman named Elena, the hair stylist, who was due to be flying in from Panama City. She had disappeared the previous week into the depths of Southern Panama's Darien jungle, from where fair ladies sometimes don't return.

As well as being one of the best wedding stylists in Panama, she was an adventurist hiker and didn't heed the warnings to stay away from the Parque Nacional Darien, which shared a border with Colombia. Despite it all, despite the official warnings that the area had always been, and still was, thick with paramilitary groups, drug gangs and random kidnappers of both American tourists and super sexy gals of all nationalities, Elena decided to hike.

The Darien jungle was the only gap in the Pan-American Highway which otherwise stretched from Prudhoe Bay,

Alaska to Ushuaia, Argentina. No highway existed in the jungle between Colombia and Panama in both countries' futile attempt to eliminate drug trafficking.

Irrelevant but interesting, this darkest of dark places was also home to the Tropic Star Resort on the Pacific Coast. It was the number one deep sea fishing resort in the world, host to the rich and famous. I hoped that Elena had been whisked away by love, onto the movie-star-of-the-moment's vessel and was trapping prize Giant Cubera Snappers, not falling prey to the horrifying alternative.

Lovely Elena, hairdresser to the Panamanian stars, should have known better.

"This is so terrible. Not just about the hair. I mean she was an amazing woman. She won't be forgotten." Olivia was already referring to her in past tense. Six weeks before, the bride-to-be had spent three days down in Panama City having her hair done by anyone with a comb and a blow dryer. Now her best of the best was gone.

"Olivia," I offered, trying to mitigate the possibility of her tears. "You look beautiful with your hair in a ponytail. We'll find someone else. It will be okay.

"Lexie," she said, clearly now past the point of no emotional return, "you've seen the pictures. You know that not just anyone could begin to attempt that."

True. I had seen the pictures of the proposed hair-do, and it might have been for the best that Elena had gone missing.

"You must have kept all the ratings of the other stylists you saw. See if you can get number two."

Olivia softly said, "I don't want number two. As somebody I can't remember at all once said, there is first place and then there is losing."

And Nico was certainly the loser in this one.

At Coral Cay, sitting five around a table was a tight fit, we were ready for the onslaught of Olivia's dictation, with binders out and pens poised. Marianna and Amanda had already been there for a bit, giggling over watered-down fruity drinks in scratched plastic cocktail glasses.

Olivia slammed her binder on the table and immediately apologized, quietly whispering some mantra under her breath. She put on her Buddy Holly glasses, which I hadn't seen since she had pretended to need them as a writer.

She was about to take everything out on her bridesmaids. To be honest, we had started to get used to it.

The hair issue was just the tip of the iceberg, it seemed.

"So it's crazy down here, I know, and there are a million moving pieces and I can't thank you enough. I mean really, what would I do without you except curl up and die. Just so you know," she sweetly said, "I'm not mad at any of you. We just have situations that are through the roof nuts. Marianna." Olivia said, smiling.

"Okay, yeah. Okay?" Marianna answered like she'd been caught out stealing.

"So, travel arrangements? I thought you'd checked all travel arrangements for personality conflicts, et al?"

"Yes," Marianna apologetically answered.

"Well, it turns out that my parents, who haven't spoken for 20 years, and their respective spouses ended up on the same flight."

"I just got confused with your mom's new name. But they weren't on the same flights from Boston, just from Panama City, and the seats were as far apart as possible."

"It's a 30-seat plane."

"Sorry," Marianna looked into her drink, ready to cry.

"It's okay. I know I'm getting crazy, but it's like oil and water. Or oil and vinegar. I don't know. Really more like gasoline and a lit cigarette. Toads on toast."

She checked something off in her book. "So then, Amanda, there is another little issue with my mother. I'm not mad, but you switched things around and now have my mother where I'm staying. I can't be running around naked with my mother sitting on the deck. So, change it around and you switch with my mom."

She was determined to be without the hint of a tan line and had booked herself into the luxury clothing optional resort.

"Can't I switch her with someone else? I don't want to be naked." Amanda clearly thought she was being punished, and maybe she was.

"You don't have to be naked. You have to be convenient!"

"I don't want to see naked people. There are almost three dozen people who can move there...."

"Fine," Olivia snapped, pursing her lips.

Phil, who hadn't screwed up, was just enjoying the show, with a wry smile on his face. Olivia triple checked everyone's plan for the day, but the last screw up was mine.

Though she had snapped repeatedly at everyone through this process, she had somehow been able to not lash out at me. Never a snarky word, an evil look, a passive-aggressive email. But that was about to change.

"Lexie," she said softly, contemplating if she was going to treat me as she'd been treating others. The answer became obvious. "Really, not smooth hosting last night. I'm taking you off running this morning's bird watching. Phil, start memorizing birds. I know that there's a bare neck umbrella bird and like twenty others. I just cannot chance it." Olivia said, peering at me over the top of her thick black frames. "I'm sure you understand."

She smiled, but Olivia was gone.

10

MAD ABOUT MAX

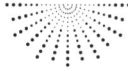

*T*he biggest lesson of my trip so far, besides not to ever go snorkeling, was never say that things can't get worse because they can. Olivia floundered off in her boat with the other bridesmaids to the bird watching event and left me to take a water taxi back home.

Logistically I couldn't care less, but I was hurt that I was taken off bird watch duty. They truly were astounding peaceful creatures of which I had memorized every name and fact. The purple throated mountain gem, white-tailed emerald, and black guan were among my favorite.

All I had to do was wait in my cabin for the police or Olivia to beckon. More than likely, both.

It would be virtually empty when I got back to Mariposa del Mar, everyone having been shuttled off to the unbelievable San San-Pond Sak Wetlands of the La Amistad UNESCO Biosphere Reserve. It just didn't get better than there.

Completely disenfranchised, I trudged up the dock to find that the restaurant was not empty; one solitary soul was sitting facing the sea. She was wearing the kind of enormous hat that you only see in 1930's movies or silly couture runway shows. The items of the gift baskets I'd work so hard to put together were scattered around her like Christmas.

Boy, was putting together those baskets a pain in the patootie. Snorkel gear, pre-sized jelly shoes, both a flashlight and an oil torch, a bottle of Krug champagne, suntan lotion and an abundance of condoms. Incorrectly sized fins. Water, maps, floppy hats, cover-ups, etc. Red Ray Ban Wayfarer sunglasses, a six-pack of Panama beer, bath oil. A flash drive with music to remember the couple by. Nothing except the beach tote was monogrammed, as statistics said any other monogrammed items get chucked within six weeks post-event.

She was reading the schedule of events for the wedding while drinking a glass of champagne topped with a sweet Panamanian fruit called the *mamon chino*. The unbelievably silky red hair and porcelain skin of Max, Nico's estranged wife.

Is God playing a joke on me?

Is it something I did in another life?

If so, please believe I'm sorry. For whatever it was.

When I reached the table, she apathetically smiled, saying, "Hey, you."

I'd had a good half dozen conversations with her over the past few years, but she usually pretended to forget my name, as if she was too good to remember. She did make me incredibly insecure.

"I'm Olivia's friend, Lexie."

"Of course you are." Her aristocratic British accent was intimidating in itself.

She snapped her fingers like only the incredibly rude posh population of English do. Flozzie, the bartendress/owner made her way over, as Max asked in perfect Spanish, *"Una copita de champán, por favor?"* As Flozzie left, Max explained, "I just ordered you a glass of champagne."

Yes, I'm not stupid.

You are truly horrid.

But how and why are you here?

"When did you get here, Max? I thought the airport was closed...because of weather..." There was not a cloud in the sky.

"Separate rules for private jets, of course, for incoming traffic. Maybe two hours ago? I can't do commercial anymore. Don't you find it tedious?"

No, I love flying coach, shuffling through first class with all the people who are pretending they don't see those of us in cattle class.

Don't let her get to you.

I didn't answer, nor did she expect me to. She continued, "I see that Nico's luggage isn't here. Is he somewhere else?"

I hated lying but it had become a necessity since the day before. "I don't think he liked it. I think he moved to the La Lapisita resort."

That hotel didn't exist, but what could I say? I hadn't lied since I was 14 and was caught forging notes to school asking to be dismissed from class after lunch. Now I was turning into a two-faced so and so.

"We didn't know you were coming, Max. Nico didn't mention."

"He never does. Like everyone's supposed to know his mind and bend to his beck and call. We are trying to reconcile once again, for the sake of our son. He asked me to come. I thought about it, and why not? I've never been to this strange island before. And this place is...quaint...in its way..."

I looked at her plate. She'd picked a bit at my favorite Panamanian breakfast tamale: cornmeal, seasoned chicken, and raisins, presented in banana leaves. Not up to snuff, obviously.

"Anyway," she said, observing me as if I were help. "I think I'll pass on this bird watching trip. Not my scene, lovely. Check out the island. There must be some staff who can take me around. I'll find Nico later. I always do. Being soul mates is rarely easy."

She walked away towards what should have been Nico's cabin without looking back even to wave goodbye.

11

DON'T LICK THE FROGS

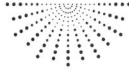

I felt like a doorman at a five-star hotel. We'd called a water taxi for Max, but she wouldn't wait outside, so I had to fetch her when it arrived, and then still wait ten minutes for her to appear, looking like a model out of a REI catalog.

"Thanks, you!" she said as she left in the boat.

She must have remembered my name, right?

Soon I saw that I wasn't going to get the afternoon rest I'd so coveted, as Detectives LaGuardia and McDonough walked into the restaurant and over to me. McDonough simply said, "This isn't looking good. Do you want to come with us, Tall Girl?"

No.

I want Nico to magically sit up and say, "God damn third-world medicine. Now I've missed the party."

"Yes," I weakly said. "But can you remember my name is Lexie?"

LaGuardia chuckled, "Of course we know your name is Lexie. Lexie Milano, with an Italian last name. We give everyone we're fond of a nickname. Which is why Dr. Nolan doesn't have one."

They'd got the bad news about the poison while they were surfing, so they came right to get me, of course not being able to get through on my phone. They were both wearing board shorts and tank tops, two surfboards in the back of what must have been one of their personal boats.

I said yes. I don't think that I meant it, but it was now my duty.

LaGuardia sat down next to me on the boat, curiously commenting, "This wedding you are part of, it's really packing a punch on this island. The whole town knows about it. I guess there's a lot of, well, it's not my place to say. I've seen plenty of ridiculous things on this island, but having limos ferried in from Costa Rica to get messed up on these off roads… silly doesn't begin to describe."

I never passed on a chance to apologize for things that weren't close to my fault. "It's starting out a little crazy, but it will settle. We aren't all so high maintenance. I didn't even know about the limos. But I'm sorry…" It was true that I didn't know about the limos.

"You should be a little more decent to the island that's hosting you. It's not my place to say. It's not… though tourism is here to serve you, you've gone a little bit to the extreme in your treatment of people on the island. I'm not blaming you."

Who was taking care of these mystery limos?

I worried, concentrating on the scenery for the rest of the ride, cruising by rainforests and mangroves, capuchin monkeys watching you watch them. They knew something we didn't.

Paulo the herpetologist met us on the dock. I was told he was a slightly sleazy scientist, no stranger to the local prostitutes, who spent his days off with them, tanning in the open-air brothels.

"They call him Crabby Paolo," McDonough said, "and that's not because of a surly disposition or because he's a carcinologist…."

LaGuardia added, "Carcinologist is a snobby way to say crab scientist."

The research station was right off the beach, looking like a very long ranch house at the end of the widest and longest dock I'd seen on the island. We walked into the cool lobby and waited; the only air-conditioned building I'd been in so far.

The detectives spoke to each other down the hall from me, giving me time to take out the slam book. I didn't know who knew Nico and who didn't. No one liked him, but it didn't seem like anyone in the book would have any reason to get rid of him.

The only motive I could think of was general disdain of a man who was rotten to the core. Up until yesterday, people seemed to forget about his dark side, seeing they were getting an all-expense paid vacation to paradise. Generous on the surface, but ultimately about control. It was always about control with the very wealthy. Money meant nothing to him, so he used it, and people, like a game.

After a short wait, Paolo emerged from the labs, inviting the detectives and me in with gusto. Paolo ushered us into the laboratory, letting me pass before him, not hiding the fact that he was checking out my butt in surly and lecherous ways. He had gorgeous blue eyes that were so intense I immediately felt dirty, as if he had a layer of smarm covering him and it had rubbed off on me. He was way too many steps beyond bad boy. He was something you'd want to wash off.

"Nice needle, BTW. Surprised the tip could break but not

my field of expertise. That is US-manufactured, born and bred. But, you guys are on fire! It's frog secretion, uh-huh, but I have to have the guys at the Gamboa station do the final specific analysis. They're super excited to get their hands on this as soon as we can get it over. Dr. Nolan seems to be right for once.

"Durán needs to take a look before I can tell you the specific toxicology. We talked it out. He's fascinated. First item on the list as soon as it hits the station. I tested it on a few mice and they went belly up in minutes. I cannot conclude to you that it is an oophaga pumilio... your red poison frog that is... because though I stress that it's the only known poison frog in this region, but we do find new species all the time. IMHO, you should wait for the official word."

The needle tip would go out on the medical plane, which was taking "the dead guy" to Panama City, the only flight currently cleared to leave the island.

"Well," McDonough said to me, "how about that? Fascinating."

LaGuardia said, "I've seen the signs saying not to lick the red frogs, but wow, I thought that was just an inside joke to play with tourists. But this could narrow it down. How many people are going to have any knowledge of how to make the modern equivalent of a blow dart?"

Lloyd. That's your man. Take the keys and lock him up.

Suspecting Lloyd was my kneejerk reaction, but that wasn't quite fair considering the facts.

I muttered, "Well, actually, everyone I know down here does. I was teaching people about making blow darts yesterday. It was part of the entertainment."

Trying to explain the training, planning, and scheduling behind the wedding bored and annoyed them quickly. And all these fun loving guests, save a few, were in the water, masked and identically garbed.

"See, I can't swim," I exclaimed, knocking myself out of the motive pool.

"Did you see anything strange?"

Stranger than a large group of people doing a dead man's float over a school of sea turtles?

No, but Migs would have. Underwater photography was going to clean this up in

a flash. The detectives were delighted at how quickly this all was coming together.

~

MIGS WAS shirtless on the deck of his hotel, Tango Vista, the subpar quarters for Olivia's staff and exiled relations. Nonetheless, he was drinking a beer, happy in his habitat, and impressively reading a thick biography about FDR, while a dozen other random cocktailers started to get their buzz on. He knew he looked good. He counted on it.

The sound of a motor turning over refocused our attention. Olivia and Walter were pulling away from the hotel on her speedboat, leaving the resort.

"Olivia!" I yelled after her, drowned out by her motor. "Olivia!"

She finally smiled and waved. Showing up on a police boat with two surfing detectives didn't seem to tip her off to the fact that something hadn't gone quite right.

Quite convenient...

We walked towards Migs, and he smiled at me, looking momentarily jealous of the two handsome locals behind me. He was shocked about the murder, leading us immediately up to his room to look at his underwater documentation.

The door to his room was ajar and the sunlight flooded the room, illuminating chaos and destruction. There hadn't been much in the room to destroy, but everything was shattered. His two camera backs were smashed, tripods were thrown in the corner, and dozens of rolls of exposed film were strewn around the room like party streamers.

"Oh, Jesus," Migs exclaimed, immediately dropping to the floor, cradling his medium format Hasselblad like a sick child. Flash tubes were broken to smithereens, shards shimmering in the light like diamond chips.

"It will all be replaced," I said softly, offering out of Olivia's own bank account. Nico wouldn't be picking up this tab.

"This cannot be happening. This is not happening," Migs yelled at no one in particular, eyes still on his destroyed tools of the trade.

McDonough picked up a roll of exposed film and examined it, holding it up towards the ceiling. Olivia's insistence in using actual film exclusively was biting us hard in the butt.

LaGuardia put his hand on Migs' back. "I'm sorry. I really am. But I need to ask, is there any way we can save anything on that film?"

Migs shook his head and leaned against the bed in shock.

LaGuardia continued, "We're going to find out who do this."

I confirmed, "And this will all be replaced."

Migs just stared at the tens of thousands of dollars' worth of beloved camera equipment. Fun in the sun would have to wait.

12

PUBLIC ENEMY #1

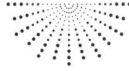

The detectives were talking intently in Spanish, McDonough taking notes all the while. The slam book was becoming an interesting tool. I could rule out Marianna and Walter's mother, who had not gone in the water. Including myself, that made three innocent guests. Plus Max, but she didn't count. So then there were 35 suspects left.

The silly slam book had ruined the mystery for me; not in a Caribbean murder caper way, but in a human way. Everyone had skeletons in their closets, but knowing them all ahead of time made me feel all the more isolated. There was no need to discover things about people if you already knew the end of the story.

It had begun as stats and FYIs and deteriorated into a serious case of Olivia dirt digging. You couldn't separate fact from filth. For instance, yes, I needed to know Colleen, Olivia's Princeton roommate, was allergic to shellfish, but I didn't need to know that she had been issued a restraining order by an ex-boyfriend in 2002. It was innocent enough, Olivia had said, and left it at that.

All the guests were gluten-free these days. Olivia's neighbor Chad didn't eat tomatoes. And Walter's movie producer friend, Theresa, didn't like any of her food to touch. That was needed information. I didn't need to know that she stripped to pay for college. I didn't have to read it all, but like a car crash, I couldn't walk away. Theresa was also allergic to bees.

After Theresa's page came Walter's, where it was written in big blood-red letters: "Walter is a serious diabetic. Confirm that he does go into diabetic shock." It seemed I had stumbled one step closer to the truth, the suspect list potentially diminishing to those who had access to Walter's villa.

"LaGuardia," I called, excited at my findings, "Walter has needles! Someone must have got one from him!"

"Or maybe it was just Walter himself. More likely the case," LaGuardia said.

I clearly hadn't thought that one out very well.

The conversation went back to English, now that I might be of some help. Migs concentrated on his experiences with Walter, whose bachelor party he'd been taking photos of the night before, much later than he was scheduled to be working. There had been a dozen people, but no one was allowed to enter his Red Frog Beach villa. Walter knew that his friends were already way too drunk and he didn't want anyone passing out or puking in his fat pad.

"Major suspect found in less than 24-hours," McDonough noted and gave his partner a high five. Probable cause didn't concern them much; authorities were allowed to detain anyone for 72 hours on suspicion.

Walter was staying in Casa Paradiso, a 2-bedroom villa at the Red Frog Beach Resort, with a private pool and all the expected luxuries. Walter wasn't around, but that wasn't going to stop the cops from having a good look. I'd never seen Walter's bachelor pad, but the beach house was probably representative of his New York City apartment.

There was certainly evidence that an after-hours man party had gone on the night before; empty beer and rum bottles, filled ashtrays (ironic for those so entrenched in the fitness industry), commemorative wedding condoms blown up as balloons, now half wilted like a bad metaphor.

While they rummaged around, I stepped outside to get an emergency call out to Olivia. I paced the length of the short pool, calling repeatedly with no connection available. It seemed like a thousand years since I'd woken up that morning.

I had failed my duties big time, and when it rains, it pours.

What could be worse than the best man being murdered? The maid of honor leading the cops toward suspecting the groom, that's what.

It wasn't my day. And it certainly wasn't Walter's.

13

GIVE ME BACK MY MAN

y usefulness to the detectives had soon run its course. After helping them come up with a list of possibilities of where they could find and question Walter, they took me back to my hotel. I'd become an annoying song stuck on repeat, insisting that they'd need me so they could talk with the groom. They told me that they had their job and I had mine, so let them get to it; I should go plan a party or something.

I guess we weren't the three musketeers.

Mariposa del Mar was empty when I returned, except for Becky, who sat reading on a lounge chair. Sitting up and giving me a huge smile, she called "Birds were a number one!"

I pretended to be on the phone and mouthed to her, "Wedding business," while holding my other hand up, questioning the universe.

My cabin was nice and cool. I sat on the bed upstairs in the loft under mosquito netting, finally getting through to Olivia, but not being able to get a word of my own in. It was a quick call. It turned out that the detectives had no intention of questioning Walter at all. They had immediately arrested him.

$$\sim$$

I MET Olivia outside of the police station. She'd been forcibly removed for what she would only refer to as a "minor scene." Her hair was piled on top of her head like a Samurai warrior and she was down to the butt of another cigarette.

We'd spent a lot of time five years ago getting her off the butts, but we could wait to work on that again until she'd get back from her honeymoon. Her reversion to chain smoking was the least of either of our problems right now.

Chain smoking, she ignored me and repeated to me in desperation that it turns out that Panamanian law stated that the police could hold someone for seventy-two hours on mere suspicion, and an arrest for up to three years with no chance of bail.

"You can fix it, can't you?" she whined, immediately regretting her tone. "Please. You're the smartest person I know."

That phrase was always the one that got me.

Though I don't think it was true.

She did cheat off me in math for most of elementary school. What a surprise to her AP Algebra teacher that she was not the genius she'd put forth. Well, you can't be perfect at everything.

But the glassy eyes of ten-year-old Olivia pleaded with me, now; Olivia was as lost as I'd ever seen her. She was looking at me with love and need, perhaps forgetting or ignoring that I was the reason that Walter was in prison.

She wasn't the pure and kind soul that she used to be, but I know that person was in there somewhere. Deep down.

I was now looking at the girl that risked her A-list junior high school popularity status by even standing next to me. She'd got me out of trouble a lot in our younger years, and if I was the only one she trusted, I'd just have to rise to that obligation.

$\sim$

IT WAS party central inside the station. The detectives and a few other officers, nearly the whole police force, were having congratulation beers for the swift success of their investigation. The island's tourism couldn't stand to have another Landis case on their hands. They'd quickly dismissed me less than two hours ago, but now they were welcoming me back into the gang. They were getting a kick out of this; Walter locked in an open cell with a six-pack of Soberana of his own.

His eyes brightened when he saw me, standing up. "Thank god you are here, Lexie. Explain to them how ridiculous this is."

LaGuardia and McDonough relived the tale of Olivia gone out of control. She had attempted to rip them a new one, yelling about their New York lawyers and how she'd make sure they'd crush all tourism on Bocas del Toro for the foreseeable future. 'What idiot,' she had said, 'would kill his best friend at his own wedding? Put your thinking caps on!' She had gone on to say that 'only a "backwoods badger-brained cop" would even for a second, look at the circumstantial drivel and implicate Walter'.

"She might have gone a little overboard," Walter admitted.

Now, she rambled on to the officers that it was impossible, that Walter had not been in Migs' room, that they'd been having a drink. Olivia tried to console Walter. She swore he had never left her side, absolutely, maybe.

She was pleasantly told that she needed to get out before they held her for suspicion as well. Before the door closed in Olivia's face, she strongly said 'contemptible vilification'.

We went over the scant, damning yet circumstantial evidence they had. LaGuardia ended the conversation with, "If it looks like a fish, and swims like a fish, it's a fish."

"You mean duck," I said.

"Potato potat-oh. Now go back to your party. And have a nice night."

I went back to the cell and clung on to the bars like I was in a bad movie. The kind of bad movie when you say things you never thought you'd say, like, "Don't worry. I'm going to get you out of here."

14

LA GRUTA

*O*livia was still waiting when I exited the station. She was pacing while on the phone with Lloyd, begging him to keep Nico's "state of non-existence" under wrap. She relayed that he didn't seem to mind and found it sorrowfully amusing, thinking that his late friend would get a kick out of it as well.

She smiled widely at me.

And then we fought.

We bickered all the time, like family, but seldom had a drag down, knock 'em out fight. She impatiently listened to my rundown of what happened in the station and she was resigned to the fact that Walter would indeed be spending the night in prison.

Then I said, "Let's go to a café and figure out how we are going to reschedule the wedding and how we can get everyone back home." There was no chance of saving the event.

Cancellation was still not an option in her crazy mind. She had an insane but convincing counter for every logical point I brought up. Between the cigarettes and the yelling, her voice was getting hoarse.

Olivia kept circling back to her moments in the police office. When she had seen that she was losing the fight with the detectives, she had begged them to not disclose to the general public that there had been a murder. Lucky for her, the police didn't particularly mind. They'd got their man, no one was in danger, and the island couldn't handle another murder in the press.

She couldn't tell the officers apart, but one of them had told her that if she wanted to go waste her time trying to clear his name, she was more than welcome. She took this as license to do what she wanted, and not the rhetorical rebuttal the detectives had intended.

Olivia took a romantic break to tell me about love. The wedding marked the third anniversary of their first trip to the island, and that was special enough for him. He had taught her how to dive here, and she had randomly taught him a few slight-of-hand hard tricks. This is also where they first said, "I love you."

He was a pretty decent guy. He really was.

The location had been a surprise to everyone, especially based on Walter's monied taste. It had been astonishing to arrive at the relatively remote location.

Olivia pulled me down the street, away from the docks, her voice cracking. "We know he didn't do it. These pseudo detectives are the laziest lazies in Lazyville, and if they're too lazy to figure out who did this, then it's up to us."

I already felt a loyalty to LaGuardia and McDonough. "They aren't that bad. They are doing their job."

"So you say…"

I followed her over to a rusty old jeep that she borrowed from the bartender at the Koko resort. Olivia navigated the small streets of the town and then drove north, on one of the island's two roads, deserted and humid, foreign insects at every step. The island was only four square miles so we couldn't be going too far.

But she might actually kill me.

By accident or otherwise.

Lighting another cigarette as we bounced down the rocky road, she said, "I'm sorry. You know I'm just not myself. Even I hate me right now."

No kidding.

Walter's best man was murdered and her fiancé was in jail, and to boot, Ryan and Emma never made it off the island.

"My oh-so-loving father found me today and refused to even come to the wedding unless I acted like an adult and let them stay. Can you believe this insanity?" Olivia took her eyes off the road and blew her smoke in my direction. "Emma probably killed Nico. Just to ruin my day. What do you think?"

I liked it better in the sun.

"So, Lex," she said, quickly switching back to semi-normal. "This was going to be a humungous surprise for everyone on Saturday, so you need to actually see the most important reason that this can't be postponed. Hell's bells, we just missed the turn."

She pulled an impossible U-turn, almost rolling the jeep, and then followed a partially covered sign pointing towards a place called La Gruta. We drove until the road deteriorated into an impassible state. Olivia's random path took us to a small statue of the Virgin Mary, masking the entrance of a cave. She had a flashlight clamped to her belt hook, running towards the entrance in a familiar way.

This struck me as 100% bad. Religious paraphernalia and

caves could only lead to human sacrifice or organ harvesting, in my humble opinion.

I was about to join the ranks of liverless ladies on vacation in Aruba, who had once said to their stupid selves, "Ooooh, an abandoned cave. Let me investigate." I was not a registered organ donor, sure that once you became one, your name went on a list, and then it was just a matter of time before the windowless white van would follow you home. The next thing you know, you wake up in a bathtub of ice with a note saying, "You have no kidneys".

We waded through a foot of water before coming to a clearing and the entrance to a bigger cave. She was the kind of person who'd go spelunking while I ate fruit salad in the cabana. I shouldn't have been surprised by this location. At the mouth, Olivia said, "Well, this is it. This is where we are getting married."

Gothic roots indeed. Mossy, dirty and inconvenient. Yet undeniably unforgettable.

She tapped her flashlight to make sure it was working and then switched it off. "So, exactly three days from now, give or take ten minutes, Colleen will pronounce us man and wife and then we kiss until this happens. Just give it a minute or two. This never happens. Only for one month every three years, does this happen every night. Thirty days every three years! That's how infrequently what you are going to see happens. We experienced it when we were here the first time, three years ago. You're going to flip your pretty lid. For sure. It's a mating thing, I think."

"What happens? I don't see." *Mass organ harvesting, obviously.*

Olivia made sure her feet were firmly planted and we stared at the cave. "You're going to love this." Her last words were drowned out by a rumbling from deep within the cave.

As if she was summoning Satan himself, she held her hands up towards the cave and smiled.

In the blink of an eye, just as the sun finally set completely, a whirling dervish of thousands of bats in rotational motion raced towards us. I screamed and dropped to my hands and knees, and into the mucky water.

Growing up night fishing with my dad, I knew about bats and sonar. Even though they were blind (cue the cliché), they would not fly into you, their interior tracking system knowing. Despite the density of their fury, they were gone in moments, leaving me on all fours, sweaty and covered in sludge. The bottom of my dress was absolutely ruined.

"What the hell, Olivia?" was the best I could muster.

She sat down next to me, wiping my hair out of my eyes. Crying and desperate, looking ever so much like my gothic best friend from high school, I understood that this was her pièce de résistance.

She took my hand, "See? Now you understand."

15

THE SCAVENGER HUNT

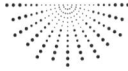

*T*he evening's activity was to be held at the Mono Loco resort, just a skip and a jump north of Bocas Town. Like many of the resorts, the cabins were over water; a dark wood walkway connected the six brightly painted cabins. The narrow boardwalks were certainly a recipe for at least one drunk reveler falling overboard. Water taxies were all queued up to take the guests on their scavenger hunt adventure.

Late, Olivia and I invaded Marianna's room, rifling through the blood red closet trying to find things that would fit us. The dresses were too big for Olivia and too small for me, but we made do. Marianna went off to host the party, and I did my best to get Olivia looking tip-top. She frowned, looking at the two sizes too big reflection in the mirror. "I guess this will have to do." She gave herself the finger.

She'd pull it off. She always did. I took her hand and looked firmly into her eyes, almost believing it when I said, "You will get your happy ending."

She'd never looked so unsure in her life, asking, "Do you really think so?"

I kept hold of her hand as we walked barefoot into the party, but no amount of reassurance from me could protect her from the sight of a smug Emma with their father.

"What? What the hell?" It was like a slap in the face. The air felt ugly. Olivia ran up to her father, again teetering on tears.

At the outskirts, Ryan stood beer in hand, understandably not knowing what he was supposed to do or how to get out of there. He still looked like a kid, with his floppy blond hair; he didn't look like he belonged at all. Though, if he was still anything like his high school self, it wouldn't be long until he was the life of the party.

In 1991, the first weekend after our magical beginning in high school, I had a major fight with my parents. I had begged to stay at home for the weekend instead of heading north with them to see the Vermont foliage. In high school, three days could change everything. I spent most of the time in the back seat of the station wagon, crying and counting every second of the seventy-two hours that were keeping me from the boy of my dreams.

Ryan and I used to meet by the back entrance before school in the morning, but returning that Tuesday, he didn't show. I waited, skipping first period. At lunch, the quad was filled on that memorable Indian Summer day. And then I saw him, smack dab in the middle of the square. He stood, one foot on a battered skateboard, surrounded by a gaggle of hungry girls, including a starry-eyed Olivia. She'd fairly fallen head over heels for Ryan. And he for her. What could I have done?

My heart broke. I had known I couldn't compete so I

didn't. Those memories weren't something I wanted to deal with.

And, back to the present, he was talking to Max.

How do I run away from here? How do I re-open the closed airport and run for the hills?

"What is Max doing here?" Olivia's crazy factor was going to hit the roof. "She wasn't even invited. Trying to be the center of attention. She always has to be the center of attention." Even in high school she hadn't acted like such a thirteen- year old.

"Her husband just died," I whispered. "Cut her a break."

She pulled me out of hearing distance, as far away as we could get. "But she doesn't know that. No one is going to know he's dead yet, right? That can't be why she's here. She doesn't need to know yet. It's not fair to her when we don't even know what happened. And Emma!! Emma, the conniving little loathsome toad. She told on me. She actually told on me. And my father, my loving father," she laughed with vitriol, "he's raised the stake. I don't get my dance unless she stays."

You've got bigger problems than that, my beloved Bridezilla.

Olivia shook it off, literally, looking like she was about to enter the boxing ring, and moved into the party, going from person to person, telling them that Nico and Walter wouldn't be joining them. She said that they had gone to join a small indigenous tribe down the Mimitibi River, as they had recently discovered a local wedding ritual that needed to be performed by only the groom and his closest friend. She was unsettlingly quick with the lies.

I wandered further away from the center of the party and sat down on the planks, submerging my feet in the warm water. Everyone was just a little sun-kissed, with slightly burned shoulders and noses, which would probably fade to brown by morning. That is, except for Princeton Colleen's husband, lobster red, in pain every time she put her hand on his shoulder. Did they have any connection with Nico?

With certain obvious exclusions, everyone looked so happy and chic, not a guilty face among them. Except Lloyd, existentially sulking, but I suspected that it was a bit of a cultivation on his part. However, I clearly remembered his entry from the slam book in bold, underline and all caps: BEWARE. HE IS DANGEROUS AND SMARTER THAN ANY OF US.

I gravitated towards wallflowers in the room, as always, maybe because misery loved company. So, despite the prospect of a less than stellar conversation, I stood and made my way over to Josh, who was again the only person standing alone.

Please smile. Please be a little charming. Please prove them wrong and save me from this party.

"You look pensive," I said, smiling. "Maybe aloof? Avoidant? Remote?"

His freckles were coming out.

He replied, "Have you been reading the thesaurus?"

"Not tonight," I continued with my terribly fake smile. "But I've been known to, which is why I'm so great at parties."

"I'm not so great at parties either. Well, this party."

Marianna started the event. Uncomfortable and unsure, she distributed her clue list and treasure map, and then announced the random partners for the evening.

Not Lloyd.

Not Lloyd.

Not Lloyd.

What?! No. Please say it's not so.

Even worse...Max.

She didn't look towards me when our partnership was announced. This was getting tedious. She leaned on the side of a cabin looking wistfully at nothing in particular, waiting for me to approach. She smiled, "Hello, you."

Forget it.

It was the same every time.

We ventured off in silence and headed north. I held the torch and read the first item to find: a whip spider, which was a horrifying beast that I came face to face with at La Gruta. They weren't poisonous, but they were jaw-droppingly ugly, and supposedly all over the interior of the island. We had received a celebratory jar to capture our arachnoid friend. We had until midnight. I guessed most would return without the spider. It was obviously a fear factor item thrown in from Olivia.

"Disgusting creatures," Max commented on the list. "I've seen them in Borneo. What's the point of this? I'm bored."

She finally spoke of her reconciliation with Nico. As much as they viciously fought, they were the only ones who could challenge each other. They once played chess for three days straight, naked. High highs, and low lows, but he was the father of her child and they'd always be together. 'Til death do they part. Ironic.

"What's this ridiculousness about this male bonding jungle jaunt that Olivia told Edgar about? It's not like Nico to agree to go spend the night with a bunch of savages sleeping in the woods. What are they really doing?"

"I don't know."

She was staring me down, and it was intense. She was beautiful in the moonlight. She was beautiful all the time. She would have made a perfect suspect if she'd been on the island at the time, not having arrived on a private jet just that morning.

We returned a good hour before midnight, all clues accounted for. Whether or not Max thought it was stupid, she was going to win and she grabbed the spider with grace and ease. "There's a Tibetan proverb," she said after dumping the creature in the jar, "there is first place and there is no place."

Olivia must have stolen that phrase from the Ice Princess.

Our prize would have been spending half of Saturday at the only spa on the island, except Phil had committed his first snafu; he'd bought the gift certificates but didn't book the appointments. "How was I to know that they'd be fully booked in this cowboy town?"

Only a handful of people returned to Mono Loco at all, and those that did called it a night shortly after. It was an unsolvable failure. The disaster of disasters. Hell.

16

SWIMMING LESSONS, PART I

*M*ax and I shared a water taxi back to the hotel. She enjoyed the ride back, not talking, but skimming her fingers through the water for the entire ride. She was two huts up from me and didn't say goodbye as she walked to her room.

With no TV to soothe me to sleep, I lay there listening to the waves and the occasional boat going by. Having a real difficulty falling asleep, I heard one or two pairs of drunken feet walking down the dock.

Rain started, just slightly. Unfortunately, no thunder and lightning to count down, so I sat up and read by the dim glow of the eco-friendly light. I had about forty-five pages left of The Dark Volume and was very glad to have the time to finish it.

I was essentially a city kid, sound sensitive in the wild, but I knew the creak of a footstep, especially one trying to be quiet on an empty tropical walkway.

Was there one set of feet or two?

They didn't seem to be moving. On the day after a

murder, this was not a good sign. My fear was split between the inability to move at all, and wondering what I had close to me that might be used as a weapon.

I made my way to the welcome basket and rummaged for the flashlight - a blunt object. I backed into the bathroom and waited for whatever was clearly lurking outside my door.

Anyone could have easily killed me with a silenced pistol or even a supercharged red frog poison syringe, without me even having to encounter their diabolical self. My breath seemed too loud.

From outside the balcony at the other side of the hut, I heard someone hoist themselves from the water onto the deck, and then nothing. Did I dare scream or was that a death wish?

I left the bathroom and tip-toed my way across the room to peer through the slats of the door and see my attacker.

Starting to hyperventilate, I put my eye to the slat, both angry and relieved that it was Ryan, who was now sitting on the deck, considering his next move.

"I was hoping you'd be up," he said and patted the spot next to him.

I opted for a lounge chair and said, "What were you thinking? You can't slink around like that after what's happened."

"What has happened?"

"You woke me up. I don't know what I'm saying. Bad dreams. When someone dies you get confused."

"Who died?"

"Someone, I'm sure, somewhere. Bad dreams." If I didn't pull myself together, Nico's death wouldn't be secret for long. "Do you know what would happen if anyone saw you here?"

"Anyone, or Olivia?" He smiled in the way that he did when he was 16.

"Do you have any idea what she'd do to us if she saw us together? Even almost 20 years after the fact?" He stood up in front of me and offered his hand. I don't know why but I took it. "I'm here to give you a gift."

"Is that what you are now? A gift to…."

"Shh. I want to teach you how to swim. It is beyond insane that even twenty years later, you still are a land shark. Remember, I grew up in the water. I want to show you that I'm not a bad guy." He stepped closer, as if to kiss me.

I was about to step away when he picked me up romantically, my arms automatically clutching around his neck before he threw me in the water.

Nothing could have been worse.

I couldn't look less sexy.

Water in my eyes, water in my nose, my favorite silk nightie ruined. I regained composure as my feet found the ground, eyes stinging and hair dripping water continuously in my face.

"Why?" I asked, and he blocked my attempt to get back on the deck.

He jumped in and stood before me. "Before you can swim, you have to let go of your fear. I'll repeat that the first step to getting you swimming is letting go of your fear."

I stood there looking at him, lit only by the light of the moon, all picture perfect. The water at night was still eighty degrees and I had nowhere to go. "Your biggest obstacle to getting over this fear is to learn to exhale underwater in a shallow area like this." He waded out further and put his face in the water. Anyone looking at us would imagine quite a strange courtship. "Just close your eyes and put your face in the water. If you don't want to exhale through your nose, you can hold it closed."

I held my face in my hands for a moment and then put my face towards the sea. The reflection of the moon seemed to make everything alright. Deep breath, deep panic, exhale. Very vulnerable, I raised my head from the water.

Ryan smiled and put his hand on my back. I lowered my face in the water again, and then once more. I felt very small. "I always liked you best, you know?" he said.

"Nobody liked me best," I admitted.

"Well, you're wrong there."

I hoisted myself out, leaving him alone, as he looked up at me with pleading eyes.

"This is certainly not the time or place, Ryan. Not the place and time. Really not ever. Thank you for the lesson, but it's time for you to go."

I walked back into my room, closing the door, angry that we were in a lockless place. I sat on the couch in my wet clothes and wondered if he'd be back. I might have kissed him if he came back, but he didn't. His footsteps faded away into the humid night.

~

DAY THREE

~

17

LITTLE BLUE BOX

*I*f I owned a Caribbean resort, I'd put double locks on all the doors, regardless of going against the grain of island courtesy.

After having terrible dreams, this time about having my organs harvested by Lloyd, I woke up in a slow, cold sweat to find Olivia staring at me as I slept, a huge, sour frown on her pretty face. Did she know that Ryan had given me elementary swim lessons?

Olivia furrowed her brow like an eight-year-old. "I'm sorry," she slowly said, "I've been pretty terrible over the past couple of days, so I wanted to come by before today gets ridiculous and say that I'm sorry and to thank you. Thank you for putting up with me. Thank you for everything you've done for me since kindergarten. Thank you for being my family. Thank you." She handed me a blue box. "I was going to wait until Sunday to give this to you, but I felt today might be penultimate."

"You always get that word wrong. It doesn't mean best. It means next to last," I chided.

"Hmm. Are you sure?"

"Yes."

I knew that blue box, just as all women did. That little blue box that was the curse of the Tiffany & Co. brand. Receiving one was always an adrenaline filled build up and an inevitable let down, not being the big fat emerald cut engagement ring as our inner princess hoped. One would then be forced to show excitement at the keychain from the silver collection or what not.

I never got that far with Salty. I would sometimes wake up, staring at the ceiling, both of us wondering and dreading if marriage was in the mix for us. I'd ask myself if he was all I'd get in this life. I was a hopeless romantic whose relationship failures lowered my expectations.

I knew there'd be no letdown this time as I held my breath and opened Olivia's box. Even in the overcast morning light, its contents shimmered: a pair of hoop earrings with three little rows of exquisite diamonds, a lovely five-figure purchase. I knew how much they cost because I suggested those for her wedding. She had passed on them for being too subtle, but they were certainly good enough for me.

"Oh my god, thank you." I excitedly put the earrings on. "This is too much. Olivia, this is too much. I mean…"

"It's just money," she said, having achieved that enviable level where wealth and extravagant gifts meant nothing.

Blood money.

Hush money.

"I mean, you've done more than I should have ever asked, and now on top of bridesmaid stuff, needing to clear Walter's name and everything.

"I've been on the phone trying to get lawyers from New

124

York, but it's 6 a.m. I've got to get to Panama City to get to the embassy. It's our best shot. It's a huge mess and it turns out that on this island, it's easier to close an airport than open it, especially when the people in charge have gone surfing. Like, are you kidding me?

"I've been up all night. And I mean all night. I just might be losing it. I spent the wee hours looking through everyone's phones. You'd be surprised at how few people lock devices," Olivia explained, with no sort of moral consciousness. "You'd be shocked at what's going on behind closed doors! Walter's uncle Gordon is having an affair with a chiropractor named James. Also, Lloyd, though he is my first suspect, does awfully good seductive texting, and Amanda is this close to dumping her husband. You think that she'd tell me, of all people."

She'd always loved getting the dirt on everyone and sharing it only with me. At least that's what she had always told me.

I got out of bed and opened the doors to the deck. It looked like a perfect day was coming, at least weather-wise.

"Don't go out there. You don't know who's listening," snapped Olivia.

"How are you going to get to the city without a plane?" I replied.

"I've got a boat that will take me to Almirante and then a helicopter to Panama City. So, you need to hit the streets, by boat I guess. The boat street." She creepily laughed. "I need you on the ground. Talk to people. Most homicides are solved within 48 hours, so *Law and Order* tells me, so time is of the essence. Someone had to see something.

"Anything. I'm sure you can find something out when you're hosting the tour. You were good with those cops yesterday. Remember. We're in it. To win it. Color me exhausted. I wish I'd have slept. I'll tell you one thing: I'm not getting married in a Panamanian prison. Don't give me a present, just figure this out. You'll be like Fox Mulder and I'll be the guy with the cigarette behind the scenes. I can't do both."

I *appreciated the X-Files reference, but why couldn't I be Scully?*

"And, okay, seriously," she continued. "I really am still banned from the police station, so you'll have to handle that. They wouldn't let me in last night. I guess you can do that down here. My face is probably on a Polaroid with a devil mustache and horns drawn on, so any entry is denied. Can't be legal. Probably. Make excuses for me. Don't worry, I'll be back for the costume party. Thanks, Lexie."

She stood up and headed for the door, then thought twice, coming back and hugged me for a long time.

I whispered, "You have to come clean."

Then she collapsed, sobbing, in my arms. We sat on the bed and she cried, not having any answers or clues. Her long blond hair was sweaty and she hadn't been sticking to her three showers a day routine. This hadn't happened since Ryan broke up with her 17 years ago.

When I finally wiped her last tear away, she begged, "You're the only one I can trust. Everyone will leave and I'll never get married. Or maybe we can at least find someone else we can implicate, like my sister or something…"

I looked deeply into her pleading eyes, utterly conflicted. My best friend was lying in my arms, as vulnerable as I've ever seen her, and then as if under cover of night, she slips in the idea of wrongly incarcerating someone else.

All for the sake of a walk down La Gruta's bat lane and an eventual piece of blood red velvet cake.

There are ways I could have saved the day for everyone else. With Olivia away for the day, I could have fought to open the airport and evacuate the wedding party before sunset. We'd still be on a plane with a killer, but it was a risk I was almost ready to take.

And then she was gone.

~

I WAS UP, so by 7:00 a.m. I sauntered out to find some coffee before heading down to the police station. Josh sat at the end of the dock next to a fishing boat, flanked by the captain smoking a pipe, and two crew members, enjoying the freshness of the morning.

Josh was in full flow when I reached him. "We were all supposed to meet here at 6:00. This was our thing: deep sea fishing. Rain or shine, sick or fine, rum or wine. Well, that's what we always said. This is very weird. This is not like either of them. Walter showed up last year when he had food poisoning, on time. It wasn't pretty, but you get the picture."

He was pulling off a very classic Kennedy sailing look; not so much looking like JFK himself, but one of the Wayfarer clad members of the entourage. The guy smoking a cigar on the high seas with our handsome president, his face half-remembered in the background of a photo in an old magazine, taken of JFK and Peter Lawford. A little bit classic, a little bit entitled, but still being that awkward single gentleman, devoid of a plus one.

Please don't ask me if I know anything, because I just might say yes.

Josh wasn't stupid and was shooting holes in every story I came up with to explain why Nico and Walter might not have shown up.

"There is no way. You don't get it. At least not without an enormous apology. At least without something." Fishing was the one reason he didn't write off Nico altogether.

"Do you know anything about that village they were visiting last night? The one that Olivia was talking about? Because my feeling is that there isn't a village at all. I think I'm going to take this boat down to the police station and see if they can help."

"No, please," I blurted out.

"No?"

So, I spilled. I desperately needed to tell a rational person about what was going on. His expression changed from surprised to shocked, to downright angry. But there was no sorrow. All of his attention was focused on Walter behind bars.

"Ok, so let's go."

He had been my much-needed confidante, but I didn't want him along. "It's kind of my gig. I just wanted to let you know."

That didn't come out right. Of course he'd want to do something. It's one of his best friends.

"You can't stop me from going, with you or without you. Do you see the boat I'm standing in front of?"

So, there it was, I had a partner. I immediately knew it was a mistake telling him. Damage control, really, and not partners, but self-preservation. I hoped he'd still be there when I got back from the mad dash to my room; shoes, money, and the surprise reaction of applying lip gloss and a quick fix of the hair. I grabbed the slam book and ran back to Josh, who had waited.

I boarded the boat in the least graceful of manner, all of my belongings scattering over the damp deck. Josh chased after the loose pages of the slam book. Watching with dread in slow motion, he tried to put the book back together, ending in a curious skim of the volume.

Oh no. I don't know what's about to happen, but it's not going too good.

"Peculiar dossier." He frowned at me, seeming very tall.

"Yeah. Well. Schedules. Budgets. Lists. Not what it looks like." My cheeks were on fire.

"I think it's exactly what it looks like. Something out of a twelve- year- old's birthday party."

I lowered my voice again. "Well, it's helpful now. Somebody in this book is, you know…"

"Well, it's obviously Lloyd. He looks at everyone like they might be his next anatomical experiment." Josh opened the book and flipped through it until he found his page and read out loud: "Josh Wright. Groomsman. Long, long, longtime friend of WF, living in Chi-town, also known as the windy city. Another trust fund baby. Waaah. Single - that's with three exclamation points by the way. Writer of boring book on the forgotten modernist John Dos Passos. Snooze-a-saurus Rex, it says here. Could be cute if he tried a little harder. Maybe mopey, maybe arrogant. Marianna, want a crack at this one? You could import him to New York."

Cleans up well? Too shy for his own good? Kind smile?

All I could say was, "I didn't write that. I just read it. And I'd never set you up with Marianna. I like John Dos Passos. I read the trilogy and everything. Look, it's all very high school, I'll admit. But there are far worse descriptions of other people in there."

He turned the pages, eyebrows betraying the shock at some of his discoveries. He tossed the book on a table and let the captain know we were ready to go.

He stubbornly stared me down and I repeated the plan of keeping the rest of the guests in the dark.

"Do you know just how in over your head you are? Beyond." He shook his head. "—I didn't mean that."

Snooze-a-saurus Rex? No, just a jerk. Marianna could have him.

18

OH SO VERY OVER MY HEAD

*M*y idea of the best way forward with Josh was to pretend that the last ten minutes never happened.

I asked polite questions regarding his flight and if he enjoyed himself at the scavenger hunt, which he did not. He tersely responded that he was paired with Uncle Gordon's sixty-year-old wife, who had sexually harassed him for the whole three hours, innuendos flowing like Niagara Falls. I could see he was dying to tell more of the story, but I knew he wouldn't.

Down at Bocas Town PD, we were made to wait for a while. The 24-hour police force was essentially only a 9-5 operation, with two shifts of phone operators who would call and wake someone up if their presence was absolutely needed, which was more or less never.

Finally, my friendly detectives emerged. "Lexie!" LaGuardia said. "Here to see your killer? And who's this guy?"

"Walter's not my killer. He's not a killer at all. And that guy is just Josh, one of Walter's friends."

"Are you here to have the same conversation again?"

Knowing what an idiot I sounded like as I got up to follow them towards their office, I said, "I think that my presence speaks for itself."

"Will you be trying to tell me how to do my job now, Tall One?" LaGuardia looked at Josh, who was walking behind me. "Does he talk?"

"Not really."

Walter was sleeping, seemingly sound. A Trivial Pursuit Lord of the Rings Edition sat on a table near the cell. The detectives had told him that if they played and Walter won, they would release him. Of course, they didn't have any intention of letting him go.

Walter began to wake up as I flirted and bickered with the detectives, asking for a few moments alone with the prisoner. Walter looked predictably frazzled. The cell was basic but hospitable enough. It even had the benefit of a screen in front of the toilet to provide a little privacy. He had a rough looking blanket around him as he whispered to us.

"Thanks for coming, Josh. No one knows I'm here, right? I am just beyond humiliated. And tired. And broken hearted." Walter's voice was gruff.

"No one knows what happened yet," I said. "I just thought you needed—"

"Cut to it," Josh interrupted. "Could you have a motive?" He moved the board game to the side and took a seat on the tiny table.

Walter weakly replied, "No. I mean, what do they think? That I thought I'd ruin my wedding by killing my best friend? That's a motive. He was a lovable Alpha snake. A very lovable snake."

"You probably shouldn't be referring to him as an Alpha snake in your situation," Josh mentioned.

"He would have got a kick out of it," he unconvincingly replied in the same way that Lloyd had yesterday. "Why isn't Olivia here?"

"She went to Panama City to see what the embassy could do. She thinks it's your best bet. And she's not allowed in here anymore anyway." I changed the subject back to the point at hand. "Walter, Josh had said that you locked him and everyone else out of the house during your party. Did you really? Someone must have been able to get to your needles. You really couldn't have locked all your friends out of your house for the entire night." I got out my pen to scribble in the back of my guest register.

What was I going to do with this information? No idea.

Walter answered, "Why not? Sure, I really did lock them out. You've seen these guys drink. I don't want to open the door to a bedroom or bathroom or who knows what. They can puke in the pool, you know what I mean?"

Money can buy anything but class it seems.

"Walter, help me here," I pleaded. "Maybe not just at the party? Who else was in your place?"

He rubbed his stubbled face. "Olivia, of course, had a key. Edgar, my college buddy, showed up earlier in the week. I had cigars with him and my dad. I mean, I guess anyone who was at the party Tuesday night could have found a way into the house. I passed out pretty early. Lloyd. Michael, Gordon, Scott…." Walter counted off on his fingers.

Back to square one, where everyone was a suspect.

Josh was serious. "They should be looking at Lloyd."

Walter continued. "My dad, some girls, that photo guy. Yeah, sure, it could have been Lloyd."

"What were you doing at that crappy hotel where all the

photos were destroyed, though? I saw you and Olivia leave on the boat. You know, they think you wrecked Mig's room. Your visit wasn't exactly a secret. And I've never known you to frequent any version of a dive bar, ocean front or not. It's not looking great. Give me something, Walter." I paused for a moment thinking about bachelor parties in general. "And what girls were at this party? Girls we know?"

"You know, girls…" he shrugged off.

Ah, those kinds of girls. Refrain from judgment, Lexie.

Josh was no help; he'd passed out early as well, not used to four tequila shots an hour. Josh woke up at 5 a.m. to realize that someone had drawn hockey sticks in red magic marker across his forehead and found his way back to Mariposa del Mar. When I asked if he remembered who was fraternizing with the girls, he just waved me off.

"That is not," Josh had said, "germane to the conversation."

I had replied, "I don't think that's the correct use of the word."

"I think you'll find that it is."

Currently forgetting that I thought he had a kind smile.

Walter brought the focus back to himself. "And as far as me being at the hotel where the photographer was staying? I needed some time out and a stiff drink to think about my friend. I wanted to be alone. I just needed to be alone, with all this secrecy and lies. I don't think we should be keeping this a secret. But thinking about that, there are about seven hotels in Bocas and we've taken over five of them. The hotel was there. I knew it was there. It was quiet. And, it had a bar."

"Here, Walter," Josh took the book from me and handed it over. "Is there anyone here who could have any reason to want Nico out of the way?"

Who died and made Josh Inspector General?

"No, no, no, no, no." I snapped the book out of Walter's hands. "There's a lot of private bridal stuff in there. And a lot of stuff you really don't want to see."

"I'll attest to that," Josh snidely added.

"It's a lot of silly comments made by silly girls, three glasses in after midnight. I'll just read the names out loud and tell me who you think might have a motive. However slight."

Please don't do this to me.

Please don't let me endure yet another person's wrath.

From behind me, Josh yanked the book out of my hands and tossed it to Walter, who moved out of my reach.

Josh confirmed, "For better or for worse, not to make a wedding pun, you'll want to see this."

Walter was flabbergasted as he turned the pages. His family didn't have near the kind of money Nico did, but he was still from wealthy Virginia stock, the kind that didn't air dirty laundry.

"Do you really think it's necessary," he asked angrily, "that all the yappy bridesmaids, yourself excluded, need to know about my brother's fetishes or that my grandmother will 'flip a flapjack' if anyone talks about the White Sox? Or that Brian has a glass eye, which isn't even true. God help us all."

"And enjoy my page," Josh said. "According to this, I may be the most boring person in history."

"Well, that might be true," Walter joked. "But everyone should have the distinct chance to figure that out on their own."

After a moment of silence, Walter's mood changed back to that of desperation. "Please, you guys. I need you. Josh, you'll help Lexie, right, if the embassy doesn't come through? Everyone's going to leave the island and I'm going to be left to rot away here."

Rotting wasn't exactly accurate. He'd have beer, enter-tainment, and passive-aggressive humor.

He started at the beginning of the book, taking time to think about every entry. "I don't know. I think Edgar had some bad business with him. A while back. I think that's water under the bridge.

"Max? But she didn't make it down. I don't think his money even goes to her. Lloyd, because he's Lloyd. But I wouldn't have invited him if Nico hadn't insisted. I honestly don't know."

"Max is actually here," I said. "She took a private jet in early yesterday morning."

"What? What? Can you have her come see me? She can get anyone out of anything. What a mistake keeping this all under wraps."

I had to agree there.

"Sure," I confidently said, "Walter, we're going to fix this."

"Don't worry," Josh commented. "I'm not letting her do this on her own."

Count to ten.

Count to ten twice.

Count to ten backwards. Then breathe.

The humidity was stifling, but Walter still pulled that blanket around him. Reluctantly, he smiled at me and said, "Thank you."

~

OLIVIA WAS BACK in speed dial mode. She took advantage of the mainland Panama cellular service and I had six voice-mails from her by the time we emerged from the station into the already searing sun. It wasn't even noon.

After a few desperate voicemails, the next ones quickly

flipped back to her role as a dizzy bride She was back to her old pleasant self when she asked me if I was still excited about the zip line excursion back over at the Red Frog Beach Resort. It had seven zip lines, 150 feet in the air, and soon we'd all be flying by macaws and silver faced capuchin monkeys.

God, how I loved monkeys. I'd recently learned that they preferred stale dinner rolls over bananas. Who knew? Possibilities included seeing a three-toed sloth if you looked carefully. A real treetop challenge, with cocktails every step of the way.

Keep secrets?

Solve a murder?

But still, host the zipline treetop adventure?

Such is my station in life, I suppose.

My plan up to this point had been merely to warn people of the danger of getting buzzed while flying across 300 meters of forest at 42 miles an hour while 100 feet in the air. At least it was safer than the drunk driving that happens after most weddings in America.

I said to Olivia, "I think my time would really be better spent elsewhere. As you said, time is of the essence…"

"Means to an end, sister, means to an end. You'll have everyone there and you'll figure out something. I know you will. See if there is enough to concoct a story about Emma, like…" The phone cut out.

"Why do you get to keep your phone?" Josh asked as I threw it in my bag.

"So I can get harassed by the queen of darkness every twenty minutes. And before you ask why I put up with it, I don't know. Years of practice."

My experience in coming up with hashtags for failing Broadway musicals didn't exactly qualify me to investigate a murder in a foreign country. To be honest, I was the person who never could "see it coming" in movies.

I earnestly turned to Josh and said, "We can't do this."

He considered this. "No, we *can* do this. There are only so many people, and we'll do it together. We aren't detectives, but it's possible that the detectives aren't even detectives here."

"Have you decided that I'm not completely in over my head, then?"

"I never really thought you….Things don't come out right sometimes. Note that in your little slam book."

19

SOMETHING LIKE SQUARE ONE

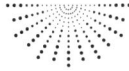

*M*igs was sitting at the restaurant when we got back to Punta Caracol, with a small brown leather suitcase on the ground next to him. I wasn't supposed to meet up with him until we headed to the zip line. I quickly put two and two together, as my heart sank, realizing Migs was going to leave.

Josh walked away without a goodbye, so I sat down with Migs by myself, only to find his aggressive flirting style had vanished. He held up his phone despondently.

"This is now the official camera of the Fowler/Parker event."

"You aren't leaving?" I asked.

Please don't leave. Pretty please with a cherry on top.

"No, but I've had my ear to the ground and know that people are being moved around to different hotels on this set of Real Housewives of Bocas drama, and I know there's room at this inn, as you Americans say. If you want me to stay and finish this job, I'm now staying here. My replacement gear is being sent here, and I don't want my kit destroyed again. You are messing with my livelihood."

"Of course. Of course. Thank you Migs." I really meant it.

"And I need a bonus."

"You'll get a bonus."

"Big bonus."

"Like you couldn't imagine."

There goes my savings.

He slyly winked, quickly returning to the Migs I knew and enjoyed. He finished his coffee, slid his sunglasses down his nose, showing off his gorgeous green eyes, and smiled that bad boy smile.

"So, I'll be right next door to you, baby, should you have any photographic needs deep into the night." He winked, got up and left the table, turning back to me just as he reached the door to his cabin.

～

I DIDN'T FEEL 100% safe anymore sitting alone in my cabin, so I took a break in the restaurant. I ordered a tall iced tea, flavored with guanabana, a fruit only found in the Bocas archipelago.

I was looking for a bit of a break, but my mind couldn't get away from the dreaded slam book I'd finally wrestled away from Walter. I tried to eliminate any suspect I could from the book, but I'd only successfully ruled out a woman named Sarah and her husband, literary friends of Olivia's. They'd moved off to Hong Kong long before Walter was on the scene, and this was their first time out of Asia since then.

Every other face in the book seemed to look back at me with devious eyes, hiding something. According to the notes in the book, everyone had secrets that I already knew. No one was innocent.

I was now paying more attention to the juvenile notes in the book and feeling increasingly embarrassed.

Edgar's wife may or may not have been a very high-priced call girl at one time. Madman Murphy was known for running down the Main Street of his small town once he reached a certain state of intoxication. Colleen's husband, also known as Scumbag Scott, was known to proposition everyone except his wife.

And Lloyd? Well, I knew his page by heart.

"So, what's your plan then?" Josh was standing above me, having magically appeared from his cabin. I couldn't believe this new, serious Josh that had replaced yesterday's nervous and shy wallflower.

"I don't know." I didn't want to look up at him again.

"No, plan? Come on, what's the plan? How should we work on this? What have you been doing so far? Let's strategize." He was pensively enthusiastic to join the investigative team.

I looked up to catch his pensive stare, but I failed to come up with an acceptable response. "I'm going to interview people at the zip line tour. One by one."

"You're serious?"

"Do you have a better idea?" Shaking him would be impossible. "Maybe Walter actually did do it," I challenged. I can't say it hadn't crossed my mind.

"Maybe Olivia did it," he snapped back.

"Don't be ridiculous." It was time to stop talking, but I couldn't. "And, I apologize if this is a rude question, but you don't seem to care so much about your friend dying, so what's your plan?"

~

"Don't care? You think I don't care?" He looked into the sky, waiting for an answer from no one in particular. "You know, I think it might be a good idea if we do this separately instead of sitting here bickering like old ladies. So, now you can go work on getting your events back on track." His normally kind face was turning red with anger, not embarrassment. I lost my partner almost as quickly as I acquired him.

He had a rabid loyalty to his old friends just like I did. The groom history recap had reminded me that Walter, Nico, Josh, and Edgar had met early on at Philips Exeter and stayed tight from then on. They all went to Washington University in St Louis for undergrad, which was considered part of the Ivy League of the Midwest. That's where Nico picked up Lloyd, entering into a dark and secretive friendship.

Nico was betting that Lloyd was going to make some astounding medical discovery that would make them both rich. But, no one truly ever understood the bond, which went way beyond making money. And they made a lot of money. They whispered secrets.

Edgar, Nico, and Walter stayed on at Washington to get their MBAs. Lloyd stayed on for medical school until he was questioned for serial killing and then left. He was an MD and a Ph.D., though where he finished his medical studies no one knew. It was possible he didn't. Josh left after undergrad and went to work for some publisher.

Hardly any closer to a suspect than I was when I started, I slammed the book closed. It was time to go. As Josh had pointed out, I had an event to run.

20

THE VIEW FROM ABOVE

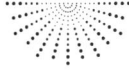

I was running late for the zip line tour, due to a never-ending conversation with Olivia, which was more of a one-way rant on her part. It seemed that the "cack-handed, maladroit and floundering" American Embassy wasn't in enough of a rush to get this fixed. But, they'd fully investigate the issue after the Bocas airport opened.

Olivia promised to be back on the 4:00 flight, determined to still make it to the costume party and to maintain the status quo.

Everything that could go wrong was going wrong. Jewel Orchids ordered from Vietnam were being held in customs, so there was a new flower crisis to fix. Olivia was putting Marianna on that one, so I could stay focused. The balance of workloads wasn't quite fair.

Migs sat with me on the dock, listening in amusement, ready to drive us off to Red Frog Beach. As we cast off, he said, "It would be perfectly understandable if you wanted me to turn right instead of left, and we went off to a little island I know where I could blow your mind, for a week, a month, who knows…"

Doesn't sound too bad.

We pulled into the marina, and the rest of the wedding guests were under the giant canopy at the Red Frog Beach resort, continuing the perpetual cocktail party. Dressed in red jungle wear, the team of bridesmaids confronted me.

Amanda said, "Lexie, you abandoned us. This is, has and will always be a four-person operation, and we've been scrambling. What do you have to say for yourself?"

The most important and inevitable question came from Marianna's mouth, "Where are Walter and Olivia? And Nico? It's like a wedding movie without the main characters." She scrunched up her face.

I remembered something that my mother had said about Marianna when we were twelve, that she always looked like she was smelling fish.

My quickness in lying was an increasingly bad habit I'd acquired over the last few days from Olivia. "They had to go to Panama City. There was some problem with the marriage license. They'll be back tonight for the costume party, for sure."

Ugh. The costume party. It remained my most dreaded event, and that included the ones where I could have possibly drowned.

At Red Frog Beach, I slowly walked through the impromptu cocktail party, answering the same question about Olivia and Walter a dozen times, looking around for anyone who looked slightly weary, guilty or nervous. There were board games scattered around and a few were partaking in those. I walked towards Lloyd playing chess with Walter's grandmother.

Lloyd. He was the stuff that urban legends were made of. I was sure he was very nice. Really.

Just as I got near him, he turned and smiled at me, saying, "I'm kind of a cliché."

I caught his dangerous gaze, starting to apologize. "I never said…"

He held his finger up to his lips, silencing me, turning and walking away.

Josh was nowhere to be seen. Becky looked around constantly, pretending to be part of a conversation with Georgie and Dave. She had been one to ask about Nico's absence, and not the other couple. Staying at Mariposa del Mar, she'd noticed his absence.

Looking around the party, the only hunch I had to go on was Edgar. He wore an everyman polo shirt and khaki shorts ensemble, had lost a little of his hair, and sported a small but noticeable paunch. He was talking intently to Uncle Gordon. His business with Nico was a long time ago. *Maybe.*

Walter Sr. made it through the crowd, charging at me like a linebacker. He wasn't as good looking as his son, but twice as imposing.

"A word, please," he said to me, as he dragged me out of the crowd into the harsh sun. "Where is Walter? Is he being remiss in his responsibilities? Is he getting cold feet? It's been 24 hours since anyone has seen him. I went by his villa and he's gone. I need my phone."

"I don't know where the phones are. Please believe me."

It was true. It was a bigger mystery than Nico.

"Then I'll take a boat to town and buy a new one. Not exactly a foolproof plan your group has."

His eyes bored into me, and I stared up at a man who was a good half foot taller than me. At my height, I was not used to being talked down to in the literal sense.

"Everything we've told you is true. Olivia woke up this morning to find that there was some wedding paperwork they hadn't been taken care of in Panama City, so they flew over there. Your son hasn't jumped ship. He's as devoted as ever."

Livid Bridesmaid Phil was the next one to drag me away with unnecessary force, leading me farther away from the party.

Walter's father called after me, "And where's Nico?"

How could it have only been noon?

Phil waved Walter's father away, scolding me. "You've got to keep this on schedule. You know how difficult it is to keep this group together. They're like a gang of drunken squirrel monkeys. Get going! I'm coming with you. You need support."

"I'm going, I'm going," I said as I walked towards the dock to take the short trip down the coast to the zip line entrance. Migs was still waiting on the boat to take me away. Maybe I'd run away from Phil and let Migs take me to his remote island after all.

"Lexie," Phil asked. "Are they really in Panama City?" He knew Olivia too well not to wonder.

I had no words but nodded, exasperated, getting into yet another boat.

∼

THE SOUNDS of the rainforest seemed subdued while the three of us quickly walked down the path. The sight of the zip line tour professionals calmed me immediately. I realized that I hadn't been breathing.

Two guys were already carrying coolers up to the launch deck, filled with bottles of champagne for pre-embarkation. I pointed out to Leo, who was in charge of the operation, that I had serious safety concerns, as most people would be half in the bag already.

Leo looked like another ex-pat American who'd rather have been somewhere else. I wondered what his life was before he traded it in for the tropics.

He lightly punched my arm and said, "You don't need to lecture me on safety, tall one. When our tours are cocktail-heavy, we close the Tarzan swing, the treetop challenge, and the vertical rappel. We just hook them up, let them fly, and then someone re-hooks them at the next stage. Seven zip lines are usually enough for anyone who, as you say, is half in the bag. And we do turn around anyone who's clearly had too much. Of course."

He hadn't really satisfied my safety worries, as I brought up the example of Aimee Copeland, a twenty-year-old who had been zip lining in Georgia. She'd fallen into a lake and got a case of necrotizing fasciitis, commonly known as the flesh-eating disease. What would happen if one of our drunken sailors slipped into some rainforest lagoon below?

Leo, far less patient with me than Carl from the snorkeling trip, barked back that more people die of being hit by lightning twice than dying in any zip line accident. "No one has died here. And," he finished, "that girl Aimee Copeland lived, as do 80% of necrotizing fasciitis victims." We had both done our research.

Phil had somehow wrangled a glass of champagne for himself, having decided that he wasn't going to the be one going up. "I'll man the fort down here."

Though they were steep and creaky, I was not afraid of the stairs up to the zip line, almost a hundred feet above the comfort of the earth. I was more apt to jump out of a plane than to volunteer to sit in a kiddy pool.

"Remember," he warned, yelling up to me as I arrived in the treetops. "We have walkie-talkies. We will hear everything. One word up there about necrotizing fasciitis to the tourists and you are out."

Migs was up there in twenty seconds, setting up his iPhone on a tripod he'd bought in Bocas Town for $15. His mood was effervescent. Everything was amusing him to no end.

Maybe a solitary moment, eye to eye, every guest would tell me something.

Someone's got to crack.

Besides the Dissector, the killing had to be a first for anyone at the party. It had to be. There had to be a tinge of guilt in someone. A moment of the fear of being found out.

First up was Walter's grandmother, to whom I asked, "So, what did you think of Nico?"

She squished up her nose and asked, "Who?"

I checked her off the list.

Becky, looking exhausted and straight out drunk, was up next. "Becky, you shouldn't be doing this. I think that you might have had one too many."

Between deep breaths, she said, "I. Want. To. Do. This."

She had her glass of champagne and then reached for another. She wasn't talking the marathon she usually did, and each word she uttered was slow and deliberate.

Looking a little touched in the head, Becky said, "Something's not right, Lexie. Something is not right with all of this. I don't think Walter is in Panama City. I don't think Nico wandered off to wherever. It is not right." Then she flew off, still with her yet to be revealed secrets.

"Everyone's okay," I yelled after her, my words falling on deaf ears. Her reaction struck me as strange. Her giddy, repetitive nature had been replaced by a very serious, very straightforward tone.

I was pissing off every guest who took a glass of champagne from me. Migs giggled as I sent off another offended guest.

"I'd like to make a coffee table book of only candid photos of you with every person you piss off. You're tremendous. They'd fly off the shelves."

I quizzed every guest with the same brilliant statement, "I know about the bad business between you and Nico."

Not much of a brilliant investigative plan.

Migs snapped a few pictures of me, after a few guests had flown off into the jungle, and asked, "You think anyone's going to say, 'Why yes! Glad you asked!'"

"It's subliminal, Migs. I'm looking for a moment of recognition. Isn't that what detectives do anyway?"

"In old movies. Very old movies."

Most people looked at me strangely, either not knowing him at all, or asking me what the hell I was talking about. My current prime suspect, Edgar, laughed and said, "Really? That was ages ago. Settled. Done and done. Why are you bringing that up now?"

After Edgar's launch, Migs took a picture of me, pointing out the obvious, "You're really annoying everyone."

I repeated my question to Amanda, as a bit of a joke, and she blushed, smiled, drank her champagne and was off. I didn't say anything to Walter's father at all as he stared me down.

Glamorously ascending the stairway, Max took her time, big tortoiseshell sunglasses and haute designer safari wear. She declined the bubbly and held her helmet up with one witchy finger. "Do I really have to wear this? We did this in

South Africa and we weren't riddled with instruments of the mentally ill."

"It's an insurance thing, so yes. And I wouldn't want you to get necrotizing fasciitis."

"From what?"

"It's a flesh-eating disease. It happens."

She slapped the hand of one of the men harnessing her up as if he were being fresh. "Where's Nico? Why is he missing? He does not miss a party. He knew I was coming. Where is anyone who matters?"

"He's not missing. I saw him this morning."

"You're lying. People's eyes shift down and to the left and down when they're lying. Where did you see him?"

I'd need to remember that lying thing.

"Kayaking?"

My time to investigate just shrunk to negligible.

Her eyes bore into me "That's not true, Marianna—"

"Lexie—"

"Of course." She didn't break her gaze with me, even when she yelled to the operators, "Can we get this thing going please?"

"Don't forget to watch out for the necrotizing fasciitis," I yelled after her, as she glided, bored and slightly bemused, into the rainforest. Nothing in life thrilled her.

The operator tapped me on the shoulder, walkie-talkie in hand, and pointed towards the stairs. "You've said it twice. You're out."

"Fine, fine. I'm going."

Josh was almost to the top of the stairs when I started down. "What was that about?" he asked.

"Oh, nothing. I've been fired from my duties up here, so, well, you know?"

"Find anything out?"

"Yes, I think that I did. I don't know. Maybe. Probably. Possibly not at all."

"Move it along, tall girl!" The operator called from above.

I sighed, surprised at my confession. "I guess tall has become my defining characteristic."

Josh smiled in a way that seemed a little out of his comfort zone. "I never saw you as particularly tall… just pretty."

I didn't expect that one. I never saw coming how much I needed that.

"I just wanted to take a moment to say that I was sorry. I don't know what happened back at the station with us. I don't always say the right thing," he said awkwardly, as if sorry wasn't a word in his general vocabulary. He bit the side of his lip and waited.

"I'm not doing this for my health you know. I'm not doing this because I enjoy it. I'm trying."

"You're doing this because you're a good person." His tone was kind.

"I've just been handing out champagne, and… I'm sorry too." I wasn't sure how to continue to conversation.

"So, let's talk later. I'll stick with the group for the rest of the afternoon, and we'll talk at the hotel before the party. We can calmly try to put this puzzle together. No fighting."

From the bottom of the stairs, Dave, Walter's brother yelled up, "What is this? Social hour? Get it moving!"

"Sure, okay, Josh. I could use the help." I smiled, walking down the stairs.

"But I'm still taking my turn," he said, continuing up the stairs, "This might even be fun. The zip line of course, not the…you know."

21

FLAT FOOT

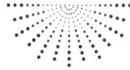

*G*oing back down the stairs wasn't as easy as going up, and I held on to the railing for the simple sake of preserving life. Between the slats, fifty feet down, an unmistakably flirty blond skipped down the yellow brick road into the woods.

Emma, in her flowing yellow dress, shoeless, walking through snakes, fire ants and other various poisonous creatures and plants, quickly disappearing further into the unknown. It wouldn't be the worst thing if she were bitten by a yet to be discovered species.

Dave, next in line, pushed towards me, muttering, "We've always been cool with each other, but you know that I want my iPhone."

I ignored him and joined the remaining bridesmaid crowd. Indicating towards Josh at the top of the zip line, Phil nudged me and whispered, "Someone's got a boyfriend."

And, in the spirit of maturity, I said, "Shut up. Do not."

The real Marianna kindly backed me up. "It's true. She totally does not have a boyfriend."

Classic Marianna. She'd scoped the single men and the competition and had decided that Josh, the mopey writer, was going to be hers.

Why couldn't he be mine if I wanted him? And I didn't.

Did I?

Out of the corner of my eye, I saw Lloyd walking down the same path that Emma had wandered down. *Blond, young and beautiful. His taste.* Was he starting over again? He'd been looking at her like she was an exquisite specimen the night before. Had killing Nico given him a taste for more?

It was not easy for me to walk quickly through the unfamiliar and dense vegetation. Our poison frog expert, Crabby Paulo, had referred to the island as a "biologist's fantasy," but I'd call it a hypochondriac's nightmare. The list of all things deadly was running through my head, but it was strictly a life or death need to follow Lloyd.

The chilling sound of a howler monkey made me trip over the trunk of a tree. The howls were only a defense mechanism, but they were chilling all the same. I fell, knocking the wind out of myself. I'd sliced my ankle open somewhere along the way.

If Salty could have seen me now.

He had a running list of put-downs about me, including my habit of not embracing adventures, not working out enough "even though your best friend owns a gym made for lazy people like you," and that I didn't take risks (which was why I was back in a job and career that I hated, tail between my legs).

It was the way he would say it, emerging from his office, "Oh look another day of you doing nothing," regardless of knowing what I actually did. He was far from perfect, but I never fired insults back at him. Though, I will admit to the guilty pleasure I received reading all of the horrible reviews of his last book, my favorite calling it a "pile of moronic drivel." He was a revisionist historian, probably working on a new book, probably a memoir, about his crazy love that never existed for a tall girl named Lexie.

Even while stumbling through the rainforest, directionless, I could hear Olivia's voice in my head, saying, *Why on earth would you have tried to save Emma? My problem would have been gone and the wedding would be on. You knew time was of the essence!*

The darkness of the rainforest was growing as I headed farther in. If I lost the light, then I would lose my direction, and I'd never find my way out.

A small green snake slithered over my feet so I stood very still, knowing not to startle; the smallest snakes often were the most dangerous. Crabby Paolo had muttered this while breathing down my neck yesterday, smelling strangely like blueberries.

That's when I heard the first scream, slightly muffled, and maybe not too far away. I started running again in the direction of the scream, and stopped, waiting for another hint of direction.

More muffled screams came from behind the trunk of a huge upturned tree, as large as any I'd seen. I touched the years of moss covering it as I climbed up and over, giving me some advantage if I needed to run. The next scream was more of a moan; I knew I was too late, imagining a knife being plunged into Emma's tan stomach.

Then I heard her giggle and say, "Shhh."

I peeked, just for a moment, and there were Emma and Lloyd, her dress pulled up over her head, and he was writhing against her. I slithered down my side of the trunk, hoping to go unnoticed.

"What was that?" Emma whispered.

Lloyd clearly said, "Nothing. Just the hundreds of danger-ous…" His voice was muffled by another moan.

That is so not what I wanted to see.

Did they see me? Was Lloyd slinking behind me reading for the kill? I wasn't going to look back. I quickly scurried towards the east, finally making it to the shore. My ankle now throbbed and I rinsed it in the shallow warm sea. I wanted to stay there, but could see the Red Frog Beach resort far up the coast. I knew I wouldn't be comfortable for long.

2 2

ALONE IN PARADISE

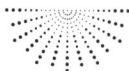

*M*ariposa del Mar was a like a ghost town when I returned; everyone else still drunk in the rainforest bar after swinging around like little silver faced capuchin monkeys. War-torn and filthy, I let one of the bartenders scurry over to the water taxi to help me onto solid ground.

It was a basic kindness that touched me to the core, and I felt tears welling up in my eyes. I didn't need help walking, but it hurt. The folks at Red Frog Beach had helped me patch it up, though the whole incident had left me exhausted. Josh would be back with the rest of the party eventually, hopefully collecting more intel than me.

I accepted the comfort as he escorted me down the dock and through the restaurant to a lounge chair. A waiter came over with a Soberana beer and a plate of warm plantain chips. I felt a nap coming on, under the detached supervision of the Mariposa staff.

Am I kidding myself that I'll be able to sleep?

"Hey, I wondered where you went," Migs called over to me, as he swam over to the lounge.

He pulled himself out of the calm sea and shook the excess water out of his hair, waiting for the sun to dry his fit body. It was something right out of a bad romance novel, with his shimmering pecs and mischievous green eyes inviting but the wrong choice.

He frowned looking at my ankle. "Wowie, zowie. That's not good. What happened?"

I left it at, "I fell. I'm not quite the essence of grace today."

Or, let's face it, any day...

"There are more important things than grace. Let me get that cleaned up for real."

Blood had already started soaking through the bandage they had patched me up with at Red Frog Beach. He held his hand out for me to take. "I've got beer and sun at my cabin. There's nothing to fear, kitten."

His eyes were... new grass green or, like dancing emeralds shimmering in the light of the discotheque? I couldn't get it right.

"How would you describe the shade of your eyes?"

"Just green..."

I took his hand and followed him to the room, part of me proud that the staff might think he was taking me to his cabin for more than a first aid consultation. His cabin was exactly like the rest of them, but his was now filled with newly replaced photographic equipment, half of it still in unopened boxes.

He walked through to the deck, "I must admit, I'd kind of like to pretend this didn't show up yet. Using my iPhone was liberating."

He took my foot, propping it up on the small table. He unwrapped the towel from my ankle, displaying the mess.

"Tell me it's not as bad as it looks?" I squeaked out.

"Ouch. Well, it doesn't look deep, I think. No, it may be positively deep, but I'll clean it up." He returned to the deck minutes later with wet warm towels and a first aid kit. "You might want to go to town and see a doctor."

"I've met the doctor," I said. "I think I'll take my chances with you."

"I like taking care of you," he said and winked. "Why don't you call in sick for the rest of the weekend and I can be your nurse? I know, I know. Don't get the scared look on your pretty little face. So, did you find what you were looking for at Red Frog Beach?"

Calling in sick for the weekend sounded like an excellent idea. Migs had another two beers in the next half hour, and I couldn't even try to keep up. We had said very little after a short discussion on the lack of ideas I had about Nico's death.

"Well, I'm taking a nap," he finally said, yawning, bathing suit hanging low on his hips as he stretched his arms. "Are you coming?"

I blushed, surprised, as I was more than familiar with his usual innuendos. He perked up at my modesty. I grabbed my beer and was quickly, but immediately regretfully, on my feet, twinges of pain radiating through my lower leg. My clumsiness was on full display as I stumbled out of Mig's cabin while he looked on in amusement. Slow eyed, he leaned on the frame of the door after I left, watching me go.

"There's something wrong with me," I joked, walking down the wooden path.

"There's more that's right with you," he said. "Bye-bye." He closed his door.

I found myself with an interesting opportunity. The

murderer still could have been anyone, after all. There were four bungalows I could search for a clue in.

Time was certainly ticking. Becky was acting strange, and Max was, well, Max, but what answers could be in Nico's former lair? I needed to bite the bullet and go for it.

Before I lost my nerve, I moved quickly down the walkway and entered Becky's cabin. Clothes were casually tossed on the couch. It looked like she'd brought enough for a month, and had obviously spent all morning trying things on and then discarding them. Most clothes still had the tags on them and based on those prices, I wondered what Walter was paying her.

Her drawers were filled with the most exquisite and expensive lingerie; Agent Provocateur, La Perla, Bordelle. She was definitely planning on getting laid this trip.

But by who?

On the second floor, next to the bed, sat a paperback copy of my book, which she had highlighted throughout in pink. In her night table, two more books about taking control of one's life, and a Cartier ring box.

For those who don't know, the Cartier little red box trumps the Tiffany little blue box any day of the week. The ring was a dazzler, easily 5 carats, square cut, presented like the Queen of England. Olivia would have freaked out if she saw the size of that dazzler.

Certainly too flashy for my taste, but I wouldn't be a woman if I didn't try it on and hold it up into the light making its way through the holes in the thatched roof. I was transfixed, as I momentarily drifted into a fantasy wedding to no one in particular.

My imagined walk down the aisle was interrupted by the easily identifiable sound of heels on the walkway. On a calm day, noises carried effortlessly on the gentle wind across the resort. It was always best to speak in whispers. Always.

My charges were back early. I fumbled to get the ring off my finger and back in the box, knocking over little bottles of powders and perfume, spilling pink crystals of something inside the drawer. I picked up the slightly cracked and weathered bottle, with a label that was half gone, labeled "Peppermint." I brushed the few spilled crystals to the back of the drawer. There was no time to clean up for real. I'd have to let Becky blame it on housekeeping. But the diamond was still there, so what did she care?

Who was the fiancé and why the secrecy? I made my way quickly down the stairs, hoping to get at least out the door, trying to quickly formulate some kind of natural reason that I'd be lounging around in her grand cabana.

The door flew open and I was as surprised to see Max as she was to see me. She always seemed taller, but she was actually a petite woman of only five feet. With her demeanor and the four-inch sandals she teetered beautifully on, she more than made up for her slightness. She looked perfect, with her red hair juxtaposed with her white bikini under her white cover-up. She breathed with anger.

She asked with her snake like tongue, words carefully spaced out, in her silky posh accent, "So these rigmarole excuses about where Nico is are completely fabricated, aren't they? Lies, right? You are a liar, Lexie! Are you a dirty little liar?"

Like a five- year- old getting caught in my own web of deceit, I said nothing.

"Lexie! What. Happened." She demanded. At least she finally had my name right. I doubted she'd forget it again. "Are you stupid, or do you think you could answer me? Because I can't seem to get an answer from anyone else."

Josh thought I was stupid. As did Walter. And now Max made up the trifecta.

"Ok. I wasn't telling the truth. He died. Of a heart attack."

This calmed her for a minute, and I swear she smiled, just a little. "Well, cocaine and Viagra will do that to you."

"I don't know what happened, exactly. We were snorkeling—"

Out of nowhere, she slapped me across the face. The lies had caught up to me

"You daft little cow," she continued. "Do you think I'd really take it so casually when my husband has gone missing? Do you know that I actually had to track down police officers on a surfing beach to find that you, particularly you, had sent Nico's body to Panama City and not thought it appropriate to tell his wife? The mother of his child!"

She laid into me for at least twenty minutes. I said nothing and did not break her stare, because I deserved it all. I just hoped I wasn't going to get another smack across the face. It was a first in my life and I hoped my last.

She knew every detail, pieced together from a reluctant team of detectives, a seemingly enamored Dr. Nolan, and a fully disclosing and now angry Walter.

Outside Nico's cabin were her packed bags; two vintage Louis Vuitton armoire trunks. A speedboat was waiting by the dock to take her to the airport where her chartered jet would fly her back to New York via Panama City to take care of her husband's body.

It looked like she'd been traveling for quite some time and I wondered who was watching their child and if she even knew, let alone cared. She was furious and insulting, wondering how I had the audacity to take on any kind of responsibility in looking into this matter?

She'd apparently riled Walter up to the point of frenzy.

The best private investigators out of London and New York were being contacted; if local authorities were not competent enough to find out who killed Nico, then come hell or high water, she would. She was going to sue anyone she could over this, including me. We had acted very poorly.

Once she had turned around to take leave of the "hell hole" I trailed behind her, finally finding a voice. I apologized profusely, mumbling excuses that had seemed valid enough for the last 24 hours, but which now seemed obscenely ridiculous. She ignored me. She'd said her peace and then she pretended like I wasn't there.

She daintily got into the speedboat, being served a glass of champagne while her trunks were loaded. She gave me the finger as the boat sped off, fading into the distance, saying, "Despicable, Lexie. Really despicable."

She never questioned why I was on the way out of Becky's cabin or mentioned why she had been on the way in.

Ironically, there was a folded note from Detective LaGuardia, pushed under my door as I finally entered my own room. "Could not get through to your mobile, but call us immediately about the red lady. Max is coming for you."

23

DRESS UP

*fter a bad nap, I woke up dreading the next event. There was no way this party was going to be pleasurable. The costumes themselves were a surprise for everyone, and it was embarrassing at best. There had been a million things to annoy me along the way, but back in the beginning of planning the wedding, I had taken a stance against this upcoming masquerade party.

Olivia was adamant that I go dressed as a red M&M, based upon a bonding moment from our youth. We had one of our few real fights, as I envisioned myself as a shapeless wallflower standing at the end of a dock, while everyone else dressed in glamorous garb, snickering at me.

Olivia would be dressed as Wonder Woman, of course. In a rare moment of defiance, I said that I would only attend dressed as a sexy Spanish Inquisitor, at my own expense. She had growled, said it was an excellent idea, and that she'd be sure to add the mustache and beard. That was just another thing to dread, thinking ahead to the night.

There was no need to compete with me. If you surveyed

100 people on the street about who was better looking, she'd somehow get 101 votes. However, everyone was competition.

My Spanish Inquisitor costume was ridiculous and immediately regrettable. Dressing for the night's costume party, I tried to cinch it in a way that might give me a hint of a woman's shape. The red capelette and full-length tunic were just sagging polyester, the tailoring merely a red shapeless sheet. I tried to cut it to knee-length with disastrous results. What did I expect for something that was purchased for $19.95 plus shipping?

Curiously, Olivia had put me at ease after I finally reached her in my panic about Max. She had responded, "Good, she's gone. We don't have to worry about that succubus. Thank the Guari-Guari for small miracles."

Though she knew better, she'd yet again tried to get into the police station for some desperate contact with Walter. I kept it to myself that through the grapevine I had heard that he was presently livid with her. And I'm sure with me as well. She currently could do nothing, so she'd be at the party on time.

A fleeting part of me strangely wondered if the last few days were all a ruse to make sure that this was the wedding that people would be talking about for the rest of their lives. Maybe Nico was alive on a power yacht sailing towards Richard Branson's Private Necker Island in the British Virgin Islands. Maybe Walter was shuttled off to some resort under the cover of night and the detectives were Broadway actors, handsomely paid and part of the joke.

Max had struck a crisis of confidence in me. What I was doing was wrong, plain and simple. There is a saying that there's good in everyone, so there must have been a decent side to Nico. There must have been a decent side of Max.

I frowned at myself in the mirror, slightly achy since waking up. I'd been sleeping on my arm the wrong way, waking up with pins and needles that had subsided but still left me with slightly tingly fingers.

The easiest explanation – my messy jaunt following Emma through the woods had hit me with a case of necrotizing fascitis. I think they'd call that a clear case of insult with injury. A messy up-do and lipstick usually succeeded in making me feel a little pretty, but not at this time. The big red blob which was me stared back in the mirror, making me feel even worse.

Like a big bouncy beach ball. Congrats, Lexie, on the alliteration.

I was the last one of my group to the bar, getting on the boat to take us to the Cala del Paraiso resort on Isla Bastimentos. The tension was heavy as we took off on the half-hour boat ride, with a vessel full of randomly clothed guests, provided gratis by Lexie.

No one was happy. Dave and Georgie were a caveman and a cavewoman, Josh was a dapper 20's gangster, and Becky looked ridiculous in a blond wig, garbed as Alice in Wonderland. She looked almost as bad as me. Truly she looked insane, manic nervousness and dark, as if she knew something.

It's the look of guilt I've been searching for.

She had murdered Nico and planned to play the week out but couldn't handle the pressure. I looked at Josh to see if he was picking up the same thing that I was, but he was looking off into the distance as the sun set.

Becky picked at her perfectly manicured nails. "Lexie," she finally quietly said. "When are Nico and Walter coming back?"

Dave continued to question, "Is Walter going to be at this one?"

"I believe," I quickly fabricated, "that he had to stay overnight in Panama City."

Dave threw his arms in the air.

∾

CALA DEL PARAISO RESORT was the strangest of possible choices to have a costume party, as all other guests at the resort were walking around naked. Playing tennis in your birthday suit all day? Not my cup of tea.

The surreal feeling increased as we walked down the torch-lit path under the full moon towards the party location. We passed one couple in the nude, holding hands, modeling non-existent tan lines. They politely nodded as they walked past, and I returned the gesture. Which of us looked stranger?

I grabbed Josh's hand and pulled him back from the others as they walked along. "Can we catch up quickly? This cut is a doozy."

"We didn't get back until much later than I thought. And I don't think I learned anything except that everyone knows something's going on." He nervously glanced towards the party.

"And I'm sure you learned that everyone's mad at me."

"Well, I'm not mad at you. Though I am concerned about your red piece of polyester fabric."

Was he flirting with me again?

"Long story."

"Let's just really watch people. There are enough people on edge. Something's got to give. We'll see something in someone!"

I really did have a partner. He may have been a little awkward and goofy, but I felt a little less alone.

Outside the massive gazebo, and in his Star Trek best, Phil was nervously smoking, having picked up Olivia's renewed bad habit. "I'm taking ten minutes out of there until I hope Olivia calms down," he said, obviously regretting he had said yes to being a bridesmaid. "How you might have put up with her for all these years is beyond me."

"She's back?" I knew she said she'd be, but I never thought she'd pull it off. She had no idea what she was walking in on. Did I?

Amanda had left the party and was crying on a naked beach somewhere; she had not checked that the entire shipment of costumes had arrived until she returned to her hotel that afternoon when she unpacked the boxes. There were two missing boxes and she was unable to track the ten costumes down.

She had made the best of it and wrapped herself in a white eco-friendly towel, which was an indefinable costume of sorts. She could have made it look like she had lathered up shampoo in her hair and pretended to be a dandruff commercial. Still, nine other guests were cavorting in civilian wear. Olivia had elegantly taken Amanda outside and screamed at her, having realized that she'd lost control of everything. Things were only going to get worse.

Inside the party, Olivia again played her perfect role of exquisite hostess, though still missing her fiancé. She was dressed as a majestic Wonder Woman, lying left and right, charming everyone. Her charisma had saved her many times in her life. Though some of us were beginning to see the light, her smile and laugh were still working on others.

Her outfit was of far greater quality than the rest of the guests' costumes, and I wondered if it had actually once belonged to Linda Carter herself. Her black wig looked wickedly gorgeous, her blue eyes luminous in a way that only blondes with dyed black hair can possess. She stood in typical stance, hands on hips, feet firmly planted in her four-inch red boots.

Marianna stood proudly by her side, as if she had usurped me as maid of honor. She was dressed as a flapper - her identical costume for every Halloween since 1998. As we entered, she made a beeline to Josh, whisking him off to the bar, taking my reluctant partner away from me.

Not like I wanted him, but where were her manners? Was he being polite to her or was the groomsman assessing all of the bridal party?

Lloyd brushed by me, dressed as Count Dracula, arrogantly dangling his fake fangs between his thumb and forefinger. He smirked and slyly said, "I'll stop being a cliché when I stop being treated like one." He then leaned over and whispered in my ear, "Dirty girl," before disappearing into the crowd.

Oh my god, he saw me seeing them.

People had made fast friends over the last few days, and little cliques had been formed while I'd been away, leaving me on the out. Phil was laughing over new private jokes with Edgar, Colleen, and their significant others; Olivia's neighbors, Chad and Tom, were comparing tan lines with Georgie; and Theresa and Brian, Walter's film producer friends, were doing shots with Olivia's mom and step-dad.

The coupling off of the singles had seemingly happened, and I was Left Behind again as the rest ascended to cuddle heaven. Emma was making no secret that she had abandoned Ryan and moved on to darker pastures with Lloyd; Marianna had affixed herself to Josh in their offending matching costumes. He'd see through her. He was smarter than that. Plus, he had detective work to do.

My biggest surprise was the sight of Ryan and Becky talking intensely in the corner. Her eccentricity was intriguing to all. I had an urge to stamp my feet like a three-year-old and yell, "Why does she get both a fiancé AND Ryan? What does she have that I don't?"

Boo hoo.

I stepped aside to leave another voicemail for LaGuardia. I had a twenty-percent success rate on even making it through, then a good half hour or so waiting for him to return my call. If I left three or four voicemails, the relevant information would be in there somewhere.

The party started to go quiet, and uncomfortably so. A whisper campaign had started, as people clasped hands over their mouths, gasping with surprise, and then underlying mania set in.

Olivia looked petrified, in the Mt. Vesuvius way; Marianna holding tight to her arm, staring ahead like a deer in head-lights. I spun around to see who was meeting her stare, and there stood Max, her face displaying a level of anger beyond what I could have imagined was possible in a mere mortal.

God, no. You were supposed to be in Panama City, mourning your loss.

Josh ran up to me and guided me to the periphery, "She couldn't get a plane chartered until the morning. She's told everyone about Nico. About red frogs too. Maybe we should get out of here. She knows everything, and I mean everything and probably more."

I couldn't move, watching the whole thing like it was a bad dream. The room exploded, everyone talking, trying to put the puzzle together.

Max then stormed across the room, past Olivia, to Becky, who was hanging desperately onto Ryan.

"You…" Max growled at the assistant. "You little gold digger. You little white trash gold digger." She slapped Becky across the face twice, paused, and then slapped her again. "What did you think? That you'd end up with Nico? Men like him use women like you and toss them away when they're bored. They don't stay around. Were you surprised when he left you to reconcile with me?"

With a strength uncharacteristic to everything I had seen of Becky, she screamed, "He was not going back to you. He hated you."

"Yet I'm here. So what? Did you figure that if you couldn't have him, no one would?"

And no one would.

Becky lunged at Max and they entered a silly looking catfight, throwing slaps and punches that weren't landing until Becky started to kick. After a few moments of shock, Walter's father and Edgar pulled Max away from Becky.

Nico and Becky? That was unexpected. I guess Nico had a thing for redheads. That potentially explosive piece of information hadn't made it into our binders.

Becky, with her Mary Janes and white knee-high socks, sat on the floor, looking for a friendly face. Lloyd picked Becky up and took her into his arms, whispering and leading her away from the limelight. She was talking to him a mile a minute while he held her. Emma was none too pleased with this; her glare at Becky being almost as nasty as Max's.

I'd been ignored up until this point, until Walter's father, holding back the wriggling heiress, barked at me, "Where's Olivia?" I quickly scanned the party, finding that Olivia and Marianna had somehow slipped out.

"She knows. She knew about Nico being murdered and

was silent. She knew about Walter being arrested and was silent. That woman knows everything," Max said, pointing her long pink fingernail at me.

Everyone looked at me for a response, while Walter's father dragged Max from the party. "Let's go to the police station," he calmly said. The party watched Max and company fade into the distance, her accusations (both accurate and not) rolling out of her mouth until we could not hear her anymore. We all stood in silence, watching Lloyd lead a wobbly Becky away.

"You lied to us?" Dave asked, completely aghast.

And then all eyes were on me.

24

SWIMMING LESSONS, PART 2

t was well into the hush of night when I returned to the hotel with Josh; exhausted, mortified, and knocked for a loop. It seemed like weeks since Olivia had woken me up with her cigarette smoke and luxury bauble offering.

In the few moments she bounced into my mind, I saw blood-red-wedding-color rage and pushed her out of my head. With her disappearance from the party, she'd finally become a peripheral part of the problem.

There had been a collective freak-out at the fête, but only a few revelers had stormed off. All of Walter's family had gone to the police station. Edgar followed them at the last minute, leaving his trophy wife to drunkenly reel around the party.

Josh stood by my side, trying to reroute Walter's angry guests away from me. This wasn't too hard as only fifteen, total, remained at the party, and some of those were close to passing out face down on high top tables.

Olivia's guests didn't seem too bothered, but they all had

opinions. Emerging from indignant irritation and fear was a flurry of accusations. Everyone had an idea, but the collective wisdom was an insistence that Walter was innocent and there was a killer among us.

The bar stayed open, as people weren't ready to go home yet. Guests approached Josh and me for hushed conversations about who the murderer might be. Even Olivia's guests, many having met Nico for the first time only two days ago, got in on the action too.

Amanda accused Edgar. Edgar's wife, in a slur, accused Amanda. Movie producer Theresa was steadfast in her observations, blaming Chad and Tom. And in a strange turn of events, Uncle Edgar implicated his wife.

But it was Ryan who stated the obvious and yet impossible. "Does everyone not see that Max killed him?"

He was right, in some respects. She'd be my obvious front-runner, but she'd only flown in on her private jet the day after the murder.

She clearly had the most to gain. But is that enough?

But did she? What about love?

As if Phil had his suspicions at the same moment as I did, he said, "Did everyone not see what just happened? Serious catfight between ice princess wife and Becky. His mistress."

Who to believe?

I remained at square one, with ten proposed suspects. After hours of discussions, the party ended at the insistence of the management. Josh's parting words of advice were that everyone should stay in pairs at all times to be safe. At least if someone tried to kill their buddy, we would know for sure who the culprit was and all would be over.

Bone-weary, Josh and I shared a boat home. "If you were a betting man," I asked him, "who'd you put your money on?"

"Edgar? Lloyd? Walter's brother Dave? Of course, Lloyd. I

honestly have no idea. Not a trace of a clue. You were right. We're terrible at this."

He didn't jibe with my Becky theory, but we'd at least have some fresh ideas to talk to the detectives about in the morning. I still hadn't heard back from them and had no plans of sleeping.

The "just regular" frogs were out, chirping like crickets. They were called peepers. One of the bartenders had told me the night I arrived, smiling and calm. That felt like a long time ago. We mumbled low, walking past my cabin, past Becky's and eventually standing in front of Josh's walkway.

He looked as if he was going to say something friendly and comforting, but stopped himself before he spoke. He then furrowed his brow and shifted his nose, contemplating if we were going to buddy up in support of his safety in numbers scheme. "You've been through a lot tonight and, well, it's going to be an early start. So sleep well, if you can."

Break up residuals made me feel rejected, but I tried not to show it. "Of course. Sleep well too."

Josh awkwardly kissed my cheek, again looking like he had something to say, but instead turned and quickly retreated to his cabin.

Becky's lights were on. Against any sane decision, I knocked on Becky's door, both sympathetic and shocked at all that I learned that night. In retrospect, like in The Usual Suspects, all the clues to their affair were there. For sorrow or success, she wanted to be left alone. There was nothing for me to hide in my cabin in the non-safety of alone.

I screamed when I walked into my room, as the shadow of a man on my couch moved. Frozen in a superannuated moment, I finally reached for the light as I heard my name muttered. "Lex…"

"Migs! You can't just…" I didn't know what to say.

He lounged on the couch, a bottle of Patron tequila and two small glasses on the table in front of him. He rubbed his eyes and smiled wickedly, sitting up straight. He was dressed casually, in a worn white t-shirt showing off his toned arms and worn jean shorts. Barefoot of course.

With snake hips, I think they call them.

"According to your partner in crime," he said, opening the bottle of tequila, "we need to buddy up and look after each other. You need someone to protect you from things that go bump in the night. No one better than me for that. What time is it?" He stretched his arms in an exaggerated yawn.

Maybe it won't be so bad for someone to hold me close all night.

"Close to three. In the witching hour." I wasn't close to being tired.

"What's the witching hour?"

"Technically between midnight and four in the morning. If you want to be particular..."

He seductively smiled. "You are so strange, in the best of ways." He patted the space on the couch next to him. "Come, sit. Have a drink."

I felt the pressure to speak but instead sat next to him. Rejection was clearly not a word in his vocabulary. Without asking me if I wanted it, or even if I wanted him to stay, he poured two shots of tequila.

"Cheers," he toasted, "to the strangest week of my life, and that's by no means an exaggeration." He flirted, and I retreated, becoming a completely nonsexual creature by his side. "Strictly as a friend, I think you should forget about finding any murderer. It's been entertaining, and I'm perversely getting a kick out of it, but I've been taking in everything that you've seen and heard. Face the fact that the right man is probably in jail. Either make plans for them to get married at the police station or jump ship. Seriously, Lexie, you're on a wild goose chase."

We said nothing, but drank a number of tequila shots in a short period of time. "Thank you," I said. I tapped my tingly fingers against the shot glass. "Do you know anything about necrotizing fasciitis?"

He chose to ignore this question and gave me a big smile. "You know, and I know you know, that all I want to do is kiss you right now. That's all, gorgeous, to just hold you and kiss you all night." He ran his hand through my hair and continued, "Unless you want something else, of course."

I flinched and moved just a little away from him.

"You're not attracted to me?" he asked in a way that showed he thought it was the most ridiculous thing in the world. And it was. His attractiveness was not an opinion. It was a fact.

"That's not it."

"I've got a second wind going. How about taking a dip, then?"

"I can't swim."

"I know you can't swim. You tell me every chance you get. I'll teach you."

"What is this? A reality show? You're the second person in two nights."

"You need a local. You need a friend. You need to know at least how to keep floating. You'll find that you are actually very buoyant. But seriously, you need to know what to do in a worst-case scenario. 'Cuz it's very possible you might find yourself in a worst-case scenario. I mean I'm not trying to scare you or anything. Not right now, at least."

Being out in the moonlight felt right. I didn't feel uncomfortable when peeling down to my underwear and easing myself into the water.

Migs walked me out to chest deep water. "Are you going to give up your quest for justice?"

"I want to. But I don't think I can."

"You're a good friend to a silly woman. Okay, you just need to be able to float on your back, you floatable you. I'm going to put my arms under your back and then you just slowly lay down. Look at the moon and remember that I won't let go until you say the word. Spread your arms and legs and relax. Not like that. Look at the stars and listen to the water. You're already floating. My hands just happen to be under you."

I would have liked to have slept right there. "Do fish sleep?"

"Yes," he responded, as he looked down at me. "Kissable you."

I closed my eyes. "You can let go now." And we floated, silent and safe, until the sun started to rise.

I said nothing to Migs when I finally waded back to my cabin. My thanking smile for a moment of calm was all the thanks he needed.

~

DAY FOUR

~

25

WHAT COMES AROUND

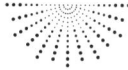

I should have guessed that I wouldn't be alone when I woke up. I should have had the fore-thought to pretend to be asleep until I was ready to meet the day. Olivia was staring at me when I opened my eyes, arm outstretched with an offering of 6 a.m. coffee.

As soon as she parted her pouting lips, I said, "No. Be quiet."

I drank my coffee in silence, not in any calm, as Olivia traded off between staring at me and tearing at her fingernails.

She took a pause. "As Thoreau said, true friendship is never serene."

She still had last night's make up on; black mascara caked on in a raccoon style around her eyes. She'd definitely skipped the shower option that morning, again, but had made a last-ditch attempt at being presentable in a preppy looking pink dress and matching espadrilles.

The smeared eyes gave me a momentary flashback to 16-year old gothic Olivia: huge teased hair, torn up stockings, and black, black, black. Black clothes, black humor, black bedroom walls. A simpler time. A better time.

I was not in the mood. "Just to clear the air, it wasn't Thoreau, it was—oh, forget it—and I would say it goes far beyond not serene."

I'd only seen that expression of apology once before. After Olivia had stopped having panic attacks over Ryan, she'd found another love of her life at a party in Princeton. He was a drummer in a punk rock band that was going to tour the West Coast for a few months, and he had invited her along.

She had no money for the ticket to Los Angeles, so after a long conversation, I lent her my credit card to pay $186 for a one-way ticket to California. Though Olivia's family had more than enough money to send her to LA, or a summer in Monte Carlo for that matter, they'd never in a million years subsidize a semester away from Princeton. If she'd wanted to spend a semester in Kenya learning from the Maasai warriors, that was one thing, but to fund her daughter slumming it with a third-rate band up and down the Pacific Coast. No way. It was on me.

When my statement came a few weeks later, I was met with only $28 of credit remaining and an $800 charge for a one-way, first-class ticket. That card was my back up in case I couldn't get a job during the semester, and I couldn't carry that kind of a balance. After not hearing back from her for a month, I eventually had to plead with her well-off mother to pay me back.

I think Marilyn Monroe said it best.
I always get the fuzzy end of the lollypop.

It had taken me a good three years to speak to her again, and much longer to forgive her. The rainy day we had finally met up, she sat across me in a West Village café, with the same quivering bottom lip, hopefully authentic, looking for redemption. Above all, love. The two of us sisters in not only superficial knuckle injuries, but in hopeless romanticism. We kept throwing ourselves out there, and we kept getting our hearts trampled on. We got each other. We understood each other implicitly, and that always wiped the slate clean.

Sitting across from her now, almost thirteen years later, I was unfortunately just as apt to forgive her.

"I'm sorry," she said.

"Really? What are you sorry for, exactly?" I snapped back. She said nothing, perhaps not knowing where to start on the long list, or truly not understanding. "You disappeared last night! I had twenty people on top of me like a mob asking me what I knew, what was being done, and where the hell you were!"

"I had a panic attack. I had to go."

"No, you didn't."

"No, I didn't. You're always right, always smarter than me, which is why I always need your help. Please, just come with me. I'm sorry. I'm sorry. I panicked." She handed over a crumpled note on hotel eco-recycled paper from Amanda, demanding that she attend a meeting of the bridesmaids at the Pickled Parrot at sunrise. There was nothing friendly about the message. No "XOXO," no "Love ya" and certainly no "So excited to see you!"

Be there, or suffer the wrath of those who have served you so faithfully.

I SPOKE ONLY one sentence to her on the boat ride to the meeting. "What's the bad business that was going on between Nico and Walter?"

She threw her hands up in exasperation and that was the extent of our conversation.

There was no chance of running into anyone else at the Pickled Parrot at 7:30 a.m., and I'm frankly surprised it was open.

Amanda was drinking a fruity cocktail with whipped cream on top, large sunglasses hiding whatever was going on in her world.

Olivia strutted over to the table, as composed as she could hope to be, and sat down with a giant smile, ready to start spinning whatever tale she had concocted.

"First I want to apologize. I should have told you what was going on. And I know people think I was putting them in danger, but I wasn't. I was doing what both the police and the lawyers were telling me, but I should have told you guys. And Interpol. And I'm sorry."

"Poppycock," Phil coughed into his hand before drinking his mimosa.

Amanda raised her half-empty drink to Olivia saying, "Everyone hates you. A lot."

Olivia tried to grin and bear it, but the group expressed they were tired, disappointed, and had been taken for fools. No one seemed scared, however. There was very likely a murderer in our mix, but they were more hurt by her betrayal than concerned with a frog poison killer. They were sick of the treatment they had been getting and went around the table, listing off the terrible things she had put us through.

Amanda was still feeling humiliated by Olivia's temper tantrum at the costume party.

Phil's major gripe was at Olivia's request that he taste every dish being proposed for the wedding dinner. "Did you think," he spat out, "that it would be okay if I died and you didn't? You said it was for taste's sake, but now I'm seeing a very different you."

Olivia weakly listed some things that she hadn't asked us to do that she'd read about, like insisting that all the females went on birth control pills so no one would be pregnant at the wedding. She mentioned that some brides had required bedtimes, and even dying their bridesmaids' hair similar shades of mousy brown to contrast her platinum blonde.

"You know me," she whispered. "I know I can be over-bearing, but I'm a good person and I know I've been terrible."

"How about you?" Phil asked me. "Do you have anything you want to add since we are clearing the air?"

There were a million things, but I shook my head no, with Phil mouthing back, "Really?"

Half of the guests were clamoring to get off the island. Rumors were going around that the airport was going to open in time for the 5 p.m. flight that day. Soon, there'd be no wedding to save.

Still, there was not one person in our group who believed for a second that Walter could be guilty. I was having my doubts, though, and Detective LaGuardia's "if he swims like a fish" cliché was hitting home a little bit.

After the humble apologies, Olivia took my hand, smiled at the group and said, "Don't worry. The show will go on. Lexie's rocked it and it's looking like she's proven that Walter is innocent. It was Becky. The police are getting ready to bring her in."

"That's an exaggeration. She's not being brought in. It's a conversation that—"

"Only because the police haven't gotten back to you...." As if that was the way law enforcement went.

Conversation shifted to how Olivia was going to get herself back into the guests' good graces, and it was clear that was to orchestrate the simple return of technology. Olivia had a grand idea about giving back the phones en masse, suggesting that she have a big party at Red Frog Beach. Walter would be free, everyone would be checking emails, and all in the world would be fine once more.

No. We insisted the only way to even start patching up the situation was for Olivia to go to everyone, one by one, apologize, return all phones, and to take whatever would be thrown at her, both literally and metaphorically.

Grasping at straws to retain some part of her plan, Olivia asked the group if they thought she could still request folks not to take pictures at the wedding, but now she was a captive of the bridal party, who unanimously said no. This was mutiny, and we were now running the ship, at least for a little bit of time.

"Would anyone be able to run the surf school event since Lexie's wrapping up the murder issue?" Olivia pleasantly asked.

Marianna took over as if she had been the one who saved the day.

I handed over the papers and diagrams I had jammed in my book.

As if solving Nico's murder was just something to check off in the binder.

I wasn't up for the break of dawn cocktail party and walked towards the dock without saying goodbye.

Olivia chased after me, "Thanks for everything." She took my hand leading me down the dock, talking as quietly as possible. "And please keep this between us, my Blood Sister. Even though I understand that the airport is scheduled to open, I've bought all the tickets on the afternoon flight, so that buys us some time. All the way until noon tomorrow. Honestly, I'd buy all the tickets for tomorrow, but I've maxed out my AmEx! I thought there was supposed to be no limit on the American Express card. It's platinum for the love of… do you have any credit left on any of your cards?"

No, of course not.

"I'm not sure I actually believed it yesterday, but I know without a doubt, with you on my side, I'm still getting married tomorrow." Before any response, Olivia turned and skipped back to the rest of her entourage.

She's gone over the line.

Understatement of the century.

Certifiably insane.

Maybe Max and I could make amends. A delicious but fleeting thought entered my mind. Maybe she could take me off the island on her chartered jet, which was surely scheduled for later in the morning. But the fantasy disintegrated when I realized that she just might be one of the guests to stay until the end. She was enjoying this.

26

YOU HAVE TO KISS A LOT OF FROGS
TO FIND A PRINCE

hough it felt like it was time for lunch, it was only going on 10 a.m., so it was as good a time as any to figure out how to get the detectives to come and detain Becky. *And set Walter free.*

I walked over to Josh's to get his final take on it. There was no answer when I knocked on his door, so I walked in like everyone did on the island. The doors to his back deck were open and the morning light was flooding in. I heard his quiet snores coming from the platform above. It was a peaceful snore, one that you could sleep next to and get into the rhythm of, not much more than very heavy breathing.

Salty's log sawing was unbearable. As my affection for him faded, we would fall asleep and then I'd retreat to the guest room, thoughts about leaving him running through my mind at a million miles a minute. On our last vacation, for my sanity, I'd eventually sneak out to sleep in the humidity by the pool, under the stars on the beach of St. John. The last two nights I booked my own room, with no resistance from the other party concerned.

Most people would rather date an alcoholic than a chronic snorer. I had read it in a survey somewhere and agreed heartily. I'd held my own survey in one of the final nights of Left Behind and the group agreed. Rather alone than with a snorer.

"Josh," I called as I went up.

He quizzically looked at me as I approached his bed. He grunted, "Is it already office hours?"

He rubbed his eyes and put his glasses on - nice thin wire rims, just slightly smudged. His hair was pointing every which way, and he had imprints from the sheets on his face. His stubble had specs of grey, and he slept without a shirt, with the cute little belly that emerges on artsy men who were once very lanky and had never the need or desire to work out. He'd have to get rid of it eventually. Just as I'd eventually have to get rid of mine.

"Why don't you sit down instead of just nervously looking at me?" He propped himself up on his elbow, "You look terrible. Not like that. You look exhausted."

For a writer, he didn't have the best way with words. "I'm going back to the police office if you want to come, and bring them back here because I can only think that it's Becky. I know you're skeptical, but she's the only one with a motive. She was acting terribly guilty yesterday. Nico was leaving her. She is the only one that makes sense."

"Of course she might, but what about the mysterious fiancé? What if Nico wasn't leaving her?"

"She kept the ring. So, why wouldn't she? And why would he want it back?" *You've got a lot to learn about women.*

The ring always struck me as strange, especially her grilling me over my book, the guidebook for the perpetually single. As long as LaGuardia could see she had more motive than Walter, I could be off the case. I didn't want to be responsible for throwing this sweet girl in prison, but as I had been quickly learning, there is often more than what meets the eye. Who's to say she wasn't as bad as the rest of them?

"I suppose it's time to talk to her?" His expression mirrored mine, discomfort. It was one thing interviewing random people on the zip line tour and making notes in my little slam book, but talking to a real plausible suspect in a dark room was another thing altogether.

"Let's do it," I said without confidence. Neither of us moved for a while. He got up to get dressed but, like an awkward teenager, asked me to wait outside.

I glanced down the dock and over to the restaurant. Max, Dave and Georgie sat at a lonely table, hunched into their coffees, whispering even though no one else was around to hear. I couldn't think of anything worse than catching Max's icy stare again. Chances were that I'd have another unpleasant run-in with her. The day was exceptionally humid, and my clothes were already damp. Hywel the surf guy had said to me that people on the island usually picked their outfit by what was least damp.

I couldn't stand the pressure of being seen by Max, so I walked to Becky's and knocked on her door. Josh could join after I confronted her woman to woman.

Once.

Twice.

Three times, clearly adding, "Becky."

Abiding by island custom, I walked in. It smelled dank and earthy, and it seemed darker than ostensibly possible. Crickets were chirping in surround sound.

I opened the doors to the balcony, immediately experiencing the distinct feeling of something crawling over my foot. With my hand on the door I froze as something crunched under my feet.

The light was let in and I saw the unspeakable horror. All around the room, hopping around, were tiny red poison frogs. Dozens of them. Frog clung clinging to the bottom of my feet.

All I could think of was the repeated warning of, 'Don't lick them, don't lick them, don't lick them…' Many of them were drawn to the light, but I backed up to the stairs, to the loft, two steps up, terrified of the chaos. Becky had gone mad indeed. I'd seen her loving those frogs on the first day.

She extracted the poison. She was close to Walter. She knew about the needles.

"Bloody hell," I heard, as Josh entered the cabin.

He hadn't made it to the bottom of the stairs before I screamed again, another frog bouncing off my head. The palm thatch above me would be a perfect place for frogs to hide out.

I moved to the top of the stairway, where the worst would be behind me, and I slowly turned to find Becky, already looking bluish and dead in the shadows. She laid, eyes glazed over, one arm over the bed, with that big old diamond affixed to her ring finger. Surrounding her body were ten red frogs, impaled with needles. Someone was sending a message.

The last murder was meant to look like a heart attack. This one was us being played with.

How could I have been so wrong?

The frogs that still breathed wanted to get out of there as badly as I did. Josh ran up the stairs and exclaimed, in the same tone of terrified quiet that I had used, "Bloody, bloody hell." It was the only phrase he had in him.

"I don't think I'm up for this," I whispered, still frozen in shock.

THE EMT BOAT showed up first, including an excited Dr. Nolan who was trying to hide how pleased he was at being involved in the investigation. He regained his composure and tried to hide his animation with medical concern. He examined the bottom of my foot for any abrasions but found nothing.

"Don't walk around in bare feet. I think you must've stepped on a frog whose glands weren't on the offensive. I think. Maybe. But seriously, you could get an infected splinter down here. It's just not a good idea."

And with that he was done with us, the living, and went up to see Becky's body, saying as an afterthought, "Your ankle isn't looking great. Make sure you come by the hospital later."

I'll take my chances.

LaGuardia and McDonough showed up minutes after the good doctor. They evicted Josh from the room but let me stay. The detectives were very serious this time around. It wasn't arrogance or laziness that had made them assume that Walter was their man; with any detachment, it had made sense. Now there were questions. Did they have the wrong man? Could there be two different killers? They'd been proud to congratulate themselves on a murder quickly solved, but as they say, the plot thickens….

They questioned me on everything I had seen, heard, and experienced in the last day. They had monumentally messed up and the future of tourism on the island was in the balance.

I had been in the water for a good deal of the night and

up at the crack of dawn and had seen no one come and go. My light sleeping had not been interrupted by any echoing footsteps. Dr. Nolan could tell that the murder took place only hours before my two-hour jaunt to the Pickled Parrot.

Though I hadn't heard either Olivia or her boat when she was so wonderfully waiting for me in my room. But no chance it was Olivia. Absolutely no chance.

McDonough started pacing the room, looking for anything out of place. After Migs had photographed the crime scene and the dead body for them, they bagged the dead frogs and needles. Most of the frogs had abandoned the scene of the crime, but one of the cops, borrowing gardening gloves and a broom from the staff, scooped up the rest of them with an occasional hello to his colleagues.

LaGuardia called from above, "Was she here with her fiancé?"

My answer was another disappointment. The EMTs removed the body quickly. I wondered who was footing the bill for her transportation to the hospital and if by this time we had a running tab somewhere.

McDonough emptied the contents of her living room and bathroom trashcans onto the floor. Flozzie, had brought in some bright lights for us to see better, which made me wonder if they really were all that eco? She also brought some coffee.

Island hospitality just doesn't stop.

There wasn't a lot in Becky's trash; tissues with blotted lipstick, two empty bottles of wine, old boarding passes. McDonough shook the garbage pail again and a pair of cheap vampire fangs dropped on the wooden floor.

I gasped.

Lloyd had been a vampire last night. He'd also escorted her back from the party before I returned.

The Dissector was back.

Granted, she wasn't technically his type, with her red curly bob instead of long blonde locks. But, serial killers evolve. Don't they? Yes, of course they do.

Walter would be free.

I had done my job.

27
WHAT A CLICHÉ

*N*ews of Walter's innocence and Lloyd's impending arrest spread from resort to resort like wildfire. The overnight terror had been eradicated. It could never have been Walter, they all said. Never. As quickly as the good news about Walter spread, the insidious news about Lloyd followed suit, accompanied by the resurgence of rumors about the co-ed murders of yesteryear at the internationally renowned Washington University.

Plus, everyone was now happy to go for surfing lessons.

Wrong had been righted and vice-versa. I'd spilled on everything I knew about Lloyd. Everything Josh had told me on day one clicked in to place. He had been cold and emotionless while standing over his dear friend's body. He'd taken Becky home, and he'd been in her bungalow. She knew Nico's secrets. It was like being taunted – the first murder with red frog poison, and then mocked with a virtual infestation of the creatures. As if to say…you've got the wrong man.

Had it been as much evidence as they'd had to arrest Walter? The groom had no motive. Technically, I suppose

Lloyd had just as little motive, except that he was most likely a serial killer. That was all the motive he needed.

Phones were returned, with Olivia's personal groveling apologies. The party would commence - "honoring Nico's hedonism." Becky's death was already merely an afterthought, but as relief spread, anger and moral indignation rose towards Lloyd. The villagers were out for his blood.

Nico was now a bit of a convenient afterthought too, but the wedding was branded as his swan song. I took a breath and looked around as adrenaline flew through the roof. The terror was over. We'd actually cleared the good name of an innocent man.

I waited in the boat outside the Koko resort, while LaGuardia went in to arrest the waiting Lloyd. The scene was remarkable. The guests had caught onto the news and surrounded the dock in water taxis, with a few folks teetering on the dock, blocking the walkway back to the police boat.

"Everyone get back," LaGuardia yelled. "Anyone not back on a boat in two minutes is staying overnight down at the police resort."

Screaming at Lloyd as he was escorted to the boat, all that the crowd was missing were pitchforks and torches. The insults being hurled were astounding, but Lloyd was able to walk calmly and quietly, and this infuriated the crowd even more.

Olivia, of course, the ringleader, stayed defiantly on the dock, confronting him. "I knew it. I knew it all along. A leopard can't change its spots."

He smiled and said, "Thank you."

$\sim$

I sat cross-legged on a desk, watching LaGuardia question Lloyd in a cell. For a silent man who usually only spoke in creepy one-liners, he was certainly one chatty person that morning.

He looked more amused than anything. "So, you are detaining me over a pair of fangs and a boat ride? I've already told you...Emma, that precocious little stalker, showed up in a water taxi outside Becky's about an hour after I left the party. Becky had calmed down, so I left with Emma.

"She'll tell you. I was with her all night in my hotel room, not sleeping if you know what I mean. I'm not one to kiss and tell, unless I'm arrested of course. Am I being arrested or are you just detaining me, anyway? This is silly. You just need to talk to Emma. She'll set this straight in a New York minute."

Maybe Emma is dead as well.

"I'm a fan of the cliché," Lloyd said, confidently. He gave me a sideways glance filled with amused condescension. He'd beat a murder wrap before. This was old hat to him. "So, get me a couple cigarettes and I'll riddle you with fact over fiction."

A transaction in Spanish that I didn't understand went down, and a box of Marlboros and some matches appeared.

"You're going to want to get this down on an official detective pad. I've always wondered if all cops are given those tiny flip books. I have some actual viable suspects for you," he said to LaGuardia.

Lloyd smoked half a cigarette, pointing at me before he went on a roll. "Though Encyclopedia Brown over there thinks she's cracked the case again, there's a lot I have to say."

LaGuardia asked, "Then why didn't you try to contact us

after your friend was arrested? You had knowledge of potential suspects in a homicide."

"Because it was really very entertaining to know that Walter was behind bars. I've never particularly liked him. And maybe you had the right guy," Lloyd said. "Except, I suppose, that he was in jail while Becky got the jab. Curious."

McDonough asked the most pressing of questions, "And, who's Encyclopedia Brown?"

Lloyd continued, "Annoying storybook child detective of our youth. Solving life or death conundrums like 'the case of the missing library book.' I think that little annoying snot nose ended every short story with 'Looks like Encyclopedia Brown has done it again.' Have you done it again, Lexie?"

Sociopaths are supposed to be charming. What's happening here?

After an embarrassing verbal struggle, I was coerced by LaGuardia into handing over the slam book. I would never get it back. LaGuardia had stood with his hand outstretched for minutes until I reluctantly and painfully handed it over for the final time. It was immediately handed over to the Prince of Darkness.

"Brilliant," he said, flicking through the well-worn pages, assessing the guests, licking the tip of his finger before he turned each page. "You girls are developmentally stunted, stuck in the time of your sweet sixteens. But—huh—Michael likes to swing? Who knew? Fascinating." He put the book down in front of him, ready to perform.

"It goes a little something like this," Lloyd started, and no one could deny his style. "One. I'm sure you've heard about my previous arrest regarding an unsolved serial killing spree from my formative college years. But A, I was released and B, if you believe I'm guilty of the previously referred to killing spree, you would note that they were all blonde women under the age of twenty-three.

"Two. I liked Nico. I'm probably the only one here that genuinely did. I made a lot of money for him, and him for me. I would even venture to say I loved him.

"Three. I'm not an idiot. I've got an IQ of 157 and I am probably smarter than anyone at this shindig, probably double that of Encyclopedia Brown over there. The lovely ladies even wrote it in this book here! If I were going to murder someone, I'm not going to be stupid enough to A—leave a party with them and B—casually leave my pair of fangs from a costume party at the scene of the crime. This is 101 here.

"All the same, Becky was very smart, though it doesn't say that in your book here. She was in MENSA. Were you? She dropped out of a Ph.D. program to have some fun. No wonder Nico was in love with her. Engaged to her—also missing from your diary. Bored yet?" he looked at me.

"By all means, no," I forced a smile. I divided 157 by 2, and knew that Lloyd had kindly clocked my IQ just shy of the lowest number in the average intelligence scale.

"Four. I repeat, number four. Talk to Emma. And speaking of Emma—just a little FYI to entertain you, I must tell you that Encyclopedia Brown watched my intimacy with the bride's sister in the woods just yesterday, right? A little voyeuristic jaunt in the jungle."

They both turned to me, and I sheepishly nodded my head. It was so out of context. All of a sudden, I felt like the convicted pervert in the room.

"Five, alphabetically going by this book, here's a list of people who would have a reason to kill Nico, which is not insignificant."

Boy, did he have a list. I lost faith in everyone that day.

I just kept learning. Becky had alluded to it in her rants that Nico was pushing Walter out of his business. Though he had been generous in his initial investment in the gym, Nico had wanted to buy Walter out. And not so generously.

"Walter didn't want this to happen, but there was a loophole in the contract that Nico was going to exploit. This had been going down for the three months prior to this trip. Olivia knew nothing about it, and Nico had enjoyed watching her excitement planning the wedding with his money, while Walter scrambled to find a way to save his business.

And Lloyd went on.

Max stood to inherit hundreds of millions of dollars, and wasn't it a coincidence that she showed up here? No one else had heard about this mythical reconciliation. Max did actually know that Becky was engaged to the Greek shipping heir. Was the time of Max's arrival airtight? Could she have glided in under the cover of night?

Nico had also taped a sexual escapade between him and Amanda, Olivia's business partner. She had a husband, and Nico simply liked having things to hold over people's heads. The world was a game to him.

Edgar's bad business with Nico was not so far in the past, not so unlike Walter's situation. Edgar had gathered a fair amount of venture capital interest around his high-tech start-up, which would manufacture energy-efficient supercomputers. Lloyd went on to explain that the company intended to build and market a family of clusters of between 12 and 972 compute nodes, connected in a Kautz graph.

Lloyd is trying to make us feel stupid.

At the last minute, and after much interest in the company, Nico swooped in and made a bid that covered all the venture capital and then some. Seeing Nico as a friend of sorts, he felt comfortable, but even I knew it was a bad idea to raise capital from one source. After they had signed the initial agreements, Nico had dragged his feet in delivering the funds, tying it up in miles of litigation.

"Not my fault," Nico had always said. "Standard practice, my friend," was how he'd ended that the conversation.

And then there was Josh. Lloyd pointed at me, "And Encyclopedia Brown missed this one right in her face. That Josh you've been skipping around with wrote a book about me, about what he thinks I did back at Washington. Speculation. No research. Nico knew that. His lawyer issued injunctions on my behalf. Pending libelous lawsuits. Potential bankruptcy. Bet your partner in crime didn't lay that one out for you. Plus, are you a little smitten, Ms. Brown? I think you might be.

Don't be ridiculous. I'd have more of a crush on Lloyd... I take that back.

"So, keep me here as long as you want, but maybe take an afternoon and look into people who actually wanted to kill him. Becky's death was not an afterthought. Talk to Emma. Use your brain. Go have another party, Encyclopedia Brown. Frankly, my dear, I don't give a damn."

Then he smiled again, picking up my binder, "Ceaselessly entertaining."

2 8

LET'S TWIST AGAIN...

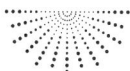

Staggering from my time with Lloyd, I humbly followed the detectives onto their boat to help them locate Emma. I enjoyed the idea of Lloyd in prison, but he certainly made a convincing case on a half dozen other folks who should be in his place. Somewhere in the world, he had to be guilty of something. There had to be some karma in the world. He probably deserved to be locked up.

We hit Emma's dumpy hotel and she was nowhere to be found. Nor was she still at Lloyd's, so we continued motoring around the island. Next stop: home sweet home, Mariposa del Mar, where I'd be retired from my brief life as a flat foot.

Just like Nico had said on the day he arrived, it looked like a bad spring break in Cancun when we arrived at the lunch party on Red Frog Beach.

The restaurant at Punta Caracol had been overtaken by a massive party of bathing suit-clad Walter worshippers dancing out a scene from Beach Blanket Bingo. Couples spilled out onto the walkway towards the cabins, laughing like they weren't one-hundred feet from the morning's crime scene. Phil's husband had written on his white t-shirt, in red magic marker, "Free Walter". He had missed the point, just a little.

The attention was all on me as the detectives escorted me towards the festivities. Walter and Olivia, the latter clad in a 50's style red bikini, danced on a table, doing the twist. She smiled widely when I came into her view. "Three cheers for Lexie! We are back on track!"

Theresa, the perpetually drunk film producer, drunkenly stumbled up to me at an attempted high five, "Ding dong, the witch is dead, right?"

She must have been poorly phrasing about Lloyd, not Becky. I hope.

Becky had done nothing worse than fall in love with the wrong man.

She was the keeper of secrets for Nico, in business and life. Lloyd was tying up the loose ends. Would the secrets die alongside her? The dirt she must have had…

The crowd happily went through their hip-hip-hoorays; patting me on the back, kissing me any number of times on the cheeks depending on their level of affectation, giving me sweaty hugs with rum punch and morning coffee breath. I tried to stay with the detectives, but the group was dragging me in other directions. I stopped trying when Max stopped me.

Max gave me a long but frigid hug. "I apologize," she smiled in her saccharine way. "You knew. You obviously knew exactly what you were doing and now all that was wrong is right. Here, slap me if you want." She closed her eyes and braced for it. "Do it. It will make you feel great."

My eyes weren't on her, I concentrated on following the trail of the detectives through the party.

Max grabbed at my hand as I walked away. "Wait," she said, looking in her bag, and then on her body. She took off a very expensive looking bracelet and put it on my wrist. "Thank you," she said again. "You've done an amazing thing."

I looked at her with some curiosity when I realized I was being tipped.

She had my attention as she whispered in my ear, "Please pass on to the authorities that it's not outside the realm of possibility that it was a crime of passion. Becky might have taken her own life, rest in peace."

I jumped up on a table, doing a little faux celebratory dance of my own, giving me both breathing room and a view to observe the party. Across the loud din of the party, the soiree detectives were listening to Emma, who was talking their ears off, shaking her head at every chance. I couldn't read a word of her lips except the repeated, "No." LaGuardia caught my eye and shrugged.

Seeing my chance after Colleen and her husband twisted by on the way to the bar, I jumped off my table, again trying to make my way out. This time Walter pulled me into a disgustingly soggy hug.

Walter was happiness incarnate, and every time he stopped hugging me, he would look at me with very pure affection and hug me again.

"Thank you, Lexie," he said, heavy into a two- minute embrace. "What you have done is amazing. Trust me, you'll be rewarded."

Tipped twice in ten minutes.

He pulled me out of the roar of the party, asking me a million questions: if I was sure it was Lloyd, and what was said, and if we could meet up later where I could tell him everything.

I was able to free myself when the detectives started walking away to the second dock.

Walter called after me as I scuttled away, "I'll find you later! I'm around! How awesome is it to say that!? Free as a bird." He then riled up the crowd in doing another chorus of three-cheers-for-Lexie.

Lloyd had been so convincing at the police station that I believed him wholeheartedly. But now, without his Emma alibi, I couldn't process it. I wondered if Lloyd would even be there when the detectives returned to Bocas PD, or if he somehow slunk out and was halfway to Caracas by now.

"Hey Lexie," McDonough said. "Have a beer. Your day is done."

That was it? Case closed?

Lloyd could use his 157 IQ and clear his own name. I wanted to get to my cabin and close my eyes until I was back in New York.

Too good to be true.

Not ten feet away from the party, I was grabbed again, this time by Ryan who looked genuinely sad and may have even been crying that afternoon. He didn't understand why no one cared that Becky was dead, and why anyone would want to kill her. He said that she was like sunshine, and I grew a little jealous. They had spent a good deal of yesterday together, and Ryan said that her love with Nico was true.

I made it to my door in silence, but Ryan stayed right behind me.

"Hey Lex," Ryan took my hand. "You okay? Your ankle? Whatever you've been doing with the cops?"

"I don't really know," I said, pulling my hand away and walking over to my terrace.

He readied himself to go but didn't. "I've been waiting to talk to you, like really talk to you, for like twenty years and I just want to find a time where we can do that before we leave."

He leaned against the frame of the door, looking down at me with big blue sad eyes. High school damage never goes away. He was still gorgeous, but I wasn't looking at thirty-five-year-old Ryan. All I saw was the fifteen-year-old who broke my heart.

The only thought in my mind was the memory of the first time that the three of us were in a car together, early on in Olivia and Ryan's relationship. We took her car to see Green Day at the Worcester Centrum. It was supposed to be a double date, but my boyfriend was grounded at the last minute, so it was just us three. We had a fun drive out, but as the saying goes 'two is company, three's a crowd.' I became chauffer on the way back, with the lovely couple scrunched up kissing passionately in the back seat. It hurt.

Ryan quietly said, "I've been understanding that there are things to say…"

"You've wanted to talk to me for the last twenty years? My name is Alexandra Martone. Match that with reading my book *Left Behind* and I think you'll only find one. Google me. You'll see."

He changed the subject. "So, is anything being done for Becky?"

"Of course there is. We feel the loss," Olivia confidently offered, magically appearing in the open door of my cabin. "So, what's going on, guys? Everyone having fun?"

Neither Ryan nor I had an answer.

She smiled at Ryan genuinely, "Can you excuse me, Ryan?"

I believe it was the first interaction that he'd had with her since their boat ride from hell, and he trotted off like an obedient little puppy.

Olivia smiled at me and gave me a little hug. She boldly put her hands on her hips, announcing, "You will be happy to know that I personally dealt with the Becky issue. Parents called. Arrangements made."

For Becky's death to become nothing more than another item on her checklist made me sad. She was simply regarded as an obligation to be dealt with.

"Honestly," I said, and even pulled out the blood sisters' card.

She smiled and cocked her head. She took my hand, "Ok, well, to be honest, Amanda made the calls. I'm not 100% sure of the details, but I know it was all dealt with in the most elegant and tasteful way."

"Is that what this party is? Elegant and tasteful?"

"Celebrate life. Woot!"

We looked outside for a while.

"You know, I was thinking about this last night," Olivia continued. "I was watching *Scream* on my computer again last night, and no one was too upset about their friends being killed. They had a big party too. It's what people do."

Watching a horror movie in the middle of this mess?

I changed into a decent dress that I had yet to wear; all bets were off with coordination of clothes to events. Olivia stood next to me, as if she didn't trust to leave me alone, and excitedly regaled me with all of her amended plans for the next two days.

It's all back on.

"You, my love, my Thelma to your Louise, my Rizzoli to your Isles, my Cagney to your Lacey…well, you know. Come back to the party for a little bit. It's not just for Walter. It's for you. You, Blood Sister, saved the day."

I caught Ryan's eye on the way back and he kindly smiled. I'd kicked myself in the head for years for making the decision not to tell Olivia that I had met him first, that I had fallen in love with him. Though, despite the way he was looking at me, I knew we never would have been together.

Olivia dragged me back to the party, Walter presenting me with a bottle of extravagant champagne and pulling me up on a table to dance. "Chug it, Tall Girl."

I took a sip.

"Ok," Walter said, punching me in the arm. "I've got to make the rounds, but I'm going to find you later."

He left me dancing badly on top of the table, bottle in hand, still being celebrated by the group that had called for my blood the night before. The world was caving in on me and I was getting dizzy. I made my way off the table and made my way to the rear of the restaurant.

There were questions, there were cheers, there were people trying to shove alcohol down my throat. When I passed Olivia, she held up a glass of champagne, yelling, "It's a scream, baby."

Embarrassing.

The rear dock at the edge of the restaurant was my light at the end of the tunnel. After extracting myself from a criminally witty conversation with Chad and Tom, it was home sweet home. Tom poured his cocktail, with diabolical laughter, over Colleen, and I was immediately forgotten about. Quickly making my way down the dock, I begged a bus boy to call me a water taxi.

Out of sight, out of mind.

It wasn't too long until the water taxi arrived and I scuttled in, grabbing a life vest as usual. Using the little Spanish I'd picked up, I asked to be driven around the island, no port of call in mind. I didn't know where I wanted to go, except far away.

"Hey," I heard and saw Josh just behind me. "Can I come too?"

I couldn't fathom a conversation with him where we didn't talk the case, but I was up for a 'just regular' adventure.

29
BUSINESS AS USUAL

*J*osh didn't seem to sweat, his white shirt strangely remaining crisp and free of wrinkles or dampness. His style made me want to buy a pair of Wayfarers.

"Where are we going?" He asked.

"Just around the island. I need a little silence," I calmly said.

Ten minutes north, there was little to see as far as human civilization; mangroves, friendly yachters waving as they passed, and those dolphins of questionable intelligence, riding astride the boat. Hotels were small, few and far between.

The surfing side of the island calmed me; run down bungalows with a couple of people surfing here and there. We passed Hywel's surf camp which would be over-run by our group of drunk cretins soon enough.

Hywel was one of my favorite people I'd met on this trip. He told me that most of Bocas' waves weren't for beginners, but his camp was off a lazy little beach, where people were happy if they could ride a two-foot swell at the end of their week.

We were getting closer to Bocas Town when Josh pointed to a largish resort portside and asked if I wanted to stop there for a late lunch.

It didn't fit in with the rest of the island. It was a major resort hotel with volleyball courts, pools, two restaurants with decks, and bikini-clad babes getting massages on the beach. It didn't belong, and I hoped it would stay the exception, not the rule.

I could see the original charm of the island that Olivia and Walter wanted to share, and agreed that it should be preserved. It's a place that for all intents and purposes was lost. Despite recent events, I loved the island and hoped for its anonymity going forward. Everyone seemed pleased to be here.

The taxi pulled up by the dock, where two staff members in white outfits helped us out of the boat; ladies first of course. The restaurant was welcoming, and they escorted us to a seaside table and handed us menus. They assumed we were on a romantic vacation together, and why wouldn't they? This would have been the natural course of things, had the wedding not been tainted by a double homicide. At the very least, it looked like a date. In a parallel word, after some tedious wedding event, a single man would ask a single woman for a drink somewhere away from the party, where they could get to know each other. Maybe they'd smile. Maybe they'd laugh. Maybe they'd kiss. Who knew?

I looked up at Josh, who was thoroughly engrossed in the menu. He ordered a bottle of French Rose for us, chilled in a cheap bucket, and he held up his glass. "To good work."

I met his toast. "I didn't do anything right, to be called good work. But thanks. And cheers you."

"I really didn't do anything, period."

Silence.

"So, you've known Olivia since when?" Josh asked, cordially.

"Five. Kindergarten."

"You're not very alike, are you?"

It that an insult or a compliment?

"We were. Once upon a time. We really were." Hopefully, down deep, we still were.

We struggled over small talk about where we'd grown up, how we knew everyone, and the small talk you that you have to do. After an extremely awkward pause, he asked me what had gone down at the station. And what Lloyd had said. I told him what I knew, though with caution and abbreviation, now that I was fully briefed on this regular guy named Josh.

Josh listened intently and held up his glass again. "Well, here's for putting Lloyd behind bars. Where he's always belonged."

I reminded him, "He's been arrested. Not charged."

"Well, here's to the right direction."

That I could get behind.

I wasn't 100% surprised when he asked the secondary question of the week. "So, is it okay if I talk to you about your book?"

I don't want to rip you apart. Please don't ask me about Left Behind.

I'm not sure why everyone wanted me to go through the story of the formation of the group. It was already spelled out in the book that they'd read.

Unlike speaking to Becky about my previous philosophy in terms of herself, Josh wanted to know more of what brought me to the precise moment of self-realization. A lot of people had bought into what I wrote, so I couldn't really tell them that I'd discovered my entire philosophy was damaging and didn't work for beans.

The whole process was going to make you feel worse and eventually more insecure. That is something that I never actually said. Josh had chosen the wrong people to pick him apart; Nico, Walter and some of his newer, more successful literary friends. He didn't leave his house for a week after they were done kicking the crap out of his soul.

"Did you learn anything from it?" I asked.

He smiled, "Yes. To pack up all my stuff and move to a land very far away."

He had a good humor about their insults, and I was sorry that he was the punching bag for the group of idiots that he hung around with. He did believe that it had made him a better person.

I still needed to stay credible, so I went with the story that it was my strong choice to leave Salty, in search of what I confidently deserved, instead of the opposite; that I stayed with him out of fear that I wouldn't meet anyone else.

He has to know that I wasn't Left Behind.

"I think you're fine," I said, realizing that what I had said sounded cold. "You're a good catch." I supposed he was. I admitted, "I don't know if I agree with my book 100% anymore."

Through the entire lunch, I couldn't stop thinking about Lloyd behind bars. Not my business, really. It was convenient to believe it was him, and not Emma, who was lying.

Josh ordered another bottle of wine, which was much more than I'd drink normally in an afternoon. After another toast to justice, I asked, "Speaking of books, why didn't you tell me about your book?"

He returned with a question. "What book?"

"The book about Lloyd. The one with the injunction order that Nico hit you with."

Unexpectedly, he laughed. "That's a bit of an exaggeration. You're talking about something from over ten years ago. I told Walter about wanting to write a book about Lloyd. Walter can't keep a secret, and the next thing I know I get a cease and desist from Nico's lawyer on The Dissector's behalf. That was it. I'd done maybe two or three weeks of work on it. Lloyd seems to be grasping at straws, don't you think?"

Grasping at strings? He seems to have thrown a whole ball of frazzled yarn.

After agreeing through silence to change the subject, he told me with animation about his newest endeavor; a biography of another modernist writer named Fernando Pessoa, out of Portugal. He wrote under seventy-five pseudonyms.

"Sorry," Josh said. "I know that it is all very boring."

It wasn't. It really wasn't.

On the way back home, I looked at him in all sorts of "what if" situations? What if I had met him in a bar? A library? At work? At a bookstore, like in the movies. But in all honesty, I don't think that anyone in the history of dating ever met anyone in a bookstore...

What if he wasn't a friend of Walter? Hadn't seen our slam book? What if I hadn't read that born-again Christian sci-fi best-seller, spelling out all my pathetic faults and vulnerabilities? What if he were likable at all?

There was nothing left to say.

30

THERE WAS A LITTLE GIRL

*J*osh and I rode back to the resort in silence, engaged with nature as we gazed deep into the mangroves we passed. At one point I put my hand on his shoulder, pointing out a three-toed sloth high up in a tree.

"I don't see it," he said, squinting as he looked up into the tall trees.

"They don't move much. You could easily mistake it for a coconut."

"Oh, ok. I do see it."

He spent the last few minutes of the ride asking the difference between the two-toed and three-toed variety of sloths. I found myself very happy to have something to talk about besides murder and my book.

In the restaurant at the resort, Emma sat at a remote table, lips pursed, reading the *Frommer's Guide to Paraguay*. She'd seemingly purchased the wrong tour book. Part of me expected Josh to ask me for a last cup of coffee or glass of wine.

"Thanks for the company. I think I'll take a nap before tonight's party." Josh shrugged, I have no idea why, then turned and sheepishly walked back to his room.

You're a strange one, Josh.

I returned to my cabin and tried to nap myself. But sleep was no longer in my DNA as I lay on my back, under the mosquito netting, with my mind still racing. I took a long wash in the solar shower, which turned from lukewarm to cold in minutes, but I got out feeling squeaky clean and relaxed. It was late in the afternoon, and no one was knocking on my door or dying so that was good.

Poor Becky.

I hoped she'd inspire a more sympathetic outpouring of emotion back in New York. Where she came from was a mystery to me, but I hoped that she had a lovely family home somewhere, with parents who were still together and a group of friends who loved her dearly. I hoped there were hundreds of gym executives who she visited with Nico and Walter, who were surely charmed by her quirky ways and enormous smile. I hoped that she would have a huge turnout at a celebration of life ceremony. Filled with music, poetry, and tears of hope. Down the line, I'd hit up Olivia and Walter to set up a scholarship in her name. I didn't remember what Lloyd had said she studied.

I ran my hand over the beautiful red clothing in my closet. Most of it I hadn't worn, including the wetsuit, which is unfortunate as it is an item of clothing that can make anyone look good. I prettied myself up the best I could for the evening's dinner cruise, picking the most beautiful dress I owned and putting my hair up as best as I could. Then, mocking my belief that I could actually be free from Olivia and obligation, there was a knock on the door.

Behind the door was a bleary-eyed Emma, who at least

had the courtesy to knock. She could hardly look me in the face, "Can I talk to you?"

We went back to the restaurant for what would turn out to be my first of two dinners. That ten extra pounds was quickly going to reach fifteen. Emma still was amazingly beautiful, eating her burger while getting ketchup all over her childlike face, wiping it away with charm. She repeatedly looked at me, almost ready to talk, opening her mouth then closing it a number of times. She threw back half the burger, looking like she hadn't eaten in weeks.

"I feel bad," she said. "Really bad. I shouldn't have come to Panama. It was a huge mistake."

"No, you shouldn't have come." In an instinctual defense of Olivia, I continued, "It's not too late for you to leave. You've done horrible things in the past, but this is really beyond what I could conceive."

She was inconsolable about Becky's death, though I don't believe that she'd ever actually spoken with her. She looked at me, wiping her tears on her arm. "I can't get a plane ticket off the island. I've tried. Not yesterday, not today. I thought that coming here with Ryan would be the ultimate revenge. I could finally truly even the score. I really believed that."

"Even the score?" I was curious. "You've ruined every major event of Olivia's life. I know she was terrible in the past, but her sleeping with your boyfriend, who you didn't even love, five years ago does not warrant putting a cloud over every major achievement she's had. Seriously, Emma, you are warped."

"There are things I don't think Olivia told you. You really don't know, do you?" she asked rhetorically before laying her story on the table.

Olivia and Emma Fowler had a serious case of rotten. My first observation of this had been when Olivia was fifteen, and Emma was ten. Olivia had stuck so many M&Ms up Emma's nose that her parents had to take her to the hospital. I watched Olivia do it, while she was supposed to be babysitting her little sister. I quietly told her to stop it, but she didn't listen.

Emma was ritualistically tortured by Olivia all throughout their childhood. Then one dreaded day, Emma grew up and came into her own as a woman freshly scorned.

Emma admitted to being terrible as she confessed to me. There had been a lot of stealing of boyfriends once Emma became of dating age, but nothing was irreparable until Emma reached the tender age of 25.

She'd been moving up the ladder in her dream job in movie production, becoming the Director of Creative Development in a very respected indie film company.

"Olivia went through a lot of work to get me fired," she said. Through questionable connections, Olivia had somehow been able to get Emma unceremoniously dismissed for embezzlement. She hadn't. It could never be proved. A friend recommended bringing a wrongful dismissal suit against them, but what good would that do?

The gossip started and for all intents and purposes, she was blacklisted. Whether or not the elder sister had planned it to go that far, word had gotten out and Emma could never get a job in film again, instead flitting from one administrative job to the next, being subsidized by rich boyfriends who couldn't care less what she had done. After all, she was great eye candy.

No. I had never heard that story.

All she'd ever wanted, from the age of seven, was to work in the film industry, and that dream ended up dead in the water, thanks to Olivia. Emma considered every event she had terribly tainted to be partial payment for her sister having completely killed her dream.

"Olivia could always go forward with her life. I gave her obstacles, and Olivia gave me endings."

Showing up at her sister's wedding with her first high school love made them even.

"I know you are right. I've got a feeling that I might have gone too far with this one. So, I made up for it. She doesn't know it, but I've made everything right." Emma started crying again. "But I can't do this. I just can't do this. I can't be responsible for someone going to jail over a stupid wedding. I was with him. I was with Lloyd last night. He didn't kill anyone…Not in Bocas Del Toro, at least."

"I don't know what's wrong with you Fowler women! This isn't you sending your sister an apology! This is putting someone behind bars in a Panamanian jail!" Though it was a new level of terrible for her, I wasn't 100% surprised. However, Olivia…

I believed Emma. Her story rang true. This would be an unbelievable weight to bear for years, and a month ago I wouldn't have believed that Olivia could be so devious. Everything had changed.

And if she couldn't trust her best friend, who would she trust with that deception? No one.

The little sister was possibly just as morally corrupt. Emma seemed completely surprised that my next plan was to take her down to Bocas PD to fess up. The idea of helping Lloyd out was completely alien to her. The Fowler moral compass was back in debate. She had merely needed to confess her wrongdoings to me, but she had no intention of doing anything about it.

Her flawed logic was that she'd still be able to give Olivia the wedding of her dreams, and eventually the cops would figure out that Lloyd was innocent, so ultimately no one was getting hurt. In her head, all ill between sisters had been put to rest, even if Olivia never knew. Emma could leave the event in peace and never speak with her again. But, I knew she'd have to tell Olivia one day. She'd want Olivia to know her sacrifice.

She could just walk away. Could I ever do that?

"Well, I'm going to go down there and tell them what you did, anyway," I threatened as if I were her high school bully. Reluctant and in tears, she allowed me to bring her down to the dock and order a water taxi. I was so sick of water travel. A nice windowless van with a gas leak sounded better to me.

"I'm going to have a panic attack," Emma dramatically announced, as I escorted her onto the boat, telling the driver we were in a hurry.

She looked sick as she sat in the back, further excusing herself. "You know, I was only sleeping with Ryan for like two weeks before I came down here. He was not part of the original plan. Me showing up was going to be torture enough, but I ran into him and told him I'd love to have him as my guest at an old friend's wedding. He just never asked who the old friend was..."

She started to dry heave over the edge, finally continuing, "He asked about Olivia, I think as small talk. Just once. But you? You came up a lot. He's been thinking about you for quite some time." She put her head between her knees and shut up for the next twenty minutes.

That last part was nice to hear. Ryan had made it into my dreams quite a few times over the last fifteen years - a few times a year, not as a nightly obsession. The dream was always the same. I'd run into him somewhere randomly, where he might be in town just for a day, but he'd happen to have that day free.

We would do everyday things like going to the beach, maybe seeing a movie, checking out a used record store. As the day would progress it would become very clear that we had never been out of love. We'd drive around town in a rickshaw built for two, taking selfies of ourselves at various tourist locations.

It would all become very obvious to the both of us, yet I would always wake up right before the kiss. No matter how hard I tried, I could never force myself back to sleep for just a little more time, for just one kiss.

No, not again. Not in this lifetime.

In desperation, I thought about calling Salty, asking him to help get me out of this tropical mess of a crime scene. His logic would be to just meet halfway in Miami, where we could just sleep for a week, his hand on my stomach in a way that didn't make me uncomfortable. The week would be followed by his inevitable half-assed request to get back together again, followed by a passive-aggressive jab at what he perceived my life hadn't added up to.

No.

Let the past remain the past.

Comfort be damned.

Not in this lifetime.

PHYLLOBATES TERREBILLIS

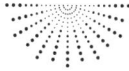

a small group of tourists stopped to watch outside the Police Station as I dragged an unwilling Emma towards the front door. She stamped her feet and eventually sat down on the filthy street getting ready for a full out temper tantrum.

"Do you want to be a YouTube viral sensation?" I barked after one of the onlookers took his phone out. She wiped dirt across her teary face and followed me into the station.

I lead her through the station to present her to the detectives. The atmosphere in the station was semi-serious and filled with cigarette smoke. Lloyd was outside of the cell, sitting on a desk, deep in conversations with the detectives and Crabby Paolo.

The Dissector pulled his glasses down the bridge of the nose, assessing the fact that I finally looked like a real female. "Well, you sure do clean up well."

Do I really?

This seemed to be the consensus, but Lloyd couldn't hold

back. "Has Encyclopedia Brown solved the case of the three-toed sloth in the bramble?"

Emma stepped out from behind my shadow, looking at Lloyd with adoring terror, whispering, "Hi."

Lloyd took a deep drag of his cigarette and turned away from her.

Emma immediately came clean about Lloyd's alibi, while tearing at her fingernails.

A family trait it seemed.

She stared at Lloyd the whole time, and despite her quiet pleading, he remained the Iceman. No words directed in her direction whatsoever. He directed his speech at the detectives only, suggesting that their best plan would be to let him stay in prison the rest of the weekend, allowing the chance for the guilty party to get sloppy and overconfident.

"It's the best plan that I've heard," Lloyd casually threw out there. "Plus, it would be a great favor to me. I can continue working on the case, and stay as far away from this group of nitwits as possible."

Emma swore to the group, and specifically to Lloyd, that she'd keep it silent. There was only half a chance she wasn't lying.

My heart had gone out to her when she had told me about being fired, but it didn't mean that I actually thought she was a good person. As if I didn't already know it, I was clearly seeing there was something inherently wrong with the Fowler family.

"Let's consider," LaGuardia said, "detaining her as well."

Panamanian law was certainly convenient.

Though it was obvious to the room that they were joking about her impending incarceration, terror quickly spread over her face, immediately looking at Lloyd as her savior.

Lloyd slyly smiled and shooed her out the door, "You may withdraw."

As soon as Emma left, Lloyd's expression immediately transformed to that of detached entertainment. He and Paolo metamorphosed into two little boy science geeks as they disclosed the newest bit of information that had been uncovered: the poison found in Nico was not that of a red frog at all.

"Phyllobates Terrebillis," Lloyd said, with great respect.

The frog in question was a golden dart frog, indigenous to the Pacific coast of Colombia only. Unfathomably, a quarter of a gram of pure toxin from the one-inch terror could kill a man in minutes. Its maximum capacity of one milligram could kill ten people.

The weapon of choice had not been a red frog; it turned out it would take days to kill a man, if ever, if it went untreated. She'd have to be examined but the smart money was on the same cause of death for Becky. Red frogs had been losing some of their toxicity over the years, and so an injection could possibly be fatal over many days, but no one could die in an instant. It was going to take a much tougher frog than that. It was an exceedingly clever bait and switch.

"Do you understand, Encyclopedia Brown, how much more interesting this is than the wedding?" Lloyd smirked in perpetuity.

"Can you stop calling me that?" I asked.

"Do something to change my mind. Your involvement up to now has been limited to randomly walking into the wrong facts and having things dropped in your lap."

The Dissector was right. I was a complete fraud, and I knew it from the start.

The detectives looked like they might come to my defense,

but they didn't. As usual, I swallowed my pride and listened to Paolo's discourse. One would have extracted the poison from the yellow frog and stored it as a solid crystalline salt, with a stable shelf life of up to three years. It would resemble something like pink bath salts to the untrained eye. Even touching it could make your arm numb for a week.

Who were these golden frogs fighting?

Lloyd was right. Things did keep falling into my lap.

"I've seen it," I told them, all of a sudden understanding the tingly fingers, still not quite right. They'd only started to subside, but I was still overwhelmed with a new sickness. The pink crystals I'd spilled when snooping through Becky's drawer could have killed me. Forget swimming and skiing and all the things I avoided for safety's sake. It's all out there. The poison had been left in clear sight. Did that mean no one else was going to die?

"I've been poisoned," I quietly said, and filled them in on my clumsy spilling of the Victorian bottle. "I'm dying."

Paolo assured me, "You are not dying. You merely touched a few crystals. If you were poisoned with a lethal dose, you'd have been dead in ten minutes yesterday. Ghastly stuff, really." He took my hand in a way that made me feel dirty, looking at my fingers, which displayed nothing in particular. "Just fine…"

LaGuardia's metamorphosis into a respectable policeman of note was complete. He told Paolo and me to go with him back to my resort and to see if the poison was still there. I was nearly out of the door when Lloyd called after me, "Do some good work, Encyclopedia. Show us how a junior ranger becomes a real grown-up one."

Tired, frustrated and finally pushed a little bit too far, I lunged at Lloyd, knocking him off the desk and to the ground where I put my hands to his throat. While I was able to get a satisfying look of terror from him and a few moments of strangulation, Lloyd quickly disarmed me by getting a swift kick into my ankle wound. The wound pulsed as I slumped away from him across the floor.

LaGuardia took him by the neck and pinned him against the wall, "You never hit a woman. What's wrong with you? You never do that. She's helping us. She's helping you. You don't do that."

Lloyd looked surprised that they weren't laughing, while Paolo helped me off the floor. It was clear that an apology would not be forthcoming, so I pulled myself together as best I could.

Lloyd finally opened his mouth. "I think you're really making a mistake if you aren't really wondering about Josh, just because you're running around together or whatever you are doing. Aren't you curious why he's been so keen to be involved?"

"Josh and I already talked about that, Lloyd. There was no injunction. There was a cease and desist on a synopsis. You're the one grasping at straws."

He snickered and waved me away, dismissing me in the manner he got rid of Emma. "And may Encyclopedia Brown be on her way."

∾

IT IS A COMPLETELY regular thing for police to return to the scene of a crime, even when they've arrested a suspect. After all, they've got to build a case, review a scene, and account for every detail.

Despite the normalcy, my heart was beating triple time and my breath was short as I took Paolo and LaGuardia toward the second floor of Becky's quarters. Only the staff was hanging out when we returned, but every creak of the dock, every boat that motored past, every unknown animal noise made me feel like our guilty party was watching us intently and close by.

The crime scene was gone; the mattress was replaced, the room had been aired, and all evidence of frog inhabitants had been eradicated. Flozzie would be ready to rent it out after the terrible wedding party left on Sunday. We had all donned latex gloves, but Paolo still didn't want us going anywhere near the night table. Hands shaking, he secured and bagged the bottle and placed it in his kit, so they could take it back to the lab.

"Leave the bottle," LaGuardia whispered. "If that is the poison, the guilty party knows it's there. It's all we have right now, the hope that someone is going to want to reclaim it. I'll send an officer up here to act like hotel staff and watch what goes on."

"I think that's a very bad idea," Paolo said while returning the bottle.

I agreed, wondering if the absolute last place the criminal would go back to would be to the murder weapon at the crime scene.

LaGuardia threw his hands up in exasperation. "They may not come back to get it. They probably won't. But if they do…"

Paolo pleaded, "Let me take it to the lab, look at it, and see if we can replace it with something benign that at least looks the same."

A short, heated conversation spoken in Spanish concluded that they were going with Paolo's request. There would be no more murders from frogs that night.

32
PRETTY IS AS PRETTY DOES

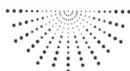

J was well aware of the late afternoon hour when I escorted the gentlemen back to the boat. I felt a lot safer as they parted, though I stayed in full view of the waiter and bartender in the empty restaurant.

I had caught my reflection before we had exited the cabin and, despite it all, was holding on to the compliment from Bocas PD that I "cleaned up well." Sun-kissed and black hair always held its own against blood red dresses. There would be a dinner cruise that night, on a yacht out of Panama City, with "certified American staff" as advertised on their website.

Was that a good thing?

In a few hours, they'd be picking up passengers from their resorts, but I had to go see Olivia first. Besides my now limited bridal party duties, I wanted to take a good look at her and see if she really was the person that Emma had claimed.

After avoiding the group of naked people playing tag at Olivia's resort, I entered her somewhat somber chambers. A platinum-haired beauty was working on Olivia's hair, thus far teased and higher and blonder than it had been that morning.

Olivia caught my reflection in the mirror and smiled. "This is Carmen, right from town! Who knew? She is seriously stupendously talented and has already made suggestions for making tomorrow's hair even better."

And with that, I knew that the old Olivia was back.

Carmen gave a brief wave, which allowed the bride to turn and look at me. She clasped her hand over her mouth. "Oh Lex, you look so beautiful, like I knew you would. You look like true love personified."

She rushed to me and held both of my hands as she took me in as if she hadn't seen me in years. "She is beautiful, and therefore to be wooed. She is a woman, therefore to be won. That's Shakespeare and don't tell me it isn't because you know that I know that one." She then let go of my hands to give me a high five.

It was true. She loved her Shakespeare and especially her Henries; this one being from *Henry VI*, a play that aptly starts at a funeral. Through years of what I now saw as subtle backhanded abuse, I was never fully able to believe any compliment from her about my looks.

When coming into my own at the tender age of seventeen, she had taken me aside at a party, where I'd been having a blast. Olivia had said, 'It's so nice, Lexie, that all these guys seem to have crushes on you. It proves that guys do care about more than looks.'

On the kind side, she often set me up with guys, as I was never much good at dating on my own. On the mean side, she never set me up with anyone above what she probably considered my level. She dedicated her book to me. She'd helped me relentlessly with my book. But she never thought it really counted.

Back in the now, she twirled herself around under my arm, landing back in her pampering chair. "Finally," she said, "we are ready to get this show on the road. And you're beautiful, these islands are beautiful and I'm beautiful. Was that too narcissistic to say?"

Emma was on my mind as I tried to smile. "It's never stopped you before."

She looked at me quizzically, as if that was a move in the game that she hadn't expected, and turned back to the mirror while Carmen piled teased curls on top of her head. "I'm going to let that one pass."

Our conversation was staid and formal while she did her final prep for the party. After Carmen buttoned up the back of her dress, Olivia turned to me and furled her mouth, "Spit it out, ding-dong."

Lloyd was innocent.

It's what I wanted to tell her, but my jaw stayed clamped shut.

The news would send everyone running to the airport when Olivia's finishing line was so close in sight. There was a deep vulnerability behind her big blue alpha eyes, and I found myself reverting to the bad habit of wanting to forgive her. Like Emma, I thought I'd give her the same secret present; a normal and calm wedding. Also like Emma, perhaps this was my final gift, and I'd let myself drift away from Olivia after our return to New York.

"I know that I asked you before," I sheepishly said, "but are you sure you didn't know anything about Nico finding this loophole in his contract with Walter? It was going to let him buy Walter out, for like hardly any money at all." My words were slow and clear. I watched Olivia's expression change from surprise to defiance to anger.

"That's ridiculous. I'd certainly know about it," she snapped. "Why would Walter want to do that? Nico was his best friend and best man. And what's the point of telling me now? Who cares anymore?"

"I'm telling you because I'm your friend, Olivia."

"This is the worst wedding ever," Olivia said, turning away from me.

Clearly.

～

I WAS BUMMING Olivia out big time, and once on the dinner cruise, she abandoned me, transforming like usual into the charming hostess. After a few people smiled and raised their glass to me, all my hero status of the morning was forgotten. My fifteen minutes had come and gone. No one approached me for clever small talk and my anxious claustrophobia set in.

"Woah," Amanda said from behind. "I'll so be happy to have half a day off tomorrow. We should be getting overtime pay."

You have no idea.

She smiled at me and offered a glass of champagne. I was sick of drinking but took a small sip when we toasted, also thinking that if I just held the full glass no one would offer me another.

We observed the rowdy party in silence. "Amanda, people are whispering that you and Nico had an affair. And he had pictures or video or something? I guess this was one of his things? I don't want to upset you, but I just thought you should know."

"People are saying that, huh?" she nonchalantly said. "I didn't know it was common knowledge, which is unfortunate. I'm paying the price, though. I told the hubby months ago, rather than have Nico holding anything over me. Supposedly I've been forgiven, but all I'm saying is that it's a good thing there's a couch in our cabin."

Now I was pissing Amanda off too, and she quickly made her way into the party.

Not guilty? I think. Is it safe to cross her off the list?

The seating plan had been changed by Marianna, who'd become the de facto maid of honor while I had put myself in harm's way. I'd been turned on.

I had been reseated with some of the people I liked the least; Edgar and Mrs. Edgar, Colleen, Joe the nephew who was the only person under twenty-six at the wedding and strangely still wearing braces. Still clinging to my half-assed investigation, I sat down next to Edgar, who was yapping it up with some chic couple whose names I no longer had the energy to remember.

"Edgar," I interrupted. "I never really got the chance to say sorry about Nico. I know you guys were close." Mrs. Edgar didn't acknowledge me.

"It certainly is a tragedy," Edgar said, lacking much expression. "He will certainly be missed." Our talk ended there, and he returned to his jovial conversation.

Doing what all socially awkward people do at parties when no one is talking to them, I pulled out my phone, finding a text from LaGuardia: 'Poison has been replaced with a saline compound. No worries if anyone gets jabbed now!'

That's some good news at least.

I scanned the room again, preferring to withdraw rather

than try to participate anymore, but was startled to meet Josh's stare.

He was not alone in the corner of a party. Josh sat next to Marianna, who had her hand casually on his, laughing in the easy-going and feminine way that she did so well. Perhaps he had explained the comic side of John Dos Passos, rarely, if ever, seen.

Josh had tolerated me, and maybe was actually entertained or impressed by me when trying to solve a murder, but I wasn't suitable for nighttime flirtations. Despite the fact that the general consensus was that I 'cleaned up good'. He cleaned up pretty good too. I'd always been a sucker for a man in a seersucker suit.

He was Lloyd's prime suspect, and it was beginning to come together. Josh had been one of the very few people staying at Punta Caracol last night. He had a motive. He didn't want to buddy up with me for safety, despite his own instructions to the rest of the gang.

Everything Lloyd said was ringing true in my ears, including the fact that Josh had been trailing around with this amateur flatfoot for the duration of my less than successful investigation. I quickly turned to Edgar, pretending to be part of his raucous conversation.

Walter hit his wine glass with a fork, and the silence took over. Walter stood center stage, flanked by Olivia playing a perfect first lady. He appeared to be as in love with his own voice as he was with Olivia.

"I'll have to admit," he loudly announced, "that this has been one hell of a week. Intensely horrible, and yet filled with love, yes love. And back to spending my evenings with you," he continued, followed with laughter. "I need to dedicate tonight to my eternal friend Nico and my brilliant assistant of five years, Becky. I can't believe that Olivia is going to be my wife tomorrow, but tonight belongs to the two people in my life who are so tragically gone."

The room applauded like it was an award ceremony, not a slapdash intoxicated memorial speech. He went on for far too long, so the guests returned to previous more interesting conversations in whispers.

The food was bland, like all dinner cruises, no matter what ridiculous amount they paid for it. Dessert was followed by the inevitable dancing. Couples flocked to the dance floor while I poked at my undercooked crème brûlée with a fork.

It's time to go.

I nodded goodbyes to various folks as I made my way to the back of the boat, hoping I could find a member of the crew to take me back to land with a lifeboat or a jet ski or frankly anything that floated.

"Are you going?" Josh said, following me in the dark. "Can I come with you?"

I was too polite to say no.

33
SWIMMING LESSONS, PART 3

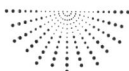

I felt relatively safe leaving with Josh because I knew that the poison had been replaced as part of the detectives' questionable trap. I didn't want to chalk it up to my sheer stupidity. Josh would sacrifice Lloyd to the gallows and return to Chicago, having committed what was looking like the perfect crime.

"I hated that party. You look like you hated it, too," he smiled.

I could hear my deep nervous breaths over the sound of the motor. I looked back at the giant yacht that was slowly disappearing out of view. My heart was beating double time and I was sweating through the polyester of my ridiculous Inquisitor costume.

Josh continued, "You know, I was thinking that maybe Lloyd didn't do it after all."

Was this going to be a Scooby Doo moment?

Would he confess his master plan and then kill me too?

We walked towards our rooms and he said, "Okay, this sounds stupid but I'm going to say it. Put your bathing suit on and meet me in my room in five minutes. I'm not going to be the only man at this wedding not to give you a swimming lesson. But you need a real swim lesson, not some half-baked instruction, not so subtly masking an attempt at seduction."

Hmmm. There was more than one way to skin a cat, that is to say, he could drown me just as easily as poison me. As was par for the course, the restaurant was almost empty, with a few drunk locals doing shots with the bartender. I could only assume one of the men at the bar was the drunk undercover police officer LaGuardia had promised. He caught my eye, and I hoped it was true.

"I understand your fear of drowning, but what else is the fear about? It has to come from somewhere. Sharks? Giant octopus? Drowning is a very real and valid fear, but you have a better chance of dying by bee sting than being killed by a shark. That's true."

I softened at his use of statistics. "I don't know why I'm afraid."

"I don't foresee you becoming captain of the swimming team anytime soon, but I would like to give you the skills needed so that if you fell out of a boat, you wouldn't die, and that doesn't include an early morning extended back float in three feet of calm water. I'm guessing there won't be the same number of men lining up to teach you how to swim on a nightly basis when you get back to New York."

How do you know how many men are lining up to teach me to swim in New York?

Okay, yes, maybe none.

Definitely none.

He had the back door open when I got to his room. He was searching for something in his drawer. He was wearing black board shorts and his shirt was off. He turned around and tossed me a pair of blood red goggles. "You're going to need these."

We walked out to the deck and sat down with our toes touching the water.

"Now spit in the goggles."

"Gross," I said. And spat.

"Now wash them out with salt water. The goggles won't fog up that way." He then put them on my head and checked the seal. "Come on." He hopped off the deck into the water and I followed. Though the water was warm a shiver ran up my back. Josh took my hand and led me farther into the ocean.

"Taste the water. Then spit it out. Get used to the taste."

I couldn't have looked less sexy if I tried.

Very academically, he patiently taught me to tread water, which I've been told is just like riding a bicycle, but I wouldn't know about that. After I had mastered that pre-school task, he explained the doggy paddle.

Humiliating.

"Okay," he said while swimming about fifty feet from me. "Paddle to me."

"I can't," I said and did nothing for a while, staring at him. "I can't."

"You can. You're hardly going to get your face wet."

"I look stupid. You look regular."

I started treading water and then swam to him; goggles and cupped hands letting me swim at a snail's pace. Slowly but oh so surely, I reached him. If he was teaching me to swim, he was saving me, not killing me. He wasn't the killer. I stood up in front of him on tiptoes, spitting out the water I'd collected on my long journey. "I did it."

"You did it. Of course you could do it."

"I did it," I said again.

He cocked his head and did a half smile kind of smirk, silent for a moment, like he was conjuring something very witty to say, but simply repeated, "You did it." He held out his hand to shake.

I took his hand, "Thank you."

Not giving me back my hand, he bit his bottom lip while looking at me inquisitively. Slowly he pulled me closer to him and kissed me, sweetly. I kissed him back, with increasing intensity.

We waded back towards his terrace, kissing every few feet. We reached the deck and he helped lift me to the edge, where I turned around and sat, kissing him while he stood between my legs, his hands growing more confident with my body.

"Do you want to come inside?" he asked.

I kissed him back and said, "Yes?" though it wasn't a question.

Back inside he threw me a towel and we both dried off. "Do you want a drink?"

"Yes?"

He poured two glasses of wine and brought them over, putting them down on the table next to me. He started kissing me again, his hands running through my damp hair. In between kisses, he whispered, "It's been a while. You know?"

Still kissing him, I replied, "Me too."

He reached over and picked up our drinks. We toasted without saying anything in particular. "Do you want to come upstairs?"

I said nothing, but slowly removed my bathing suit, and stood naked in front of him.

He took a step back, looking me up and down, finally saying, "You are so beautiful."

I walked up the stairs slowly, with him closely behind. I lay on his bed as he took his shorts off and lay next to me. Before kissing me, he rested his hand on my hips and whispered, "This is going to be great."

And it was.

~

DAY FIVE

~

34

WH'APPENED?

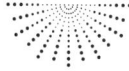

There was no Olivia watching over me when I woke up, but there was no Josh next to me either. I had slept so soundly that I felt quite guilty when I opened my eyes, the ceiling fan and ocean providing the perfect hypnotic calm. I pulled the white sheet around me and sat up, cheeks flushed as my mind replayed the events of last evening.

After a beautiful few hours, we'd stayed up until just before dawn, sharing secrets and telling stories, falling asleep tangled up in unfamiliar warm limbs.

"Josh?" I called, in as demure of a voice as I had in me.

No answer.

Suddenly very conscious of my nudity, I looked for something to put on, finding nothing, so I pulled the sheet tighter to head downstairs to meet the day. I crossed my fingers, hoping that I'd find Josh returning to the room with some coffee, not murdered, lying across the sofa surrounded by a group of red frogs.

A new day began, and I was still alive.

Josh was neither dead nor present on the ground floor, terrace doors open, sun shining on the almost full bottle of wine. My red bikini was in a corner on the floor. I put it on quickly, much more aware of my body's imperfections.

I quickly walked to my cabin, dreading the thought that anyone would see me. What was there to be embarrassed by? That someone might think that I was actually having sex? Laughter from the restaurant seemed quite distant, but I could see with clarity that it was undeniably Olivia lording over a small group, which was my first taste of lemon for the day.

I took the time to make sure I still "cleaned up good" and slowly walked down the dock to the restaurant, heart beating, unsure of what I was going to say when I saw Josh.

Josh was sitting across from Olivia, drinking coffee, joined by Dave and Edgar. Olivia was super animated, enthusiastically telling a story, making everyone laugh. All of her darkness seemed to have left, and she infectiously smiled at me.

"Hail, hail, the gangs all here!" For my eyes only, she whispered, "Floozy." Then, of course, she winked.

Who says floozy?

I dragged a fifth chair to the table, squeezing in between Olivia and Dave, joining the happy group who were busy telling embarrassing stories about Walter in a game of one-upmanship. Josh was less at ease as I sat, catching my eye quite often but always looking immediately away, blushing every time. It hadn't felt like a one-night stand, but I'd never had one before. Conceivably, I had already experienced the beginning and end of us. It really hadn't felt that way.

There was big business to take care of though. In the flurry of the "situation", no one had stepped up to the plate to replace Nico as best man, so Olivia was begging the remaining groomsmen to come together and save the wedding. Dave and Edgar were giddy as schoolgirls with all kind of ideas; each was met with an exuberant "yes, yes, yes!" from Olivia.

"Josh is the writer. He should be the one to give the best man speech," Dave suggested.

"Ha," was Edgar's response. "Do you want everyone to fall asleep? Have you heard him speak in public?" Everyone laughed, even Josh, and it was quickly decided that brother Dave would assume the responsibility, and he could be relied on to embarrass Walter just enough, as was every good groomsman's duty.

Olivia ruffled my hair like a puppy, hugged me close and asked, as casually as if she'd run into me at a NYC coffee shop, "So, what are you doing today?"

The idea of choice was something that I had forgotten existed. I wanted to protect myself and go home.

"Work on my speech for tonight?" I asked, waiting for the other shoe to drop.

"Why don't you go to that spa in town? Go for a few hours. Put it on my tab. Don't worry about the speech. It will be brilliant. Just have a relaxing day." She kissed me, lingering on the cheek and asked the guys, "What's the woman version of 'brother from another mother?' Come on you strapping hunks of male, there's work to do."

Free will to write what I wanted?

She'd already rejected two different speeches I'd given her drafts of, as well as heartily rejecting my writing of her vows. I'd worked like a dog on them for hours, not understanding that it was an audition of sorts. It was too comedic, she had told me, and went with Phil's heartfelt composition, riddled with sentimentality and a much more extensive vocabulary.

She led the guys towards her speedboat, bouncing along in her flirty way, letting them know exactly what they'd be doing and that they'd be reporting to Marianna in a bureaucratic fashion. She referred to a new, crisp thin notebook.

Josh shuffled away, looking over at me apologetically and confused. He gave a smile and a shrug before joining the fellas.

Back to our habit of uncomfortable partings.

Once in the boat, as Migs was helping the guys aboard, Olivia waved, yelling loudly over the motor, "See you at four!" I'm pretty sure she also winked and mouthed the word 'floozy' again.

~

WORDS DID NOT COME EASILY. The papers in front of me were stained with coffee and scribbled out paragraphs. I was in no mood to write a speech about true love. My scribblings came off like they were penned by a bitter and heartbroken spinster. Or a cat lady.

'Cat's really do kill mice and insects,' my friend Deb had asserted as she tried to convince me to adopt a kitten. 'You're going to be living near the river. You'll be happy with a feline friend, with the rats and the hobos around.' Deb had become a full-on cat lady just that year; three kittens, one bedroom, and a 47" TV.

I'd fight it as long as I could. I was a dog person anyway. I put my head face down on the table and tapped, waiting for inspiration.

I'd missed yesterday afternoon's pamper party. A massage and a facial sounded great. Time permitting, a mani/pedi to take care of the ripped claws I was sporting would be an absolute luxury.

I can clean up good twice. Just watch me.

It was a Saturday, and flocks of Panamanian tourists had arrived for a sunny weekend, so the water taxis were in hot demand and it would be an hour's wait at the resort. The bartender offered me his means of travel, a very local boat to take on my own.

It had no glamour, consisting of a hollowed-out log with an outboard motor. After taking instruction, confirming, reconfirming and then confirming again, I had the skills to get to town. The motor puttered and turned over, and I lurched south towards Bocas Town.

35
RELUCTANT WOLF. THAT IS, ALONE

I cut the motor two-hundred feet from the Bocas Town Marina, having failed to come up with a better plan of how I was going to make it to the dock without having an accident. Suddenly I felt like I was inside a watery pinball machine and I realized all too late that I was going way too fast.

I panicked and in trying to find a way to slow the log down, my primitive vessel capsized. No goggles, no ability to stand, and no Josh welcoming me to swim to him. I grabbed onto the exterior of the capsized log, with a serious sting in my eyes, spitting and coughing out seawater.

I wouldn't say that my life flashed before my eyes, but there was one single thought that flashed through my head. If was going to die when I was thirty-five, then my midlife crisis happened when I was seventeen-and-a-half, which meant it probably was all to do with Ryan.

A group of men about to board a very elegant sailboat were entertained by my bad fortune, but all the same, rushed over to the edge of the dock. The tallest looked at me hugging the log boat, "You have no idea what you are doing, do you? Just bring over the rope and I'll help tie you off?"

"Tie me off?" I asked in a state of dismay.

"Tie off the boat. Just swim over here."

"I can't," I cried as the tears ran readily down my cheeks. I felt humiliated. The group of men was howling with laughter and my doggy paddling skills had escaped me.

"All right. Enough is enough," one of them said, taking off his polo shirt and jumping into the water. He helped pull me over to the ladder up to the dock. I was drenched in my pretty dress and my shoes were nowhere to be seen. He tossed a used towel over to me and I dried my face and hair. Before the tall man had finished saving my boat, I thanked them and walked off, not wanting to endure another minute of mortification. I hoped the scorching sun would dry the rest of me off soon.

He called after me, "Hey, Tall Girl. You shouldn't be twiddling around in a boat like that if you don't know what you're doing. You'll drown."

As I walked down the dirty streets, I discarded the life jacket onto the pavement. I walked into the only tourist store that was open and found a pair of flip-flops, which I could not buy because the vendor wanted money for them, of course, and all of my cash was floating off to a new Caribbean vacation. After a desperate discussion in his bad English and my terrible Spanish, he gave me the pair and waved me away.

I frowned at the state of myself in the reflection of the spa's window. I looked like a refugee. I couldn't take the potential looks of disgust I imagined I'd get from receptionist and clients alike, so I headed for my home away from home, the police station; the only place I felt remotely and somewhat consistently welcome. Plus, I needed to borrow money.

LaGuardia shut the door in my face as I tried to enter their office. "Give us a minute."

So much for being welcome.

I couldn't make out what they were saying but the conversation was heated and loud. A good half hour passed until the door was opened, as McDonough threatened Lloyd, "What I'd really like to do is release you and get you out of here. Let your friends throw you to the wolves. You are speaking stupidities."

Yesterday's comradery between the detectives and Lloyd was seemingly no longer. While LaGuardia was fuming, Lloyd looked only vaguely frustrated, jaw dropping when I walked in. "What happened to you? You look like the girl from that horror movie The Ring, with the hair and—"

LaGuardia interrupted, "Stop it. Remember what we said."

"Okay, but Encyclopedia—"

"No."

Lloyd looked at me uncomfortably, but with no disdain. "Did you know that with this golden frog poison, a bird would die immediately, but it would take up to fifteen minutes to kill a tiger?"

"That's not what we talked about. Say it." LaGuardia hit the back of his head.

Lloyd looked at me curiously, with an emotion I hoped was compassion. "Ok. I'm sorry. I'm really sorry for how I've treated you, Lexie. And not just because I was told to apologize. You're not half bad." He'd clearly been given a talking to.

Hastily taped to the wall were over a dozen pieces of paper, listing the probability of each of the wedding guests.

Everyone was a suspect. The slam book had been thoroughly gone through and lay discarded on the floor. There were percentages scored on post-it notes on each taped-up face.

I understood the detectives' anger, as I commented while looking at the wall, "How could I be at 3%, Lloyd? I didn't go in the water. Neither did Walter's grandmother. And Max at 5%?" I started to grow confident of my font of knowledge. "It has been confirmed so many times that her plane didn't arrive until a full day after Nico was killed."

Lloyd had reverted to his casually entertained state. "Possible pay off. She has the means. She has the motive. And perhaps she had the opportunity. It's a corrupt world."

His logic was either sheer madness or utterly genius. Olivia was listed at 15% for the sheer drama, Josh was in the lead with 33% and Walter was unbelievably still listed at an 18% chance of being the guilty party.

LaGuardia explained, "This *pendejo* is insinuating that we took a pay-off and let Walter come and go as he pleased, through some secret tunnel that he's dreamed up."

Lloyd pleaded his case, "I cannot keep repeating myself when I state the fact that this is a very corrupt world and a very corrupt country, and it's not outside the realm of possibility." Lloyd had even listed himself at 12%, explaining that Emma might not be the most reliable alibi and that he may or may not have a history with homicide. "Everyone lies," he finished. "I wouldn't rule me out."

"Becky at 6%?"

"I hear that Max made a silly but somewhat plausible case for the murder/suicide scenario."

Now I've heard everything. Literally.

I no longer felt bad letting the investigation go. It was their job, and from what I could tell from hearing about the recent Landis case around town, they were good at their jobs. Lloyd was undoubtedly a better investigative asset than I'd ever been.

"I'll also tell you," Lloyd started to gossip when I was readying to leave, "that Walter cheated on Olivia with that movie lady, Theresa. He cheated on Olivia on more than one occasion as far as I am cognizant of. The relevance? The relevance being that everything is relevant. Right?"

I didn't see that coming.

What was I to do with that information now?

Countdown to seven hours until the bride becomes the wife.

After I stopped reeling, I simply turned and left.

Lloyd followed me out the door and down the hall. He was allowed to walk out of his cell, as long as he stayed in plain sight.

Island courtesy.

"Hey, I am sorry. I really have a filter missing. It's a problem. You might have noticed. I didn't have the inclination to sleep last night and was thinking about you. I actually am sorry for treating you so terribly. Whether I've called you Encyclopedia Brown or Peeping Tom, both have a keen investigative eye of sorts. Encyclopedia Brown always solves his cases. Every one. All I wanted to say is that I read your book on LaGuardia's iPad last night. He'd read it on Wednesday. I wanted to say that I don't think you are Left Behind."

"You don't?" I asked. No one had said that for a long time and Lloyd was looking at me like some strange version of a friend.

"I'm comfortable in saying I don't agree with your book in basic theory. I don't agree with having a group of people lay out every minuscule thing that's wrong with someone. I do appreciate the effort of your parable, but it all doesn't matter.

"People are getting divorces and hating each other all the

time. It's not a metaphorical rapture. No matter what or who or why, everyone gets it wrong until they get it right. And right comes at all kinds of times.

"And, just to make things clear, this is not me hitting on you. It will never be the right time for you and me. Too tall, too sad, too smart. Yes, I did say smart. You're pretty pretty, though. You really are, and you don't even know it. But you're not blond. You've heard how I like blondes." He ended in his creepy tone and then added, "Nico was right, I need to get a filter."

I accepted his apology and offered one last fact of my investigation. "I think you could take Josh down to 10% or so. He's not your frontrunner. He said that the book litigation thing was an exaggeration. Was it?"

"He would say that, wouldn't he?" He smirked and walked back to the pleasure of his cell. "Who's your front-runner?"

It's wrong until it's right. I like that.

36

A ROSE BY ANY OTHER NAME
WOULD STILL SMELL

nother boat ride was out of the question. I couldn't think of anything worse than traveling, but I wanted to get up north to the empty Bocas del Drago beach to concentrate on the speech, my final responsibility.

Restaurant Yarisnori was my last pure and fond memory of Olivia; a four-hour dinner on Monday night with just the two of us, pleasantly nostalgic about the past and unabashedly optimistic about the future. We were friends totally devoted to one another. Blood Sisters. It was the one place to write my speech that made sense.

I hadn't seen a taxi cab on wheels all day, but I'd seen plenty of scooters for rent, and some even included a helmet in the price. LaGuardia had lent me a wad of crumpled cash, so I was good to go. The proprietor was also selling fruit smoothies. He gave me a three-minute driving lesson before sending me on my way.

It was smooth sailing navigating through the small town, but a half-mile on the road toward Bocas Del Drago the surface quickly deteriorated, slowing me down to walking pace. I was running out of time. The covering of overhanging trees darkened the journey; the only noise came from my decrepit, puttering scooter and the dangerous creatures that lurked just off the road.

I pulled over at the sign for La Gruta, the bat cave. There were a number of cars pulled over on the side of the road. I made the short walk down the path, passing the Virgin Mary.

At the entrance to the cave, a small army of locals stood around talking to Amanda, who was crying.

"What is this scary place?" she sobbed, aghast. "It's just weird here. I don't like it. Not at all. It's really weird. I screwed up again. It's not my fault, though. It's not my fault."

Covering the muddy path right through to the cave was supposed to be rolls of AstroTurf to protect the guests' feet from dirt and disease. It was nowhere to be seen.

"Look at this," Amanda said. She put a pair of kitten heels back on, stood on the mud, and quickly sunk into the ground. "Everything is going wrong today. Please help us."

I suggested layers of Hefty bags. I didn't have the mental capacity to mess around at the bat cave and I had been relieved of duty until that night. Guilt overwhelmed me, but I rejected my natural urge to stay and try to fix things. I was quickly on my way, muttering "I have to go," as I went.

When I finally reached the North Shore, my ramshackle appearance didn't faze anyone. I suppose it was easy to assume I was just another surfer without access to a proper showering facility.

I had nothing to write. There were definitely good things about Olivia. I could still see that. She was funny, she could make everyone laugh, and her laugh was infectious. So, I started with that.

She had asked if I could speak for ten minutes, but I convinced her to decrease it to three. People lose interest, they fidget, and their minds wander and start daydreaming or, conversely, dreading what Monday's return to work would bring. Short and sweet was the best plan. Leave them with an indelible impression.

What else to say? Vindictive. Undermining. Pathological with an increasing need for anger management. Bossy. Insensitive to homicides of friends and associates. Perhaps homicidal in her own right.

Or to use her colloquialism, she was a shitbird.

Maybe I just didn't love her anymore.

Three plates of fried shrimp later, I was uncomfortably stuffed and no closer to writing a decent paragraph.

My window of opportunity closed.

~

THE AIR HAD TURNED from hot and dry to tangibly electric by the time I got to Olivia's door. The sea had been far too tranquil on the journey to be anything but a bad sign.

The sky was heavy and foreboding, dressed in dark, greyish tones. The humidity was stifling in the still air and I was drenched with sweat. The black clouds in the far distance were completely still. A violent thunderstorm was going to finish off the week, and I couldn't think of anything more apt.

A control freak still can't control the weather. Mother Nature cannot be manipulated.

I stood silently in the doorway to Olivia's room. The tension mirrored that of the weather - so thick you could hold it in your hand.

She was frowning, sitting at the vanity, hair done up in an

over the top steampunk fashion, crossed with a heavy helping of southern belle on the side. She had a terrible miniature derby hat pinned askew to the right side of her head.

Oh Olivia, what have you done?

She wistfully stared at herself in the mirror. "Tomorrow, this will be over. I've planned this for a year and a half and it will be gone as quick as Thanksgiving dinner."

Thank god.

I caught her eye in the mirror. "You've got a whole new life to jump into. You can go back to throwing your amazing annual Halloween parties. Those are extraordinary and take up months of planning."

She snorted. "If you like, I promise to aim the bouquet towards you, but be careful because you will be standing near a cliff top that overlooks a beach with a wicked riptide. How much do you really want it? Kidding. There's no cliff." She wasn't having fun.

The make-up artist forced Olivia's face back in her direction. "I spent a little time with Josh this morning. I told him to be gentle with you, that you'd just been broken up with."

"I broke up with him!"

"Well, in your way. But you are tender, my gal. You need some looking after. And I didn't say much, really, but Lex...do you really want your rebound guy to be one of Walter's friends? Imagine how awkward it will be seeing him at our parties. It wouldn't last. And that's a good thing! I'm just trying to protect you in your current emotionally unstable state."

She turned, to the annoyance of the make-up artist, and looked me up and down for the first time. "Oh my," she continued. "You might want to take a shower. What happened to you? There's some cream in the bathroom to put on your torso. It will help you get into the dress. They say it will hurt less with lotion and powder." She powdered her torso.

On the bed, her outfit was laid out: a white Victorian corset with a silk and tulle full-length skirt. It was terrible.

Knowing she wanted to pay respect to her gothic roots, I assumed she'd be donning a slinky, black, low-cut number. She squeezed into her corset and the make-up artist started lacing her up.

"I don't care if I can't breathe. Please lace me up as if I've had a few ribs removed." The make-up artist pulled tighter, despite Olivia's squinched up face. She demanded to be laced in tighter, screaming every beloved obscenity she had in her stable.

"You're going to faint, Olivia," I warned.

She smiled weakly, then pointed to the closet to reveal my dress; an exact replica of hers, but in blood red. Swooning in Victorian hysteria, she looked at me fondly, "You know how the guys go wild for you in red."

∾

MORE DIRT than I thought possible was running down my body and into the drain. Soap stung my ankle. I had nothing to redress the wound, but at least it would be covered by the dress. My fingers and toes looked like I hadn't changed the polish in a month.

I started crying for the first time since I'd arrived on the island. I was exhausted and my body was worse for the wear. Most importantly, I couldn't give Olivia the Emma style present of hiding everything bad from her in order for the wedding to go off as perfect as possible.

Olivia was marrying the wrong guy. She didn't know him

at all. Between the cheating and the business issues, he was hiding who he was.

Olivia helped me into the red atrocity of a dress, which looked more and more like a bad Halloween costume than a gown for a lady in waiting. We looked in the mirror together, and I couldn't hold onto the secrets any longer.

"This is bad news, and a big part of me doesn't want to tell you this at all, but Walter is cheating on you. With Theresa, and with others back in New York. You can't go ahead with this. You're worth more. You know that."

She walked over to the vanity and sat down, color draining from her painted face. She was angry when she asked me, "How do you know this?"

Her words were carefully spaced out. Her anger was directed towards me. After listening to me spill, she asked me, "Why are you listening to Lloyd? Are you forgetting he is a serial killer?"

Despite her disbelief, my words struck a chord. She looked like she was connecting dots that went back three years. Her fantasy was being crushed.

Mirror mirror on the wall.

We sat in uncomfortable silence for the next half hour, until we had to go. She wouldn't look at me, saying in defeat, "Sometimes men have to get things out of their systems. We aren't married, yet. It doesn't count, yet. It doesn't count until tonight. Why are you trying to ruin my wedding? Why are you are always trying to ruin things?"

I'm not dignifying that with an answer.

She closed her eyes, silently convincing herself to power through. She instantly transformed as she headed towards the door.

Olivia broke the silence with a quote I recognized as

Shakespeare, "Finish, good lady: the bright day is done, and we are but for the dark."

She winked at me, raised her chin, and strode out into the night.

37
IT WAS A DARK AND STORMY NIGHT...

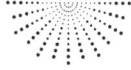

The bridal party boarded a small but well-appointed catamaran, to start the journey to La Gruta. The wedding ceremony was finally just hours away. Amanda was staring at Olivia, wide-eyed, waiting for the right time to tell her about the synthetic grass crisis, but that moment never came.

Energy vampire.

Even Migs had subdued his constant optimism and the scarcity of pictures taken spoke volumes. He was walking on eggshells like the rest of us, frowning at our ridiculous outfits.

Phil might have suffered the worst: oxblood frock coat, silk puff ties, and a pair of goggles. He was the only one talking, occasionally spouting off a litany of complaints. "I look like Jack the Ripper meets Jacques Cousteau. We look like Victorian prostitutes with their dandy pimp. We must be on a reality show. Tell me we're on a reality show. Goggles? Really? Goggles?"

Olivia said nothing on the half-hour ride. I knew that if

she talked about what was going on, it would make it real. She needed to quietly compartmentalize like she always did. The rest of the team was none the wiser that there was anything truly amiss.

The weather was holding off. For the moment.

I went below deck to try and figure out how I could possibly go to the bathroom wearing this ensemble. My skirt almost filled the tiny room on its own and I sat on the toilet with a face full of tulle.

I sat there for a good long while, enjoying the solitude. Marianna was waiting when I came out, sitting at a small booth. My advice to her, "I think your best bet is to pull your skirt up over your head before you go in there."

"You look great," she responded.

Something is up.

"Oh, come on Marianna. We both look like turn of the century hookers. You know that."

"It's niche." She was a good five inches shorter than me. Her petite stature had always made me feel less feminine. I was an Amazon to her sea nymph.

"Can I ask you a question?" she smiled coyly. I'd known her for twenty-five years, and most conversations with me were about a boy.

A man. This time a man called Josh.

"Can you back off a little on Josh? I know you spent some time with him, but I know he's pretty into me. It really could be something. So just stay away from him tonight. Is that cool? Is that okay?"

Flashback to sixteen-year-old Lexie letting Ryan get away.

Flashback to last night, letting someone in. I lost him, if I ever had him at all. I hadn't even known I'd wanted him. Maybe damaged was just his shtick.

"No problem. You'd make a great couple. You both like the Beatles," I forced out.

Who doesn't?

She won—Now I was just biding time until I could get off this island forever.

We made our way off the rickety dock at Bocas del Drago, waddling down towards the waiting 1967 Rolls Royce Stretch Shadow. There are only so many traditions one can break.

Olivia fiddled with her purse, putting on a dazzling emerald bracelet as her 'something new'. "As you may or may not know, Max was in Bogota last month. And, as everyone knows, the best emeralds in the world are known to come from the Muzo mines in Colombia."

My heart rate shot up and my skin turned clammy as she went on about Colombian emeralds, something about the 16th century and the Emperor of Brazil giving the largest uncut emerald in the world to the Duke of Devonshire, one of Max's direct ancestors. She'd visited Muzo many times and on the last visit she'd picked up the antique bracelet for Olivia.

Colombia. Max has been to Colombia, home of the dreaded Phyllobates Terrebillis. The heiress to billions had delivered the poison right to the room of her husband's lover.

I had missed everything.

The case could be closed.

Almost.

Max hadn't been on the island, but there was no doubt that she had everything to do with both murders.

Olivia touched my sticky skin as she put her arm around me. "Maybe you should let that corset out a bit, Lexie. You look like you're going to faint."

By the time we drove to the pathway leading to the cave, Olivia had regained her game face. Limousines were lined up on the side of the road heading north, precluding any other cars from passing. The entranceway to the path was lit with flaming torches, and littered with the discarded shoes.

"Hey Lexie," Migs called to me as I got out of the car. "You don't need to look happy, but I don't want a portrait of nauseous. You just need to look pretty. Pout those lips for me. Something stunning for me to remember you by."

Tomorrow it would be over. 1192.5 miles away. The end.

Olivia had no choice but to go with the flow. Kicking her Louboutins off, she walked down the haunted path and waited for her father to take her down the muddy aisle.

Amanda's choice of remedy had been desperate, and ultimately a failure. Abandoned planks were hastily chucked to the side, a failed attempt to make a new avenue on which to stroll down. There was no music. Everything was uncomfortable and wrong.

Flashes went off as soon as the bridesmaids came into sight. There'd be thirty unapproved versions of the same photo on social media within the hour.

I concentrated on looking straight ahead at Marianna's butt. Dangerous curves, as Olivia had once described her in kinder times. Marianna gave Josh a slow, sexy stare as she took her place by the altar.

He smiled back in a way I could not decipher, then caught my eye and looked away. I needed to tell him about Colombia, but it was the worst time.

He looked back though. He looked back.

Safety in numbers.

The thunder in the distance felt eerily appropriate. People were shifting their feet in discomfort on the waterlogged soil.

Olivia's father kissed her on both cheeks and handed her over to Walter Parker. She approached the officiate, whispering, and pointing to the darkening sky. I clocked the abbreviated ceremony at about two minutes flat, knowing what was coming next.

She'd have to suck it up with all the previous errors, but she desperately wanted the moment no one knew they'd been waiting for. Once pronounced man and wife, Walter kissed her passionately for a long, and then an uncomfortably long, time.

The bats were fashionably late, but finally, a different kind of thunder emerged, the kiss continuing as thousands of bats charged out of the cave. Like I knew would happen, most people dropped to the ground, screaming.

I stood my ground, staring at the still kissing couple, realizing that I'd rather be alone than end up having to live the life of lies that Olivia was entering.

Colleen was crying, kneeling in the muck. Walter's grandmother was laughing. Marianna had dramatically collapsed on her back on the pathway as Josh tried to help her up.

No one will forget this wedding. Case closed.

∽

NICO MUST HAVE BROKEN his penny bank paying for this wedding. Last night's enormous yacht waited for us a distance from the beach.

Another major snafu for the evening. The boat was too big to dock at the Bocas del Drago restaurant, which was perched over shallow waters. Passengers had to be ferried, four at a time, out to the mooring ship.

My red 1950s gingham change of outfit was waiting for

me in one of the cabins. I could now breath again in a dress that remotely fit. The deal with Walter was that Olivia could do anything she wanted in planning the wedding itself, but he insisted on controlling the reception, which he required to "just be regular".

The Red Frog Beach resort had a deep-water marina, so getting off the boat was easy. People had clamored for the three showers while they were on board, but forty minutes was not enough time for thirty-six people to get a chance to clean up.

Walter's father had immediately arranged for some hotel rooms for the guests to tidy up. Those whose clothes were not too soaked with mud made the best of it and made their way to the reception, but those who were not so lucky sauntered out in white bathrobes.

It took longer for the guests to walk to the reception from the main building of the hotel than had been anticipated. Staff had not completely set up the reception on the beach and were arguing about putting up tents or not to protect us all from the storm.

It was a disaster. Thank god for small miracles; the guests would have been waiting around for an hour had we not have already been running criminally late.

Yet, everyone quickly accepted the pandemonium and embraced the ridiculousness, immediately throwing back the vintage champagne like tequila shots. This crowd wanted to party above all.

I took the opportunity to dash into the hotel and desperately try to find some phone service. My signal strength flickered in and out as I walked into the empty bar.

They had to have good wi-fi in a major resort. I still repeatedly failed to get a call through to LaGuardia, and the perceptive bartender put a strong looking drink in front of me. At last, I was able to get a confusing text message and half a voicemail through to the detective's phone before my phone cut out, "Please call me as soon as possible. It's about Colombia. It's Max…" I don't know when exactly I lost the signal.

"I didn't order a drink," I said to the bartender. He motioned to a dark table behind me, and Max beckoned me over. Could she have been close enough to hear?

Fight or flight?

I simply froze, then I walked over to her table to sit down. "No service? It's a problem in places this remote. By the way, the bracelet looks divine on you. Just smashing, you little smasher."

It was true. I loved it. It sparkled in a way that I'd never be able to afford.

"Here," she handed me her phone. "It's satellite. You absolutely need to have one for traveling. For heaven's sake, I can't even get service in the Southeast of England."

I reluctantly took it out of her hand and just stared at it.

"Do you need some help? Do you want me to read you off the last number you dialed?"

That would be the disaster of my week. "No, no. I know the number." I couldn't remember any number off the top of my head, or even a number to make up in a split second, so I dialed Salty, the only number I knew by heart, hoping he wouldn't answer.

By heart? What a strange phrase.

I hadn't heard his voice in a month. As I reached voicemail and listened to his dry but quick outgoing message, I did not miss him. "Salty. It's me. Lexie. Just wanted to say that I was thinking about you…you don't need to call me back."

Max took a sip of her drink, slightly entertained by his name, I'm sure. "That's the man who broke up with you?"

"I broke up with him."

"I hardly knew you were with anyone. Why did you never bring him to parties?"

She had taken some notice of me after all.

It was a good question that I'd never thought about. He was judgmental and prejudiced about the wealthy, despite his secret love of conspicuous consumer consumption. I wasn't proud of him. I didn't want him to reflect on me. I didn't want him to keep me from hoping that there was someone else out there.

"Because he had the personality of a hatchet fish."

For the first time since I'd known her, she laughed. Remembering safety in numbers, I tried to say goodbye and rejoin the party but she stopped me. "Sit, have a drink with me."

"I'm the maid of honor. I've got to get back."

"It's chaos out there. No one will notice if you're there or not, and from where I sit, it looks like it's going to be at least an hour before they are nearly ready."

Though her dress was ruined on the bottom, she hadn't even attempted to wash up. Only she could look elegant in a hotel lounge with mud caked to her feet. Only she could walk in a hotel so elegantly that no one would say anything about her muddy footprints. They'd just immediately clean up after her.

"Maybe just for a minute," I sipped the drink. I winced at the strength of it.

"Thank you again for all you've done for Nico. That bracelet doesn't begin to express my thanks. I'm forever in your debt." She held up her drink to toast me. "And Lloyd?

It's really a bit of a surprise to me. He'll be staying here after we leave? He'll be prosecuted? Hopefully rotting."

"I believe so." She could wait a week until she saw him wandering the streets of New York and freak out then, far away from me.

That was really the extent of what we had to say to each other, both sipping uncomfortably. "I guess you should go. You're right."

I jetted out of the hotel, looking back in Max's direction. She was walking very slowly towards the reception as well. There would have been nothing strange about it, normally.

The first bolt of lightning crackled in the distance. It was time for the party to begin.

38

'TIL DEATH DO US PART....
(BWAHAHAHAHAHAH)

*T*ents went up, cabanas were dragged to just outside the dance floor, and beautiful Panamanian woman in slinky red dresses distributed 'just regular' looking cocktails.

The reception was cleaning up well. Ground torches created walkways for people to stroll along as far as the white beach's rock outcropping. Those with fit bodies had loosened their bathrobes, showing off underwear and abs. Uncle Gordon, going commando, was flashing to the delight of everyone, excluding his wife.

The food? Another major mess up. It wouldn't be served until way after the dancing.

The seating arrangement had devolved to "every man for himself", and I was exiled to the outer banks of the wedding party table. Josh was held in Marianna's captivity, and though I tried to rearrange to get closer to him and tell him what was happening, there was no time. Edgar pulled me down next to him, as festivities officially had begun.

I caught Marianna's eye, who's expression was very much, "Back off. I warned you."

My speech was second in the line-up; after Dave and before the groom himself. Dave took his time, long-winded speeches apparently running in the family. He started at age three, progressing at a snail's pace, making sure not to miss any of Walter's many stellar achievements.

This gave me ample time to avoid Max's quizzical stare. She'd smile, and I'd look away immediately, understanding that she knew I might have become a major liability to her. If I had to go to the bathroom, I'd be sure to take a buddy. I hoped that after the speeches I could sneak out and make it to Bocas PD. With any luck they'd have another cot, and I could shack up with Lloyd until my plane took off.

I had no paper, no pen, and nothing to say. A champagne glass and the microphone were handed to me.

Champagne was being poured decadently. They had chosen 1995 Charles Heidsieck "Blanc des Millénaires - Rare Millésime." Olivia had learned through her recent proximity to the jetsetters, to never choose Dom Perignon or Crystal as it screamed 'regular person'. This champagne was rated as the only perfect bubbly in the world, I'd been advised, at a whopping $170 per bottle.

I did gaze upon her with something that resembled fondness. Like the saying goes, I loved her, but I did not like her.

"Hi. Okay," I began, eyes upon me, the group waiting to hear me praise love. "As Fitzgerald once said, or something like this at least, 'In our twenties we think that love will save us, in our thirties we think our friends will, in our forties we learn that friends won't save us any more than love did.'" I looked up at the confused crowd, "Kidding. Really.

"I've known Olivia since she was five. I fell in love with her courage, her sincerity, and her wild notion of self-respect. I mean... I love her for believing this is the beginning of everything.

"I'm sure that Walter felt the same way when he met her. Truly original. Truly alpha, in the best way, but you can all tell that from this delicious wedding. Determined. Though this wedding began with tragedy and disaster, it ends a roaring success, and a celebration of good lives lived. I think.

"We've been through a lot together. She was always so ambitious, so beyond anyone. And people like her deserve a sidekick, which I've been for these past thirty-five years. And that's ok. Really. Alphas pull sidekicks along into strange situations and vicarious living. But sidekicks can be brilliant in their own right; Watson to Sherlock Holmes, Tinkerbelle to Peter Pan, and even Chewbacca to Han Solo. Sidekicks get to be very witty, even Chewbacca—but who knows what he's saying. We are the women behind the woman. So, Olivia, I thank you for the experience.

"There's a saying that you let a man chase you until you catch him. You know what I mean? And in a very movie moment, Walter kept trying to buy her business as a ploy to get to know her. She never sold the gym but she won his heart. Look at how perfect they are! Beautiful, funny, driven. The couple of the year no doubt. A courtship to be envied. They make a splash, you know? They are to be known.

"Walter, you are a classy caring guy. You proposed to your now wife at Macchu Picchu at sunrise. That's pretty great. And from what I hear, you did it using a Shakespeare quote, which you know she loves. She does love those quotes. We've been quoting and misquoting for decades now. Walter got it right. He always gets it right, and that's why she loves you. Well, one of the reasons."

The drunken guests had been made uncomfortable, yet they kept their gazes fixed on me, wondering if it was going to get worse. I looked around the room and spoke from my adrenaline-filled, palpitating heart.

"Walter, you will learn this about Olivia. She may not always be around, but she's first on the scene when you need her. She's always been there. She'll be there for you. Despite it all. Forever. Or some sort of forever. You know what I'm saying? Olivia, I love you, but I think I'm done. I am done."

I put the microphone down, avoiding the eyes that were still focused on me, except for Josh. He met my intense stare, through which I asked him silently to rise from the table and come with me.

I walked through the reception towards the torches lighting the way down the beach. I hoped Josh followed for many reasons, including not wanting to seem very conspicuously rejected.

Maybe I needed to be rejected in front of everyone.

Who cares if the world knows?

I ducked into the furthest cabana and waited. Immediately out of view, and shortly out of mind, I heard the distant raucous laughter in response to Walter's opening line.

If I learned nothing else from the week, it was that the party would always go on.

The signal was weak on the cell phone, but it existed. I made it through to LaGuardia twice; I could hear him, screaming amongst chaos, speaking loudly into the phone, "I cannot hear you. Text me!"

Raindrops sporadically hit the canvas roof. It wouldn't be long until the skies opened up. I lay on the lounge looking up at the ceiling, waiting for a return text from LaGuardia on what to do.

Josh cautiously entered. His pants were rolled up and he had left his jacket at the table, tie gone from his white shirt. He sat far across the tent from me.

"Don't worry," I said. "I'm not going to bite you."

"Huh?" he asked, grabbing for the bottle of champagne on ice. He took a deep breath and almost smiled. "I just wanted to say, I don't think you want to bite me. It's just...this is going to be a little awkward isn't it?"

I didn't need that.

"Save it, Josh. It's about the poison, that's all. This is not about you and me."

The phone rang, and as I answered, I continued to Josh, "And why did you even come here if you thought I was trying to seduce you?"

"That's not it at all. It would be okay if you... no... weddings depress me. They make me shut down," Josh continued to mumble as I concentrated on trying to give LaGuardia every detail.

"Hold on!" LaGuardia yelled, moments into our conversation. "Could you not throw any more chairs across the room please?!"

He let me know in no uncertain terms that there was no way that anyone could make it down to Red Frog Beach at that moment in time. There was a soon-to-be-legendary bar brawl at the Pickled Parrot, drawing all of the policemen that they could find, including the pseudo undercover cop at Mariposa del Mar.

BPD was dealing with broken bottles, knives, and a drunken British bachelor party gone out of control. "Don't go back to your hotel. There is no officer there. No one has been watching Becky's cabin for at least an hour. It's mayhem down here. Come to the station. Someone will let you in." At least that's what I think he said before thunder boomed above us and the call dropped.

I was trying to fill Josh in on everything to get him ready to protect me while at the same time I tried to convince myself that Max had no idea about my knowledge of her involvement. Max didn't know that I knew about the poison, it was very unlikely she overheard me, and she was probably giving me her phone out of her version of a genuine gesture of kindness.

"I don't know. She's pretty savvy. Let's get out of here," Josh said. The night before, those last words had a different meaning altogether. He stood up and offered me his hand. "I'm still in this until the end"

I was thankful, but wondered what the end would be? I stared up at Josh, adding him to the list of things that would be out of my life sooner than you could say Red Frog Beach.

Enjoy yourself, but don't lick the frogs.

Clammy hand in clammy hand, we walked back towards the reception. The crowd had thinned out, and most of the older people had left, along with Edgar, his wife, and Max. After all, the party was over, an unforgettable failure.

Without expression, Olivia had her head on her step-dad's shoulder, swaying uncomfortably to and fro, watching Walter walk up the hill. The distance to the bathroom was a good five-minute walk. If I knew Olivia, and I did, she was surely wondering what he might actually be off doing.

Ryan suddenly sprang from the last group of revelers and grabbed me, apologizing to Josh, "Of course you can spare her for one dance before she goes. I'll have her back to you before you can say lickety-split."

Josh was too polite to say no, and Ryan wouldn't have cared anyway. He pulled me to the center of the dance floor, and I closed my eyes for a moment and went with it. I could be the fourth Mrs. Ryan Lawler.

"You're kidding about that guy?" he asked.

"There's more than meets the eye... I can't dance Ryan. I still can't dance."

"Sure you can. You're dancing now." He whispered in my ear, "I have to tell you. You've always been the yardstick by which I measure all women."

I could have shot myself down, but I didn't. I had danced with him in high school, only once, at our senior prom. He'd already danced with all of Olivia's other friends, so I was last on the checklist.

We danced a little too close, and he ran his fingers over the bottom of my hair. 'Lexie,' he had whispered. 'What am I going to do without you?'

At the time it made no sense, and I pulled away from him, leaving the prom crying, sitting on a bench on Commonwealth Avenue until I regained my composure. I had not seen him since.

"I have to go now. Tomorrow we can do this, Ryan. Tomorrow…"

He wouldn't let go of my hands and Olivia was staring at me with dismissive anger. She was lost. But it was a journey she'd have to go on alone.

Josh and I didn't look like a passionate couple leaving a party together, but no one else bothered to watch us walk towards the marina anyway. As the rain started in earnest, thunder clapping above us, Josh hit me with a non sequitur. "Did you know twenty-five percent of fatal lightning strikes happen near water?"

We could have actually been good together.

39

THE BUDDY SYSTEM

*he marina was not well lit, but you could make out two water taxis and their drivers debating whether they were going to take their chance in open seas during a thunderstorm. Still holding hands, we walked past the row of yachts rather silently.

The taxi that brought us to the party was still lit up marking it as available. We were about to be at the finish line when Josh quickly pulled me out of sight.

"What?" I said, quite audibly.

Josh whispered, "Max and Walter are in the boat."

I really was one of those people who never saw it coming.

We stood still, trying desperately to hear their voices. There was a lot of talk about what they'd do when they left the island and plans they were making.

"I'm still not so sure, Walter," Max's voice trembled a bit. "I swear when I brought up Colombia, something flashed across her fat face."

"Why would you ever bring up Colombia?" Walter snapped.

"Because it's irrelevant. Red frogs. From here. They are poison. That's all."

"Stop being so paranoid. This is all fine. I need to get back to the party."

"Lexie knows something."

"She thinks she knows something," Walter replied. "The girl's an idiot. She can *think* whatever she wants. I'm going."

Our best shot was just to nonchalantly walk towards the taxis, hoping to slink away into the night. We offered the driver a hell of a lot of money, even for US standards, to take us immediately to town. Wobbly getting in, I took Josh's face in my hands and kissed him, in case anyone was wondering about our intentions. He kissed back just enough, but maybe just a moment longer.

For no one's benefit at all.

It was normally a fifteen-minute voyage from Red Frog Beach to Bocas Town, but the water was choppy and visibility was pea soup. I said, "All this rain. I feel stupid. It seems very obvious."

As soon as the water taxi reached the dock, we ran towards the safety of the nearby police station. It was a five-minute walk, which turned into a two-minute run, for us to arrive at a closed station.

"Impossible." I pulled on the door handles and shook the locked doors. "Could this fight really have called in the whole Bocas police force?"

"That's only eight people."

"They said someone would be here. And Lloyd has got to be in there…."

"He's in a cell. Who knows?" Josh answered. "By Tuesday, Lloyd might be mayor of this town."

I tried LaGuardia's phone as well as the Emergency 104

number that connected simply to a recording in Spanish that I didn't understand.

"Let's get out of the rain," Josh grabbed my hand and we ran down the main drag. The open-air restaurants were closed or closing. A small group of drunk tourists ran through the rain, singing some German song I'd never heard. There was more laughter and music, but in what direction?

I ran into the lobby of an originally named over-the-water hotel called *Bonita Vista,* which meant very simply in Spanish Nice View. It was small, quiet, and comfortable. There was a bored looking woman sitting behind reception, halfway through a dog-eared copy of *Cincuenta Sambras de Grey.* I think you know what I mean.

We took a room with ocean views so we could watch for the return of the police boats, hopefully sooner than later. Annoyed that we had interrupted her reading time, the receptionist quickly gave us a key and pointed to the stairway.

Though the outside of the hotel was quaint and tropical, the inside resembled the typical American McMansion. Deceptively vast, off-white and devoid of any personality.

We scurried up to our corner room on the second floor, which was well appointed with crisp white sheets and red blankets. Sterile, yet romantic.

As soon as he locked the door, Josh turned the lights off. "Better to see the incoming boats with the lights off, and for us not to be seen at all."

I was shivering, from fear and wet, and I needed to get out of my rain-soaked clothes. I excused myself to the bathroom and stripped down. Looking at my reflection with only my blood red underwear on was laughable. The plush red robe (I couldn't escape that damn color) was comforting, and after drying my hair, I returned to the room. I made a vow to myself to retire red from my wardrobe until far into the foreseeable future, however well it might suit me.

Josh was looking out of the French doors and across the balcony. "Good idea," he said, and walked to the bathroom, locking the door behind him.

Only the night before, we confidently stood naked in front of each other. Now we were hiding beneath fluffy bathrobes, locking doors.

My calls to LaGuardia were never going to get through in this weather, and my phone was desperately low on battery life. I went back to the window, watching the odd water taxi docking now and then.

"Who was that guy anyway?" he asked, not looking at me. "The guy who wanted you to dance."

"A very old friend. Maybe a very old boyfriend. My boyfriend before he was, well... Olivia's boyfriend years ago. She doesn't know. Don't tell her."

Josh joined me in his bathrobe by the window. I didn't look at him as I asked, "Do you think that we should take a taxi over to the Pickled Parrot?"

"I think we'll be safer here," he said. "That fight can't go on all night."

"I'm really cold," I said and went over to the bed, keeping my bathrobe on as I slipped into the sheets.

Josh pulled a chair over to the window and silently watched the water. "I should be honest with you. What Lloyd told you about me was true. I did write that book. I feel I should come clean at this point."

My eyes were heavy, so heavy, and despite the drive to get out of bed and ask him more, I drifted off to sleep.

A CALLOUSED HAND, hard over my mouth, slapped me out of

my sleep. I came eye to eye with Walter, who was straddling me, pinning my arms to the bed. My kicking legs did nothing.

He pulled me out of bed, dragging me towards the French doors and maneuvered himself behind me, hand still over my mouth, restraining my arms behind my back. His years in the gym had served him well. The giant ticking clock told me it was 3:30, so his new wife was fast asleep, with that annoying wheezy snore.

I whipped my head around looking for Josh, who was nowhere to be seen.

I had been so wrong about him. Fatally wrong.

Teeth and pencils, I remembered. A friend of mine who taught self-defense had told me that to buy a few minutes to try to escape a perilous situation, all one needed were pencils and teeth. I refused to stop struggling and sunk my teeth into the palm of his hand, which allowed us both to get a momentary scream out.

"Knock her out," I heard from behind me, in the unmistakably posh British accent which belonged to Max.

He wrapped his arm around my neck in the traditional sleeper hold and though I was able to get one more squeak of a scream out, I felt the extreme pressure on the back of my neck and knew I was passing out.

40
SWIMMING LESSONS, PART 4

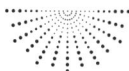

I had a hard time opening my eyes when I came to, but I knew I was on a boat. My lips tasted like salt water. The rain had let up, but I was still drenched, shivering in my waterlogged bathrobe. My wrists and ankles were tied to the table.

Coming into focus, I saw for sure that Josh was one of the good guys. He was shackled next to me, in complete terror and disbelief.

Boy, had he picked the wrong girl tonight.

Marianna would have been plying him with some ginger massage oil she'd picked up in the Bahamas last summer.

With the hundred plus boat trips I'd made that week, I had a good idea of where we were going - south from Bocas Town into the canal between Isla Solarte and Isla Bastimentos.

Once you passed the main town of the smaller island, civilization was sparse. The two islands were essentially national parks and purely desolate. The channel was maybe only a kilometer wide at best but was the definition of the middle of nowhere.

The motor was cut, so we were just bobbing out there in the dark among the currents. Being somewhat protected between the two islands, the waves were not nearly as bad as they might have been. The surfing beaches were probably raging with ten-foot swells.

This was part revenge, part fun for Max, who looked like she'd been waiting for years to do something like this.

Walter put his arm around Josh. "I am really very sorry Josh. I tried to think of a way to save you from this, but I just couldn't think of one…I have to do this."

Josh carefully replied, "You know that there is undisputedly nothing that we wouldn't do to just go back to shore. You know we wouldn't say anything to anyone. You know you can trust me. You've always known that."

"Do you really think he has to go?" Walter asked Max, nixing me from the possibility of retrial.

She gave Josh an assessing stare. "Yes," was her simple answer.

Max moved over to me and untied my ankles, unrolling the dingy gauze bandages. She looked at the cut as if it had offended her in some way and bent down to look at it, before taking a sharp small stone and reopening the wound.

It was a searing pain and a strange choice of deadly assault.

Walter then held Josh's arm rigid, while Max took the same stone and cut the inside of Josh's arm open, incising a decent sized wound. Josh gritted his teeth but did not utter a word.

She started ruffling through a backpack. "You've watched a lot of TV, haven't you, you little smasher? You're looking for a bit of a Scooby Doo explanation, am I right? About you crazy meddling kids…"

"Was Becky always part of the plan?"

"Don't be stupid. Yes, she was. I want my money. I went through enough for that money. Believe me. Walter gets his business back. We're free of Nico's terrible ways. He was a bad man. Full stop. It doesn't run deeper."

Bad man? Pot. Kettle. Black.

She pulled out the vial of golden frog poison and smiled.

I knew it wasn't the actual poison and wouldn't kill me, but I did repeatedly note to myself that I was in the middle of the ocean and no good could come of that.

"But good on you for figuring out the Colombian frog. Of course, you know how it works?" She illustrated as if presenting on a cooking show.

I nodded. "So Walter gets his business, you get the money, plus the satisfaction that no one would know that Nico left you for a good woman?"

She ignored me and handed a needleless syringe to Walter. "I'm really sorry, Josh," he frowned. He jabbed the needle directly into the fresh wound.

Josh howled with pain and every muscle in his body appeared to go rigid. Paolo had said that the poison bottle was 100% sterile, but it now seemed almost improbable that there would be no trace matter. It was the same haggard Victorian bottle marked Peppermint, probably too old and broken to not be porous.

Even if it was, sterile the fact that it was only alcohol and sea salts didn't make me feel that we'd been saved.

"Don't you think," I pleaded, "it's going to look like more than a crazy coincidence that we go missing, or wash up dead?"

Max smiled as she prepared the second syringe. "You left

the party happily locking lips together, leading to what clearly was to become an anonymous shag in a stolen boat. Anything could have happened. It's been a terrible week for tragedy."

"Sorry, again. It's just circumstance," Walter said, as he dragged Josh's pain-stricken body to the short swim deck at the back of the boat before tossing his body overboard.

Through the darkness, I couldn't see Josh's body at all.

Max kneeled down in front of me again and jabbed the syringe into my ankle. The pain was so intense, so raw, so like nothing I'd ever felt.

"You see, poison in an open wound. No needle marks. Should they find your body washed up somewhere, you'll just look all mucked up."

The sting was cold and overwhelming my body.

"Cause of death? Drowning. The poison is just a bonus for you figuring it out."

Bonus for her that even if Dr. Nolan looked, there'd no longer be any trace of poison at all.

"She's the one who can't swim, right?"

Without a word, Walter tossed me to my fate. The motor was ignited, and the boat slowly headed north.

Have you ever screamed underwater?

I pushed out most of my oxygen but held my mouth closed while I sank and made my way up to the surface, spitting out salt water and trying to tread enough to get some breath.

Knocked down again and again, it was adrenaline and surprise survival tactics that let me rise again. Everything seemed purple underwater, above water, when I closed my eyes. Was Josh around?

The ache of rubbing alcohol running through my veins

made my limbs heavy with excruciating pain. But I wasn't going to die.

"Josh?! Josh!" I choked on water. My treading water skills were on the verge of useless. "Over here, Josh!" He too was treading. "Josh, take the bathrobe off. It's weighing you down."

My sore muscles struggled with my own double-knotted robe and I wiggled out of it. I turned on my back, remembering that I could float. The harsh current still knocked me down. Josh had been right about that.

"Lexie, I can't get to you. The current is against me and keeps knocking me back. I'm not far. You're going to have to swim with me. Remember you know how to do this." His voice seemed so distant. "Ride the wave when you can. Let it take you."

I couldn't tell how far away he was, and I was feeling enormously sick with the amount of salt water I was ingesting. Finally, I could see him, and soon I could touch him.

"I can't do this," he said, defeated by the time he was barely in my reach. "I'm going to drown. Leave me."

"You are not going to drown. It's not far. There are islets. And we can find one. We can walk on coral reefs. The water is warmer here. Like you told me, reefs can't be deep. I can help you."

I put one arm under him, trying to keep him afloat for the few moments I could. We tread water again.

"Josh. You're going to have to help. We are not going to die. I don't want to die."

We followed our swimming routine for what seemed like days, but it could have been minutes; he would swim ahead just a little, I would doggy paddle in dog years out to him, and he would pull me for just a bit.

My body felt bruised between the alcohol and salt injection and being banged about by a fierce current. I was crying and sucking in more salt water, but we moved on, slowly and surely.

As soon as my toes could hit sand, I dragged him on to the shore of the tiny islet, just large enough for two people to expire. We could see the land of Isla Bastimentos, not too far, but impossible at the moment.

After a fair amount of hyperventilation, I vomited and vomited until nothing was left and I passed out. Before I faded away, Josh took my hand in his. It was finally safe to go to sleep.

~

DAY SIX

~

41

BUT WHAT ABOUT LOVE?

*S*and flies and a sore neck welcomed me as I sat up, exhausted but firmly awake at the break of dawn. Signs of the storm had disappeared. Our islet was tiny, with gentle waves just about rolling up to the tip of my toes. It was warm and the world was calm. The rising sun would burn off the mist in a few hours, but for the moment all was beautiful.

Josh was still sleeping, curled up on his side, hair matted with sand and sea salt. I felt a fondness for him and kneeled down beside him.

Though scared, I ran my finger down his arm, whispering in his ear like a familiar lover, "Wake up, Josh. It's time to move."

He opened his eyes, staring up at the solitary palm tree on our island. "I'm so sore," he said, not meeting my eyes, fixed gaze on the slightly swaying tree.

We were closer to land than I had thought, and the water never rose above my knees. Josh followed me, copying my path as I successfully avoided jagged rocks. I was in last night's terrible red underwear with ten pounds of extra stomach weight, but it didn't matter. Josh's black boxer briefs were of little consequence. We both could have been naked, and neither would have noticed or cared.

Once on the beach, he walked ahead of me and I struggled to keep up with his speed, sand grinding into my wound.

"Stop," I said, in a gravelly dehydrated voice. He kept walking, so I gathered all the energy I could to catch up with him and grab his arm. "I said stop, Josh."

"Ok, I've stopped," he said, pursing his lips.

"I feel sick enough and I really can't handle the silent treatment. What is wrong, Josh? I've been wracking my brain since I woke up alone yesterday, and for the life of me, I cannot understand what I've done to get this wall of ice from you."

"I just can't do this, Lexie. Look, I like you. A lot. I could be crazy about you, but I just... I can't do whatever was going on with us," he scratched the stubble on his chin and walked away.

"Do what?"

"I mean your three nights of swimming lessons. I just can't do it. I can't be your rebound. I just don't have it in me. I don't want to deal with the awkwardness of running into you at parties around town, at friends' weddings, etc. etc. because it happens. I just don't. Want. To do it."

His speech was too similar to Olivia's talk with me yesterday to be a coincidence.

"We're adults, Josh." Regardless of the adrenaline butterflies in my stomach, I wasn't going to lose any self-respect. "Deal with me like I'm an adult. If you can't..." There was nothing more for me to say. I turned and walked north, every step shooting daggers through my leg.

We walked for an hour, possibly two, Josh finally doing the chasing, and I was the one who wouldn't stop.

He called after me, "Adult, you said? Lexie, we're both children. There's a reason that we're both Left Behind. We're both children and no good for each other. Probably no good for anyone. We've been through a lot together in a very short period. We should just finish it out and be on our way. This is way too intense for my boring life."

He isn't right.

With a dramatic turn on my good ankle, I sternly replied, "No. I don't accept that. I was not Left Behind. This week has confirmed that everything that I wrote was wrong.

"We weren't Left Behind. We are not weird. What I hope is that we are unique and simply hopeless romantics, who just might not give up searching, who have an underlying faith that what is right is worth waiting for. You are hurtful and mean and just please don't lay your insecurities on me. It's all wrong until it's right."

I waited for a response that never came and we walked. Navigating around a particularly difficult mangrove, a welcoming lodge on a hillside appeared like a desperate oasis. We made our way up the steep hill and collapsed on the porch of the chocolate farm hotel.

Predictably, there were no phones or electricity in sight, but the proprietor helped us as best she could with cups of cocoa, coffee, and bathrobes. After she made the round trip to her house further up the hill, she handed over an ancient cellular phone.

I finally remembered a phone number that wasn't Salty's - that of Detective LaGuardia. I'd dialed it enough times in the last five days, after all. His phone was finally diverted to an exhausted operator who said she'd try to track him down.

He returned the call a half-hour later, and I spilled every last detail.

All there was to do was to wait to be eventually picked up. Josh had passed out on a lounge chair on the deck, part of a pair with red cushions facing the sun. The innkeeper noticed my disdain and escorted me to an empty room, where I lay down on the bed and drifted off immediately.

∼

A TRIO of concerned individuals woke me up at some point late in the morning. Ryan sat at the foot of the bed, LaGuardia behind him with an eyebrow raised, and Dr. Nolan looking far too pleased to be a part of the most intriguing crime to happen on the island in years.

"Looking good. I mean, considering," the doctor noted, slipping my arm into a blood pressure monitor. "Murder most foul, case closed."

LaGuardia filled me in on the events of the last six hours. While I had been tossing and turning, they'd been stuck in a high society nightmare. They'd tracked down Walter, having breakfast in bed with Olivia, and now he was locked again in a Bocas Town jail cell awaiting transport to Panama City.

"So," LaGuardia said, "so there is good news and there is bad news. I've been told by the night watchman at the marina that someone matching Max's photo motored up at the break of dawn in a speedboat. A half-hour later a sixty-foot power yacht showed up and was out of there quicker than you can say…well, it was quick."

And she is gone.

"Don't worry. You look worried. I'm a good detective, but my guess is you'll never see her again, and my jurisdiction ends at the airport. Panama City knows, but…"

"It's a thousand miles to Aruba," I randomly thought of how long it would take for her to reach the closest Caribbean island. It was harder than I thought to speak. How far was it to St. Barths? Was she cocky enough to show up to the wintertime haunt of the rich and famous?

The doctor cautiously pulled back my comforter and frowned. "That's a pretty nasty wound. There are some unusual strains of marine bacteria around here, so let's get you to the hospital and on to some antibiotics to stave off what I can. Necrotizing fasciitis is a nasty infection."

Twenty percent fatality rate, I remembered. Would I be lucky enough to be one of four out of five that survived?

Dr. Nolan saw that it was way too early to be joking, "Kidding. Maybe I don't get out enough..."

~

THE MOTION SICKNESS was kicking my ass. I sat with my head between my knees on the boat back to Bocas Town, Ryan's arm around me. He had gallantly scooped me up in his more than capable arms and had carried me onto the boat. The town came into view and he coaxed me up and took my hands.

"I know this is not the right time, Lexie, but this could be the last time I get the chance to talk to you. I'll be honest in saying that I hadn't thought of you in quite some time, but seeing you here, well, I just need to understand. Water under the bridge and all those kinds of words, but what did I do in high school to make you dislike me so much?"

Earnestly looking into his eyes, I asked, "What did I do? What did you do? What do you think happened? You broke my heart without a word and fell in love with my best friend.

She was head over heels so I never told her. That's what friends do."

"Didn't know? Of course she knew. She came up to me at the dance you couldn't make. You wanted out. Big time. That's what she said."

The events of my last three years of high school suddenly added up. As a sophomore, it was as simple as that to take something personally and then part ways for good. Back then, if you dated someone for two weeks, they were considered a boyfriend.

I only had two weeks with him. How different would life have been?

He brushed my bangs out of my face, softly smiling. "It was always you, Lexie. You were always the one."

42

SEE YA, WOULDN'T WANT TO BE YA...

A Spanish soap opera played on the twenty-year-old TV attached to a rusting arm jutting out from the ceiling in the antiquated hospital. There were no subtitles, and though I couldn't understand anything except, "*Lo siento*," I could get the gist of the plot.

Someone had broken someone's heart. The story never gets old.

Dr. Nolan had given me twelve stitches and some apple juice and then left for the beach. Hours went by slowly. The Bocas del Toro airport would be fully functioning, and the guests would be landing in Panama City soon, where they'd scatter to get their transferring flights. New friends would soon be forgotten. Everyone would dine out on the story for a few weeks, and then it would fade away as a footnote.

As the sun began to set, a giant bouquet of flowers entered the room, followed by Olivia, almost as if she was sending them as a reconnaissance mission. The rosy filter that I had looked at her through my entire life had lifted and

I saw her clearly. She stood stark in the fluorescent light from the hall, all warts on show.

I doubted that she knew how to give an earnest apology. She sat in a chair in the corner; smiling, hurt and broken. We were silent for a long time.

She softly said, "Looks like you were right, huh? Boy, were you right."

What was the point in bringing up thirty years of questions and hurt now, when she'd soon be out of my life forever? I had read somewhere that it was infinitely harder to break up with a dear old friend than a serious boyfriend, and I now understood.

"He tried to kill me, Olivia. You get that, right?" I searched her face for something genuine. I did think it was in there.

"It's crazy, right?" she asked, as casually as if I said that I had walked in on Marianna having a threesome in a wedding cabana.

"Olivia, I will always love you in my way, but I don't think you are a good person. That's what I've learned on this trip. Repeatedly. I think that there is a good person somewhere inside of you, and I hope you find her. One day."

Yesterday, she wouldn't have put up with it. But it wasn't yesterday.

"Are you okay?" she asked. I do believe that her concern was real.

"I will be." I looked out the window and we sat until the sun went down, then Olivia arose to meet her beloved night.

"When words are scarce, they are seldom spent in vain. That was Shakespeare."

"I know—Goodbye, Olivia."

She looked like a scared child. "I'm not going to say good-bye. I am going to say, 'See you later'."

"I am going to say goodbye."

I don't know if she believed it. She looked at me fondly and eventually left.

The nightmare was over.

43

EPILOGUE: FALL SEVEN TIMES AND STAND UP EIGHT (JAPANESE PROVERB)

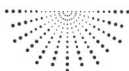

*y ankle got a lot worse before it got better, but I thankfully didn't have any flesh-eating disease.

I stayed Mariposa del Mar for the next few days after being released from the hospital, mostly sitting on my deck; foot raised, sun shining, enjoying the dolphins. Regardless of what I perceived as their lack of smarts, they were doing something right. It was wonderfully quiet and would be until the next day when the weekend crowd arrived.

The two bartenders played dominos, while occasionally bringing me food and drink, treating me like I was some kind of hero. Between Walter's family influence and the fact that no one even knew that Bocas del Toro existed, there was not even a mention of what had happened in any newspaper. Tourism would be as it ever was, and guests would be none the wiser.

None of the wedding guests had come to say goodbye, but the room had become home to a decent spread of gifts when I came in the door. Migs had given me a selfie of he and me in a frame, taken from when I was passed out in the hospital, with the note,

"So I'm off to Costa Rica, beautiful lady. You don't know what you're missing. Or maybe I don't. My loss completely."

Flowers were everywhere: from Ryan, from Edgar of all people, from Princeton Colleen. The biggest bouquet was from Lloyd, barely legible card attached, saying, "You can run, but you can't hide…" Whatever that meant.

Never to be outdone, the most extravagant get-well-gift was from Olivia; better than the Tiffany blue box, better than Cartier red, there sat her 4-carat engagement ring in the Harry Winston black box.

She had attached it to a letter that went on for pages, ending with, "When I look in the proverbial mirror, I am invariably dissatisfied, nay disgusted, at what looks back."

I crumpled the letter and threw it on the floor, remembering that the line was from a love letter an ex-boyfriend had written to her years ago. We laughed for hours at the time, back when we were good.

"PS – how can I explain how deep my apology to you is…"

If I said it once, I'll say it again.

Nothing sparkles like a diamond from 5th Avenue.

I tried it on for size, and I'd be lying if I said I didn't do that on more than one occasion. I had absolutely no idea what to do with it.

"Asshole tax," I could hear Olivia comment in my mind. Maybe. Cash it in and live the life of leisure for a decent amount of time.

LaGuardia came by for lunch every day, shooting the breeze more than talking shop. Our terrible week was in the past, and he wanted to talk about pleasant things like surfing and low-calorie piña coladas.

No one else visited, but he let me know that Lloyd was still around and thinking about moving down here permanently. He was considering investing in the growth of Hywel's surf camp and opening a medical research laboratory. There were things on the island, he had said to LaGuardia, that didn't exist in textbooks or research.

There were things that didn't exist in reality. And there were a few more stragglers who just hadn't got on the plane yet.

"It's a hard place to leave," LaGuardia said after his first visit for lunch at the hotel. "There's something quite special about this place."

That much was undeniably true.

That same day, as LaGuardia was leaving, throwing the remnants of his fish lunch off my deck, he said, "Stick around on the island. We could use you. You're a natural. I see investigation in your future."

My future?

Going over the week repeatedly in my head, I concluded that I was probably the worst investigator in the history of investigations. Hands down. Without the distance of time to reflect, I still wasn't sure if everything I had achieved had fallen into my lap or if I had actually solved a murder.

If a tree falls in a forest and there's no one around to see it, does it still make a sound?

At least for the moment, I was content. Walter was sitting in a Panama City jail cell with probably a half dozen lawyers working from New York trying to arrange an extradition. Max was hiding out wherever rich people go to hide. As long as she stayed there, I'd be fine.

It was late in the afternoon, about half an hour before the sun was due to set, when Josh showed up. The rays of light were shining through the clouds as if directly from heaven. There was nothing to be annoyed with anymore.

"I'd heard there were stragglers," I said. "I just didn't think that you'd be one of them."

He smiled that lovely smile he'd shot at me when I took my group on their first visit to Red Frog Beach. "I had some stitches too, you know, so I decided to stay for a night at a hotel in town, which became two, and now I'm still here.

"Every night I'm still down here, the more I'm embarrassed I am for what a complete idiot I was, or am, or will try not to be anymore. I think that I stayed this long to work up the courage to come by and say that I'm sorry. You deserve that."

It was too pretty from where I sat to be mad. Besides, it was the beginning of my chapter three in life. "Apology accepted."

"Sometimes people stay and they don't know why," Josh continued, furrowing his brow in a way I'd become just a little bit fond of. "Maybe I just wanted to stay and ask you on a date, or something like that. Sometimes people just want to stay."

A smile was my invitation for him to stay. He sat down on the lounge chair next to me, watching the heavenly light fade to sunset. I reached out for his hand, and my new chapter began.

THE END

ABOUT THE AUTHOR

I hope that you had a great time reading Drowning Lessons. If you enjoyed yourself, please consider writing a review on Amazon or GoodReads. Thank you!

The Wipeout Affair, the second book in the series is available now!
Exclusively on Amazon

RACHEL NEUBURGER is the author of The Red Frog Beach Mystery Series. As a playwright, her plays have had been produced in London, Edinburgh and New York. After 25-years in New York City, she now resides with her husband between London and St Leonards-on-Sea in England.

For news about Rachel and the upcoming Red Frog Beach Mysteries, check her out at RachelNeuburger.com.

THE WIPEOUT AFFAIR, BOOK 2

Ready to go back to the beach? Grab a Mai Tai and some suntan lotion, and join the next adventure…

Lexie Milano left her heart in Bocas del Toro, and she makes the big decision to move to the laid-back Caribbean island permanently. Piña coladas, white sand beaches, and a cabin of her own complete her picture of the perfect tropical future ahead. But if it looks too good to be true, it usually is. . . .

When the body of a beautiful local is found at an isolated surf camp, the owner calls on Lexie to help him clear his name it in this delicious whodunit. Lexie first turns to the police, but her sudden access to a treasure-trove of island secrets convinces her it's time to solve another murder on her own in this chick-lit mystery.

Favorite characters from Drowning Lessons return to grace the pages of this comedic mystery, including Migs, the handsome photographer; Lloyd, the genius with the cryptic past; and Lexie's new best friend, Detective LaGuardia. Between old friends, new associates, and the added potential of shark attacks, The Wipeout Affair will leave you laughing and guessing until the very end.

Available now on Amazon!

Made in the
USA
Middletown, DE